LEST TIDES TURN

DS LIZ MOORLAND 4

PHILLIPA NEFRI CLARK

LEST TIDES TURN

AN IMPORTANT NOTE...

This series is set in Australia and written in Aussie/British English for an authentic experience.

Like to discover more about Liz, other titles, and Phillipa's world? Visit Phillipa's website where you can subscribe to her email newsletter. www.phillipaclark.com.

PROLOGUE

The donkeys woke her.

Braying their blessed heads off instead of sleeping in one of the communal sheds they all liked to pack into, rather than sharing themselves around. Why she'd bothered to build so many shelters – and decent ones at that – was a mystery. Darned creatures made up their own rules about accommodation and just about everything else.

For the most part they were quiet at night and she waited a few minutes expecting the ruckus to subside.

Could be a fox passing through their paddock looking for something more size-appropriate for dinner and wary of a swift hoof up its backside. Probably cranky to have their space invaded.

But the noise continued and Lyndall dragged herself out of bed.

Before opening the sliding glass door which lead to the covered verandah, she pushed bare feet into boots and picked up the torch hanging by a loop from one of several hooks. It was raining and she muttered a few choice words about the creatures she normally loved so dearly, while donning an oilskin coat and shoving a hat over thick, grey, unruly hair.

Outside it was miserable, with the rain sleeting sideways

thanks to blustery winds. Motion-sensor lights managed to pierce the gloom but her torch made little difference.

The braying intensified and she hurried along the path to the top paddock. Whatever had got them going had them in a spin. At least Apple wasn't here tonight. The old pony belonging to her neighbour, Vince Carter, often visited the donkeys for company but had gone home this morning and would be tucked up safe and warm in her stable.

Wish I was.

Lyndall figured it was well past midnight. She didn't make a habit of checking when she woke during the night – which she did most nights – because then she'd begin calculating how much sleep time was left and that just annoyed her. Normally she'd settle again because these days she finally felt safe in her own home. But this night was already a write-off because she was wide awake.

'Settle, children!' She called as she let herself through the paddock gate but the wind and rain wouldn't carry her voice far. There wasn't a motion-sensor light out here and she used her torch to check the ground in front of her. It was slippery and muddy and sliding off her feet wouldn't be pleasant.

The largest shed was open on one side and from a quick head-count, all twelve donkeys were using it. They had their backs to the weather and were complaining bitterly to a wall.

'People! Nobody can stop the rain and you're in here and dry so for the love of all things good, shut up.'

One by one they noticed Lyndall and gathered around her, snorting their disapproval and nudging her pockets. There was nothing in here to cause such a carry on. No feral creatures or holes in the roof or fallen water buckets. It was donkeys being donkeys.

She waited until each one had nuzzled her and had a pat and settled again before leaving them. All it ever took was one to take affront at some real or imagined offence and begin a revolt against peace and quiet. But each of them had been rescued from terrible situations and Lyndall wasn't about to blame them for over-reacting. The dark of night was worse for some souls.

Lyndall stripped off inside the door, hanging the oilskin on its hook and her hat on another. The torch as well. She locked the sliding door. It was double glazed. Heavy. The lock went up and down into reinforced steel above and below the runners. Same as every door and window in the house.

Her pyjamas were dry despite the weather. But her feet were cold and she went in search of a pair of heavy socks, flicking on the light over the kitchen bench as she went by. She'd come back and make a drink. Something hot and with a good slosh of brandy. Maybe eat a piece of the caramel fudge Melanie brought up yesterday. Vince's grandchild was fast becoming a light in her life. For years there'd been nothing to encroach on the endless darkness of her soul but that little girl... even her grandfather... were working some kind of magic on her.

With a smile which was becoming familiar at the thought of her only neighbours, Lyndall rolled the socks on and returned to the kitchen.

It was in darkness.

I'd turned that light on.

And there was a smell. Human odour. Something not belonging here.

For the first time since waking, Lyndall's mind went to places she didn't like.

But this was *her* house.

To one side was the huge open plan living area. A dining table. A sunken lounge. She knew where every piece of furniture was.

The only light was that of the oven clock. Useless.

Lyndall inched her way back to the bedrooms. Five of them. Hers at the end of the hallway.

Before the bedroom door was another and with a quick motion – her hand against a small screen – that door silently opened inwards and Lyndall slid inside, pushing it closed behind herself.

Overreacting again?

She'd sleep in here tonight and keep an eye on the cameras. Might be as simple as a blown light bulb... except the smell had been real.

Not bothering with lights in this secure part of the house, Lyndall turned on the monitors. Ten in total. Six inside the house including a camera over the door to the panic room.

There were shadowy figures at the door she just closed.

Three, all with their faces covered and all carrying guns.

So, you found me.

Short of blowing the house up, they wouldn't get inside the room. Didn't make it any better that they were here and it wouldn't make for a comfortable night having them inches away.

Lyndall tapped a code into an overhead cupboard and reached for her rifle.

It wasn't there.

But the same human odour was.

She had an excellent sense of smell. And sight and hearing.

Pretending to fuss around looking for the rifle which she expected was trained on her head, Lyndall found the tiny alert button hidden against the grain of the timber and pressed it, then lifted the mobile phone which was always on in here. She tapped at it, heart pounding, hoping against hope she'd be able to message Vince.

'I wouldn't send that.'

How did you even get inside this room?

But even as she turned to face the man she'd not seen in decades, Lyndall knew. He'd always been able to find a way.

'Hello, Marcus.'

ONE
~DAY ONE~

This wasn't what Liz expected.

All the talking up of *Operation Nobody* had put images in her head.

'Every bell and whistle you could ever find in policing, Liz,' Pete told her more than once. 'Information systems like you won't believe and state of the art everything.'

'Everything?'

'From weapons to intel to transport. Just wait until you see our new home.'

Liz didn't actually have a home of her own any longer. After the last case, she'd finally been able to let go of the crappy apartment she'd lived in for close to twenty years. Some of her stuff was in storage and some in her sister's spare room, but the items she used on a day-to-day basis were in an Airbnb apartment in the city.

She'd chosen the apartment based on location, privacy, and access to both public transport and arterial roads. For now it would do – one bedroom, living room, kitchen, and something she hadn't had before. A balcony. A month-by-month commitment. The fact it overlooked the river was a bonus, along with the secure carpark downstairs. It wasn't a long-term solution but until she had time to find a place of her own to buy, this was more than adequate.

But the building she stood outside was disappointing.

As part of the shiny new team, handpicked by one of the best detectives she'd ever met, Liz expected a shiny new office. Maybe something on the top floors of one of the newest Melbourne skyscrapers, with room for two helicopters and a basement carpark filled with sleek, bullet-proof tactical response vehicles.

She'd have thought she'd got the address wrong, except she didn't get addresses wrong.

The building was red brick. At least one hundred years old. Smack bang in the middle of an industrial area close to Citylink and other main roads, surrounded by warehouses and empty lots.

A sad part of Melbourne and caught in between its roots and a future where this might all be demolished to become a high rise or rows of townhouses with an upmarket supermarket and token park.

Liz shuddered.

She'd had enough of suburban parks to last her lifetime.

Well, she was here now and whether the building met with her approval was beside the point. Ben Rossi had chosen it and she trusted him.

The door on the street-side of the building was boarded shut. Liz followed the directions sent by messenger half an hour ago and walked into a narrow alley between the building and the next – which was abandoned. It was wide enough for one vehicle. Three-quarters of the way along was a loading dock cut into the side. Someone imagined a truck could back in there, and perhaps some talented driver might manage, but there was room for maybe two cars. The dock consisted of a wide roller door and beside it, a normal passenger door.

If normal means as heavy as a fire door and with two security panels.

She gazed around, looking for surveillance, then tapped a short code into the bottom panel. It lit green and she added a second, longer code to the upper panel.

Then, when nothing happened, Liz trained a stare on the most hidden of four cameras she'd noticed.

With a click, the access door opened a crack.

Pete is probably in there having too much fun at my expense.

He'd been her sometimes-partner in Homicide for the past few years and was instrumental in her being offered this job. She'd been ready to quit the force and he knew it. He'd been the same. But at one of her darkest moments, this happened. A new task force so deep that only a handful of very senior officers knew of its existence.

Liz stepped into a narrow corridor and the door closed behind her. There was a single lightbulb flashing in an erratic fashion more suited for a horror film. A set of steps directly ahead were the only option and Liz took them.

Three flights up she reached the top floor and the only thing stopping her phone Pete and get new directions was the state-of-the-art security downstairs. If this wasn't the right place then the code wouldn't have worked.

So what now?

She stood on a small landing with no windows. One side was the same red brick as the exterior. Opposite was a door which was locked with two large padlocks and boarded up from her side. Liz almost laughed aloud. If this was a test then she was failing. Her first day might be her last.

She peered down the stairwell. It was gloomy thanks to no natural light and the presence of only one naked lightbulb dangling above each of the three landings. Workplace safety nightmare. She leaned against the boarded-up door, her ear pressed against rough timber as she listened. Nothing.

About to go down a floor, she reconsidered and did the same thing against the brick. It was stupid but in her strange new world she had to be ready for anything. The team – well, who she knew so far – were all resourceful and smart. This wasn't a typical unit and she had to remember not to treat anything as ordinary.

She expected the brick to be cold. It wasn't. There was the faintest hum beyond it.

Liz stepped back grinning and opened the flashlight on her phone.

'I know what's going on here.'

The light revealed tiny gaps around the brickwork in a rectangle pattern. Not normal door-sized, it nevertheless was the most likely way to proceed.

Refusing to give up and phone Pete, Liz ran her hand lightly over the area, pressing bricks. Nothing. But when she shone the light up, she found a camera. A very cool, minute camera between bricks. She blew it a kiss.

Flashlight pointing to the floor on either side of the sort-of-door, Liz found the key.

There was a floorboard which was just a little bit less filthy than the others and she stepped on it, close to the wall. Of course it wasn't as easy as that so she tried combinations. One step, two. Two steps, three. Short. Long. Tired of the games, she stepped back and held her second finger aloft in the direction of the camera.

With a soft whoosh, the brickwork moved, swinging away from her.

Pete was standing on the other side.

'Three seconds, Liz. Hold then release. Then tap again.'

From behind him, Ben Rossi appeared in the gloom.

'Liz, welcome to Operation Nobody.'

TWO

Ben had turned immediately, disappearing. Pete was grinning stupidly.

'Thought you had that, Liz. So close.'

'Glad you had some fun. What now?'

'You follow me, that's what.'

This hallway only went for a few metres and along one wall was an elevator. It was narrow but the door looked new.

'Does this work?'

'Of course.'

'Then what was that all about – oh, don't bother answering. Some test you thought up?'

'Not me.'

Beyond the elevator was a different kind of door. This one was made of a black, shiny material and when Pete touched it, the pigment disappeared, leaving an almost clear view of what was beyond.

Liz sucked in a breath.

This was where all the bells and whistles resided.

Pete reached above his head and held his palm on the surface. A panel – built into the material of the door – appeared and he tapped a code. 'Meg will set you up for your own version of this.'

'Meg? Our Meg?'

He grinned as the door slid open. 'Come in and I'll get some coffee.'

I've been watching too many futuristic cop shows and now I've dreamed one into life.

This was a whole new level of technology and an unexpected stab of doubt shook Liz. What if this was all beyond her to learn? What if the belief Ben Rossi had in her abilities was unwarranted?

She was alone. Pete was the only other person in here, whistling from the other side of a two-thirds height wall. A kitchen, perhaps.

Liz scanned the room.

It was huge. She figured she could fit her entire apartment – past apartment – in here with some space left over. Although it was open-plan, there were a couple of glassed offices at the far end and between them, a door, open to another room.

In the middle of the room was a table. It was empty with the top made of the same black material of the door she'd come through and a bit bigger than a full-size billiards table. In a rough circle around it were six workstations. Each had long, curved desks and two computers. All except the one furthest from her which had one long desk with three screens and keyboards.

Meg's. I can't believe she's here.

Liz had worked with Meg Mackie several times in the past couple of years. She was a forensic analyst who'd been seconded from another department by Missing Persons for a short-term experiment. The skills and results she brought saw the secondment indefinitely extended and Meg had been one of the officers instrumental in recently solving a decades-old case. A case which had shattered Liz, although bringing closure to her own dark past. Or some of it.

There was little else in the room. No filing cabinets or white-boards or clutter.

Or people.

'Liz?'

Ben waved from the door between the two glassed offices.

'Join us?'

Despite a flutter of nerves, she headed his way.

The thing was that Liz had no real understanding of this covert team. She'd been invited to join based upon a two-minute conversation with Ben at a park. Pete followed up with a few sparse details about something so new and covert and self-managed that nobody they knew had knowledge of its existence. That was enough for Liz to agree. She was done with the force. Or at least, done with being a detective working homicides and major crimes. Now, for all intents and purposes, she no longer worked for Victoria Police. She'd resigned. Had drinks with colleagues who wished her well but didn't really understand why a fellow cop at the top of her game who had just solved a major case would bow out.

At one point before that all happened, Pete had made noises about going private. Running an agency. Wanting her to join him.

She'd been tempted.

Anything other than the restrictions of her role where her hands had been tied during the most important case of her life.

But then Ben Rossi – formerly Detective Sergeant Ben Rossi who'd been head of Missing Persons until a couple of years ago – made her an offer.

Liz glanced at the two glassed-in offices. They were nothing she hadn't seen before, designed for the most senior staff to use. She stepped through the door between them.

This room was smaller than the first, running from the front to back of the building and clearly broken up for different purposes. She got a sense of areas for work and some for play but her focus was completely taken by the faces gazing at her from around a table.

Meg was beside Ben and she smiled and waved at Liz.

There were two people she'd never met and two she hadn't expected.

One was a wonderful street cop she'd crossed paths with over the years – Senior Constable Annette Benski. Seeing her smiling face was like a warm hug. While they'd never been close friends, they had a nice rapport and worked well together.

The other was every bit as unexpected but for other reasons.

Doctor Candace Carroll. Psychologist, criminologist, forensic expert. A profiler.

They'd met on Liz's last case. The doctor was an advisor, taking Liz's outline of a profile and turning it into a polished and eerily accurate portrayal of their suspect. Liz had mixed feelings about Candice, a keenly intelligent person who seemed able to see into her mind all too easily, but one she had deep respect for as well.

'Grab a seat, Liz. Pete will eventually bring you a coffee.' Ben grinned, gesturing at the choice of several empty chairs. 'You know almost everyone. What if we all go around and mention the important stuff?'

'Like my favourite snack if you want something done fast?' Meg asked, winking at Liz.

She chose a seat with empty spaces either side. 'Danishes and cinnamon scrolls work for you. Decent coffee – and I mean, really decent. A shot of caramel is a bonus'

'And that is why Liz will always have my undying attention.'

'And me.'

Pete carried a large tray.

'I make you decent – *really* decent coffee.'

'Oh… that's why you're here. Chief coffee maker.' Meg was doing a good impression of someone who'd just discovered the meaning of life.

'One of the most obvious of my many talents.' Pete placed

the tray in the middle of the table. Not only did it have two cups of steaming coffee, one of which Pete gave to Liz, but a platter of pastries, fruit, and protein balls. 'This, Liz, is our way of saying welcome.'

For a few minutes, the table was relatively quiet as people helped themselves to their choice of offerings. Liz sipped her coffee and it was good. A far cry from the crap served up in Homicide. Everyone else had a drink, most hot, with a couple of juices.

Is this the standard? Or just to impress me?

Pete had taken one of the chairs next to Liz and was chatting quietly to the person on the other side of him, one of the people she didn't recognise. Ben was watching the room and when their eyes met, he smiled ever so slightly. He'd always been an observer and that was part of what had made him so damned good in Missing Persons. He would pick up the smallest of clues – often ones overlooked more than once. But he was supposed to be happily living along the Gippsland coast, playing local cop with his family.

'I'll start!' Meg announced. 'My name is Meg and I am a workaholic.'

'Hi, Meg.' Everyone replied, reminiscent of a different type of addiction meeting.

'And that is it for me.'

There was a ripple of laughter until the man at her side spoke.

'Hello, Liz. I'm Reuben Barnes. Spent a decade in a senior role in an organisation I can't mention.' He looked very serious and sincere. 'Something about keeping the country secure. Starts with A and ends with O... if you really need a hint.' His expression was deadpan but his strikingly-blue eyes sparkled.

'If I fill in the missing two letters and say them do I get in trouble?' Liz asked.

'You have no idea how much.'

Liz liked him.

'Right, my turn,' Pete said.

Everyone shushed him and he tried to look put out but failed. Instead, he helped himself to the largest pastry and bit in, uncaring about the flakes which rained down.

Ben handed him a napkin. 'Everyone knows me.'

And I have so many questions about why you are here.

Not wanting to speak out of turn about the person who was her new boss, Liz just nodded. Ben winked at her and she found herself smiling. He'd bring her up to speed when the time was right.

'I have to say, Liz, I am beyond excited to be working with you.' This was Annette Benski who looked around the table. 'I know some of us are new to each other but Liz and I have known each other for a long time. More than a decade, I reckon. Never worked together directly, but I have such respect for Liz.'

'Goes both ways,' Liz said. Her earlier sense of inadequacy fading with each person who spoke. Everyone was here for a purpose and while she didn't know hers – yet – she was excited about what was ahead.

Aware of two sets of eyes burning into her, Liz turned her attention to the face she didn't know. Candace Carroll could wait a moment and being honest with herself, Liz wanted a little time to gather herself.

The woman she now looked at was the youngest in the team, perhaps in her late twenties. She wore an intense and slightly worried expression under perfect makeup and gorgeous shoulder-length red hair. Although sitting, it was clear she was model-thin and her jewellery and blouse screamed quality.

'Hi,' Liz said, smiling encouragingly when the young woman didn't respond.

'Um… sure. I'm Phoebe Renshaw. I guess you know who I am already. But anyway, I hope to learn stuff from you. And hello.'

Her eyes dropped to hands which clasped each other on the table.

'Nice to meet you, Phoebe.'

And I have no idea who you are.

Pete had finished scoffing his pastry. 'Seeing as we're missing one, I'll be him for the purpose of an introduction.'

'Please don't,' Ben urged.

'Didn't hear what you said. Any-hoo… ah, beautiful lady, come and sit next to Hamish.' Pete's voice had gone posh and he patted the empty seat beside himself. 'Hamish Mathers-Smythe. Mathers will suffice. At your service.'

'Cut it out, Pete. That's not how he talks,' Ben said.

'It is, actually.' This was Meg, but Candace, Annette, and Phoebe all nodded.

'You'll not find mention of me anywhere unless you search the world's most rich and snobby,' Pete continued. 'I am, however, outstanding at my job. And what is my job, you ask?'

Liz chuckled. 'Poor Hamish. I think I have to take his side if you dislike him so.'

Pete dropped the act with a broad grin. 'Nah. You'll make up your mind soon enough. But he will like you. A lot.'

Candace had the ghost of a smile on her lips. She was no doubt analysing them all from this meet and greet session and perhaps that was what unsettled Liz. There was no logic behind her feelings for the other woman, which hadn't changed since they'd first met. Liz was drawn to her on a level she had yet to understand, but was deeply wary of revealing too much of herself.

Not that I ever do to anyone.

'It appears to be my turn,' Candace said. 'My background and passion is understanding the human mind and psyche. I've worked in several fields, but all relate to profiling and I believe I'm only just beginning to accomplish my best work. I have an open-door policy to anyone who wishes to explore their own path.'

The last words were directed to Liz. The doctor's eyes were sincere and Liz offered a small smile in response. If they were going to be on the same team – again – then it was time to stop being so guarded. Candace had only ever been encouraging and kind.

'Your turn, Liz,' Pete smirked. 'Spotlight on the newcomer and all questions welcome.'

'Why don't you do the honours for me? Keeping in mind that I'm within arm's length, more or less, unlike poor Hamish.'

Pete's eyes lit up. 'You bet. Okay, my name is Liz Moorland and I'm one of the finest detectives this country has ever produced. I am keenly intelligent—'

'Stop it, Pete.'

'Empathetic, fearless. You don't want to be in my sights because I am relentless.'

'Okay, I like the last bit.'

Liz felt the heat rise in her face and all eyes were on her as he kept going.

'Furthermore, I had the good fortune to have the best partner ever to grace the halls of Victoria Police.'

He was grinning again.

Liz nodded, her face serious. 'That bit is true. Vince Carter was an exceptional cop.'

Everyone burst into laughter as Pete dropped his head into his hands.

THREE

The team had dispersed, taking with them the tray and empty plates and closing the door to leave just Ben and Liz.

'Why am I here?' The question had haunted Liz for weeks but was more urgent now she'd met everyone and been drawn into this new world. Some of the people she'd met were understandably included. Pete. Meg. Candace. Reuben. Others, not so much.

'You heard Pete. He'll speak on your behalf when you won't. Your skills are pretty clear to me and considering the differences between the people who have joined, I need someone who can do their job without hand-holding.'

'Ah. So I'm good at following orders?' She couldn't keep the grin off her face.

'Sure. Believe that if you want.'

'So far I'm seeing specialists. Meg. Candace. Pete – if you want someone who knows how to sneak around dark alleys – and Reuben must be bringing some security or similar skills? I'm meant to know who Phoebe Renshaw is. And as much as I love and respect Annette… well, she's a dedicated beat cop.'

'You forgot Hamish.'

'I can't begin to form an opinion on him because according to

Pete, Hamish is some kind of James Bond style character. He likes the ladies and they *lurve* him.'

Ben chuckled. 'Make your own mind up once you meet him. He'll be here a bit later. As for Annette? She's a solid police officer. More than solid. She's exceptional and was wasted where she was. She's not only reliable and steady but enjoys digging around in files and the like.'

Liz agreed with his summary but was a bit surprised Annette would leave the job she'd loved for so long.

'And Phoebe. Clearly you don't spend time on TikTok and Instagram.'

'I know enough to use them in an investigation but that is where it begins and ends. Is she an influencer?'

'Of sorts. She has a true crime channel and while it comes across as superficial and light entertainment, despite the subject, there's actually a lot going on in the background. Phoebe has helped Missing Persons find kids taken by a relative, sent intel to various cops about a range of crimes and managed to do so without raising suspicion from those who tipped her off.'

'That's clever. Really clever.'

Although she came over as nervous and shy. Doesn't quite fit.

'I want to bring you up to speed and then you choose who you think can help you on your first job.'

'Which is?'

'Finding Kyle Moorland.'

Liz's heart jumped.

'Think it's time we tracked down your father for once and for all and brought him to justice. Don't you?' Ben pushed his chair back. 'Like a quick tour?'

Long overdue.

'Will I have to pass more tests to access the bathroom, for example?'

'I'll leave Candace to explain her reasoning behind the little puzzles she sets for us all.'

'Candace? I thought it was Pete being annoying.' Liz followed Ben out.

'Not this time.'

The main room was humming with activity. People were at their workstations and only Meg looked up with a broad smile. If she was part of this new unit then Liz knew it was important. Meg was one of the most intelligent people she knew and one who could see patterns where no one else did. Digital forensics might be her background but she'd more than crossed over into other areas of policing since Liz met her a couple of years back.

'This is Nobody Central or the hub,' Ben said. 'The expectation is that we will become staffed enough to have twenty-four-hour attendance. That's a little way off but is my focus. Finding and then recruiting people who are not only brilliant in their field, but complement the existing team is, well… not easy.'

'But you are looking beyond the force?'

'I am. We'll sit down soon and go through the structure so you have a solid understanding of where this all sits. It isn't exactly what you'd expect.'

Liz had that impression from the beginning. The evening Ben had suggested she might want to consider his new unit there'd been a hint that it wasn't an ordinary covert operation – not that any of them could be called ordinary. Today was proving she hadn't even touched the surface in imagining what she'd agreed to.

Ben's phone buzzed and before checking it, he led the way into the area where Pete had been earlier.

'I'm going to see who wants me, so spend a few minutes exploring. Through that door you'll find restrooms, showers, a couple of sleeping areas. If you want another coffee feel free to grab one and come and find me when you're ready.'

He was gone in a second and Liz gazed around.

This was a kitchen area as well appointed as a luxury home. Double oven. Convection stovetop. Large fridge and freezer and when she peeked inside each, Liz was taken aback by the quality and quantity of food inside. There was a bar fridge – stocked – beneath a counter, and glass fronted cupboards with a range of cutlery, cups, and glassware. A high-end coffee machine was the final touch and she found herself shaking her head a little.

Who on earth had financed this? Not the kitchen, but the unit.

She opened a door to a narrow passage. Several rooms went off either side including change rooms with lockers, bathrooms with showers, a storage room, and three sleeping quarters. These had double beds, a small desk, and a television.

Far out. Am I in some peculiar hotel?

After visiting the restroom, Liz returned to the main room, instantly aware of a change of mood out here. Meg stared at Ben over the top of a monitor as he spoke on the phone just a metre away. Pete had his hands on his hips, listening intently. The rest of the team were paying close attention.

Ben glanced at Liz and waved her over, putting the phone onto speaker.

'Mate, Liz is here now.'

The gruff voice through the speaker made the hair on Liz's arms stand up. Vince Carter was one of her oldest and dearest friends, and a colleague and mentor when she began in the force. They'd been through good times and hard.

'Lizzie, its Lyndall.'

'What's happened? Are you alright. Is Melanie?'

'Yes. But something is terribly wrong. Lyndall has disappeared.'

Ten minutes later the entire team gathered around the table in the middle of the room. Liz was still processing Vince's conversation – what she'd heard of it. The distress in his voice was the worst part because Vince Carter wasn't one to show emotion.

'Have to admit the last thing I expected to be doing in our

first week of operation was finding a person known to some of our team. At least, someone who isn't a bad guy.'

Ben ran a hand through his hair. He was at one end of the table and Reuben had taken the spot at the opposite end. He'd said nothing after the call had finished, unlike Pete, Meg, and Annette, who'd immediately got into a conversation. Even Candace had joined in, although only with a few words of comfort.

'Who doesn't know Vince Carter… or of him?' Ben glanced around the table and only Phoebe raised a hand. 'How about Lyndall?' This time it was everyone other than Pete, Liz, and Meg. 'Who wants to fill in some details out of you two?'

If Pete says one smart-arsed thing about Vince—

'I'll let Liz talk. She knows them best.'

All eyes moved to Liz.

'For Phoebe's information, Vince Carter is an ex-Sergeant of the Victorian Police Force. Uniform his whole career. He retired a few years back and lives with his young grandchild up along the Razorback up Lerderderg State Forest way.'

Phoebe nodded between scribbling in a notebook.

'Lyndall is Vince's neighbour – the only one within sight. Both live on acreages but hers is pretty big. She's a good friend to Vince and Melanie, who was orphaned last year and came to live with Vince. Lyndall is like a grandma figure.'

'A killer grandma,' Pete muttered.

'Sorry, did you say she's a killer?' Phoebe's eyes shot up.

Annette answered. 'There were rumours she'd taken down a man who was after Melanie before Pete got to him.'

'Oi. Of course it was me.'

Pete and Liz exchanged a quick look.

'What else do we know about Lyndall?' Ben asked.

'Not much, really,' Liz said. 'She knows how to use a rifle. According to Melanie, Lyndall was a famous artist at one point. Vince thinks something bad happened to her close family years back. And then there's the other thing.'

Phoebe stopped writing and looked up. Everyone was listening.

'She has a panic room in her house.'

People began talking at the same time. Ben held up a hand and the chatter subsided. 'I've never met Lyndall but I know Vince. The fact he rang me, a person he believed is running a small unit in Gippsland, shows how little he trusts anyone but a few. Liz, he didn't call you first. He thought you were travelling after you resigned.'

Liz bit her lip. She'd lied to just about everyone she knew for the past month while she sorted out her new life.

'Dunno why he didn't ring me.'

If Liz had had anything throwable it would have gone Pete's way, but she chose to ignore him. The ongoing mutual dislike between her two trusted partners on the force – one old, one not quite as old – got exhausting and now was not the time. But Pete winked at her. He was just lightening the moment in typical Pete fashion.

Ben continued. 'Lyndall disappeared overnight from her house. There was no alarm and no sign of forced entry, from Vince's investigation. And the panic room door is unlocked and ajar. Meg, Liz, Pete. I want you to head out there now please. Reuben, sort out the surveillance. Phoebe, help me look into who she really is. Annette, there's files coming over. Mostly about the case last year with the shooting but it is about the only time I can find Lyndall on our system.'

'And me?' This was Candace.

'Start building a profile. Help Annette and we'll all feed you every crumb we find.'

'I love crumbs.' Across the table, Candace gazed steadily at Liz. 'We'll find her. There isn't a person here who doesn't want to see a quick resolution.'

So why do I feel so uneasy?

FOUR

The landscape flashed past as Pete took on the role of driver for their debut case. This was a huge upgrade from the cars of both their pasts and was fitted with more equipment than Liz had time to take in. Best he drive until she had a chance to familiarise herself with a dashboard unlike any she'd seen.

'Any idea where the lights and sirens are?' Pete asked.

'Seriously?'

'He says that every time he drives one of these, Liz. We've all driven them.' Meg was in the back seat, laptop open. 'I think Pete is a repressed father.'

'Hello, I'm right here. And I'm not repressed.'

'So you *are* a father?' Meg asked with complete innocence. 'Can't imagine any woman being so desperate as to let you—'

'Okay, okay. As far as I know my glorious genes have not been passed on.'

'Yet you insist on doing the dad joke thing as though you long for a gullible child to dazzle with your glittering humour.'

Pete glanced at Liz. 'Tough crowd today.'

Liz wasn't in the frame of mind to joke around. Pete used his awful sense of humour to relieve tension and most times, she'd join in.

Not this time.

Meg closed her laptop. 'Do you have anything on this so-called panic room of Lyndall's? Is it just a room with a heavy door and locks? Anything I should look out for?'

Shuffling a bit so she see Meg better, Liz shook her head. 'It's the real deal. Properly built into the house during construction with reinforced everything. Even has a hidden alarm which makes this even more worrying.'

'And where in the house?'

'All the bedrooms are down a hallway, away from the living areas. Lyndall's bedroom is at the very end and the panic room is just before it. '

Meg tilted her head. 'See, there's a whole lot of info not readily available to me and that sucks. I know that Lyndall shot the bullet which killed that dreadful man but there's next to no trace to back up what I've been told.'

Pete glanced at her in the rear-vision mirror. 'The finding was that the kill shot was from my rifle. Thing is… she shot first. Felt the bullet zip past me while I was still getting him in my sights but I made damned sure I hit him in the same spot before he went down.'

'Pride?' Meg grinned.

'Actually no. The mind does weird things under pressure and it was Lyndall's aim that showed me where to shoot. Lyndall always struck me as *good people* and something kicked in and made sure she didn't get any heat over this. Gave me plenty, but she was a civilian protecting her useless neighbour from a killer. No need for her to suffer.'

So much to unpack from that.

They weren't far from Vince's place. Pete slowed as the road narrowed and began to wind in long curves. The sides dropped away, one to farmland and the other into a deep valley filled with bush, and beyond, even higher ridges. A road snaked off and Pete took it. There were few homes along here and none for at least a kilometre before the vehicle slowed and turned into a driveway.

Meg leaned forward to see. 'Is that Vince's house on the left?'

'Yes. His land goes back a fair way but is too steep to use, apart from a little orchard higher up.'

They drove past an almost-new cottage with a patch of grass and some vegetable gardens. A pony grazed in the only paddock, lifting her head to watch them.

'And that is Apple,' Pete said.

Surprised he cared enough to remember, Liz drew in a long breath to settle sudden nerves. She wasn't here as a detective. Not in the usual sense. She didn't represent Homicide or Missing Persons. 'Do we know if any police are attending?'

'Ben sent me through an update,' Meg said. 'He's asked Vince to hold off speaking to anyone else until we've evaluated the situation – not that Vince seemed interested in reporting this through the regular channels. Also, he needs Lyndall's history, one way or another. Whatever she might keep in her house about her past. Keeping things so secret might mean she had help at one point.'

'Help? As in… witness protection?'

'Just one of several options.'

The driveway was a couple of hundred metres long and increasingly steep. At the top of the hill it evened out and they passed a garage big enough for multiple vehicles and big ones at that. Liz recalled seeing the doors open and there'd been a tractor as well as Lyndall's old 4WD. But for now the doors were down. The driveway ended with a square area for parking and Pete pulled in. The only vehicle.

'Anything else I need to know, Liz?' Meg was pulling her laptop bag over one shoulder and sling bag over the other . 'About Vince?'

Pete snorted but a sharp look from Liz stopped him saying whatever crap he was going to and he climbed out, closing his door behind him.

'Vince is gruff. He'll be desperately worried which might make him abrupt. Straight to the point. But he's got a keen mind and instincts like you wouldn't believe so let him talk… even lead him to talk.'

Vince was approaching Pete from the direction of the house. They stopped a few feet apart, both with defensive body language… arms crossed, legs apart, each leaning back a little. Liz and Meg were well aware the men had a difficult relationship and until recently wouldn't give each other the time of day.

But Pete suddenly held out his right hand and when Vince took it, their handshake was firm and lasted a few seconds.

'Miracles do happen,' Liz said.

The four of them stood outside while Vince went over the events of the past hours.

'When did you see Lyndall last?' Liz asked.

'About nine last night. Mel and I had dinner up here and walked back to the cottage after. Hadn't meant to stay so long, being a school night, but the two of them were sketching and I figured it wouldn't hurt for them to finish.'

'Melanie's at school right now?'

'Yeah. She doesn't know.'

Vince's face didn't show the emotion Liz could hear in his voice. After everything he'd been through, this had to be hard on him.

Pete was gazing down at the road. The view was over several paddocks with a scattering of cattle belonging to Lyndall, and with hardly a blind spot of hers or Vince's properties. There were a few shelters for the livestock and a row of shade trees on the side away from Vince's, but otherwise there were few places a person wouldn't be seen from the house.

'Before you ask, I didn't hear any vehicles. Nothing out of the ordinary other than the donkeys going off their heads at about one.'

Pete swung around. 'Did you check why?'

Vince made a sound of irritation which might have been directed at Pete or the creatures. 'Lyndall has a five-minute rule. If they don't settle in that time she checks them. I let it go for five and they stopped but the thing is, how long did they carry on before I heard them? I stepped outside but not a sound and although a light came on in the house it went off only a few seconds later. And if that's when she was taken then…' His hands balled into fists.

'Can you take me to the panic room?' Meg spoke for the first time since Liz had introduced her to Vince. 'And show me any parts of the house which might have been compromised.'

'Sorry… Meg? If its fingerprints you want then I doubt you'll find any. Whoever took Lyndall knew what they were doing.' Vince glanced at the case she'd collected from the boot of the vehicle.

'Fingerprints are so old-school.' She grinned at Vince. 'I think you might find my tools of trade a bit interesting. Mind leading the way?'

As uncertain as he looked, Vince nodded and the two of them headed to the back of the house. Meg had a way with people. The ones she liked, she'd treat with respect and care, as with Vince. The rest? They'd believe she was doing what they wanted until the time was right and then it was game on. It made her an important part of any team, quite aside from her skills as a forensic analyst.

Liz gestured for Pete to follow her and took a path she knew led to the first of the back paddocks.

'How often have you been here?' He kept pace.

'Enough to have a fair idea of the layout. Lyndall's had me up for dinner a few times with Vince and Mel.'

'Yeah, me too, but not with them.'

Stopping in her tracks, Liz rounded on Pete. 'You've never said a word. What do you know about Lyndall?'

'Me?'

'Come on, mate. You don't have it in you to turn off the detective just because you're catching up for a meal.'

'You make it sound like a bad thing.'

'No. No, it is one of the reasons why we solved the last case we worked on and I am forever grateful for what you did. But this is different. What did you talk about? Did you see the panic room?'

Pete shook his head. 'No to the panic room. And we talked about stuff which I'm not going to repeat and before you yell at me, none of it was to do with her past. Not even a question passed my lips about her sharp shooting. Shall we check out these donkeys?'

Vince joined them after a few minutes. There were twelve donkeys in a series of paddocks joined by open gates. Each paddock had a shelter and there was one much larger shelter in this top paddock. All were busy dragging mouthfuls of hay from a huge feeder and weren't concerned when Liz and Pete walked around them. But when Vince appeared, several of them left eating long enough to greet him.

All three stood in the middle of the paddock.

'We found Lyndall's phone on her bedside table. That Meg of yours knows her stuff.'

Good. He trusted Meg enough to leave her alone in Lyndall's house. He wasn't one to trust quickly or give people the benefit of the doubt but had excellent judgement. It was one of the things which had once saved Liz's life.

'What would set them off?' Liz asked, gesturing at the donkeys. 'Is it normal at night for them to disturb your sleep all the way down at your place?'

'Not so much at night. As you can see, there are multiple sheds but Lyndall gave up locking them into separate paddocks because they want to be social all the time. But that has its own downsides, one being how quickly a small issue escalates when they're so close to each other. But people being around – strangers – would do it.'

His eyes gave away his struggle not to blame himself and Liz decided to keep him busy.

'Is there any other way onto the property, particularly with a vehicle?'

'More than likely someone could come up trails from the valley at the back, but it would take a decent four-wheel drive and a lot of fencing would need cutting. The land next door, over there—' Vince pointed toward the back corner furthest from them, 'you can just see where it begins with that clump of trees? Worth taking a look. Before Lyndall built here there was a track leading all the way to the main road. Reckon its overgrown and useless but that'd be the way I'd sneak in.'

'Pete?'

With a nod, Pete set off in the general direction. One of the donkeys followed for a while, until he climbed over the first fence.

Vince gripped Liz's arm. 'Need to talk. Before he comes back.'

FIVE

Pete jogged along the fence line, passing several paddocks each set up to Lyndall's exacting plans. Post and rail fences, a decent three-sided shelter, small water tank which kept a trough full. Even if the donkeys didn't appreciate her efforts, this property of hers would sell at a decent price when she decided to downsize.

If ever.

He shouldn't have said a word to Liz about having been here for dinner. Speaking before filtering was his thing and he was too old to change. She wouldn't let go of it and he needed to come up with something to give her. Just not the truth.

What was needed was a full-on search of the property. Uniform police, SES, volunteers, all burrowing into every nook and cranny of Lyndall's land and the thousands of hectares around it which were mostly dense bush. So far, Ben wanted this kept to the unit until early intel led them in a direction. But it might be all too late.

Pete reached the end of Lyndall's property and drew in long, shallow breaths to get his heart rate down.

He glanced back. Vince and Liz were moving out of sight, deep in discussion. Did Vince have any idea about this new unit? How would Liz explain her presence here when the world believed she'd resigned as a cop? After all, Vince had phoned Ben, knowing he was still in the force.

Lyndall's post and rail fencing was hard up against barbed wire and metal stakes. He made a note on his phone to find out who owned the neighbouring land. Why not simply remove the crap fencing rather than two boundaries?

Pete climbed over, swearing as a barb caught his pants. He freed himself and landed on both feet, then swore again as he looked down. There were fresh tyre tracks ahead and footprints which he was managing to stand on. Finding a firmer spot, he stepped onto grass and began to take a series of photos, slowly walking alongside the dryish mud and finishing at the first of the tyre tracks. These he sent to Ben.

The almost-immediate phone call was expected.

'Boss.'

'Send me the co-ordinates for those pics.'

'Yeah, still getting to know how this phone works but will do.'

Ben chuckled.

'Fine for you to laugh. Care to come out here and help? Could use another fifty, maybe a hundred bodies to search.'

Serious now, Ben answered. 'Not yet. And do you think she's just wandered off? Or been killed and left somewhere close?'

'No and no.'

'Then we use our resources to track where she's gone. Send the co-ordinates as a matter of urgency, then keep taking photos. Follow the trail, mate.' He ended the call.

'I would follow the trail if I could work this thing out.'

He'd had basic training in the software the unit was using. So far, it was untested in the field and it seemed that Pete was to be the first. He wasted a few minutes choosing the wrong apps that nestled within the program and was about to phone Meg when he found it. All it took was him opening it and suddenly his phone had a mind of its own, the screen turning into something like a futuristic navigation program. In a few seconds the words

'Connection Achieved' flashed twice and then the screen went black.

'Uh oh.'

He rang Ben who answered on the first ring. 'Got the connection, Pete. Keep taking photos for as long as you see anything worth recording. I'll get someone up there to help.'

Before Pete could ask what he meant by the connection, Ben was gone again.

There was so much to learn about this new job. Only Meg, Candace and Reuben had finished all the training modules – the basics, anyway – and the rest were playing catch up. Poor Liz hadn't even sat at her own desk yet.

He stared along the track. Who would have expected Lyndall to disappear? Operation Nobody was designed as a fast-response, no-holds-barred unit but was woefully unprepared for an actual investigation. Ben had planned to start the team on finding Liz's criminal father as a way to ease in and learn the technology and vehicles and weapons without being under pressure.

Yep. So much for that idea.

Vince and Liz left the donkey paddock and wandered in the direction of the house. Pete was out of earshot and Liz was certain she knew what her old partner was about to ask.

'You left the force, Liz. Yet here you are with Pete, and Meg. There's also a fancy SUV, only bigger than normal, which I've never seen as a cop car. And Ben sent you, although he works out of a Gippsland station.'

They stopped at the bottom of the steps to the back deck and he crossed his arms, waiting for a reply.

She grimaced. 'I actually don't know what I'm permitted to say. Today is my first day on the job and I've not even been debriefed.'

'This is a covert team?'

'Kinda. Well, completely. I'm not privy to all the details of where we fit yet.'

Vince nodded. 'And it was pure luck I rang Ben and he's involved… is he heading it up?'

'He is.'

'And why is shithead there?'

Liz caught a laugh before it passed her lips. Vince and Pete had been enemies for years and although they'd recently found a place of mutual respect, both preferred to pretend it didn't exist. The warm handshake earlier was genuine though and the rest for show. But she quickly sobered. This wasn't the time for delving into anything other than the reason she was here.

'Let's go and find Meg. I'd like to walk through the house with you both and ask questions.'

Lyndall's house was architect designed, beautiful and functional. The large, covered deck they stepped onto was built from renewable timber and took in the afternoon sun in winter, making it a pleasant place to sit. There was a table with six chairs and Liz had enjoyed a meal out here with Lyndall, Vince, and Melanie a few months ago.

This led to the sliding glass back door. There was a front door but Liz had never seen it used.

Meg was on her way out. 'I wouldn't mind asking some questions, Vince.'

'Thought we'd both do that while Vince shows us the house. You said there was a light that came on for a minute. Any idea which light?'

They stopped inside the door. On a wall were hooks with jackets, hats and the like and below it, a shoe rack and seat. Facing inwards, this area was only a few steps to the kitchen which looked over the dining area and the sunken lounge. On the left was a hallway which Liz assumed led to the laundry.

'I'd say the kitchen. That or the dining room. Both are visible from outside my cottage which is something Melanie showed me one evening.' He smiled briefly. 'We were putting Apple to bed and when we got back to the door she looked up here and saw one light on. Made me take guesses, then she made guesses and then she asked for my phone and called Lyndall to ask.'

'I have got to meet Melanie!' Meg said. 'Sounds like she has a future in analysis.'

'Or art. Lyndall's taught her so much in the last year and Mel has real talent.'

Art was high on Liz's enquiry list.

'Do you know what Lyndall's name was when she was in the art world?' Liz asked.

Vince shook his head. 'None. I know she has a difficult past, but I've only ever known her as Lyndall Smith. She told Mel though.'

'Is there a chance she might remember?'

He was protective of his grandchild and last year, when they'd both been in danger, had resisted letting Liz or anyone talk to the child who'd only just lost her parents. If he still felt that way, then Liz would need to let it go for now.

With a sigh, he nodded. 'She might. The two of them spend so much time together that she might know. But let me ask, once she gets home.'

Relieved, Liz wasn't going to press. 'Cool, thanks.'

Meg was in the kitchen, checking the lights. Flicking one then another on, then off. 'They all work. And as old-fashioned and unlikely as it is to get results, I *will* dust the switches.' She grinned at Vince. 'And those in the dining room.'

Liz stood in the panic room, both in awe of the set up and struggling to understand why it was needed. She'd known Lyndall for a long time – not well, admittedly – and this side of the woman was completely at odds with the persona she showed the world.

What do I know about you?

She'd saved Vince's life. And Melanie's. She loved her

donkeys and the handful of cows currently in the bottom paddock – all rescued from grim futures. She was tough and kind and funny. And knew how to handle a rifle at long range, which very few people did well.

Vince and Meg joined her.

'Didn't she have the rifle box outside the room?' Liz asked Vince.

'Moved it after what happened last year. Few reasons. Melanie being here so much. A fear that her weapon might be taken by the police… not that it would have stopped them if they really wanted. She felt safer moving the lock box in here and I helped her do it.'

The box in question was long enough to hold rifles and was wide open. There was one visible and a couple of boxes of ammunition.

'Thing is,' Vince gestured at the box. 'Inside there's a silent alarm button. It is designed to alert a security company and I'm the first person they would call. Nothing happened so either she didn't get time to press it, or she did, and something went wrong.'

Meg was doing something to the panel by the door. 'So this is how to get in, and really is the only way short of explosives. Although there is a code, biometrics has come a long way and Lyndall would only need to rest her open hand on the screen for half a second to gain access. Much faster than entering a code if she was being pursued but there is also a backup.'

'How so?' Liz asked.

'These things are sensitive so if a hand was forced onto the screen, it won't open. It remembers Lyndall's touch as well as her prints. But if something stopped her using her hand – say, an injury – then there is a code which only Lyndall knows.'

Vince shuffled and all eyes turned to him.

'She wanted me to have a way to open the door,' he said.

'Why?'

He sighed deeply. 'Liz, she wouldn't trust me with the story of her life but gave me the code to access the one room she felt safe in… anyway, she made some joke about locking herself in by accident and forgetting how to get out. When pressed she muttered that if she got herself in there in an emergency but was badly hurt then she'd need help.'

Liz touched his arm. 'We need to talk about her more. Can you give me a moment with Meg?'

Vince nodded and disappeared along the hallway. A moment later there was water running in the kitchen, probably for coffee, which Liz suddenly craved.

'Can you access any of the cameras?' Liz asked.

Meg rolled her eyes.

'I'll rephrase that. When can you give me something to look at?'

'Much better. Go talk with Vince and I'll let you know. And Liz? There's always a trail and leaving this door open has meaning of some kind. Dunno yet whether Lyndall made it inside or opened it and ran but it is important.'

'Wait… do you think she might be hiding somewhere?'

'Just a thought.'

And a good one. We're going to need more bodies up here to help.

Vince was digging around in the fridge. 'Milk? Might be some?'

'Black is fine.'

Liz's phone rang and she stepped away from the kitchen. Before she could answer, a shadow passed one of the windows on the far side of the lounge room. A person-shaped shadow and her first thought was that it was Pete.

But the person ducked beneath the next window so she could only see their hair which was jet black and definitely not Pete's. They had to be hard up against the outside wall of the house and working around it. Her senses went on overload and she shoved the phone, which was still ringing, in a pocket and ran past the kitchen, calling to Vince.

'You and Meg stay inside. Tell her to get Pete back here.'

'Lizzie, what on earth?'

Outside she went to the right of the deck. If the intruder was continuing their direction then she'd run into them. Her hand instinctively reached for a weapon. None. She'd not been through any of the formal training yet and for that matter didn't even know what to call herself when making an arrest. It occurred to Liz she should wait for Pete and she stopped at the first corner.

Get eyes on them. Pete won't be long.

This side of the house was on a slope and there was a small crawl space hidden behind bushes. A man was reaching through the bushes, his head not visible as he crept forward. If he got under there, would she be able to catch him? There might be a number of exit points.

As his shoulders disappeared, Liz flew at him.

Her arms grabbed around his stomach and she used the momentum from running to haul him back. They rolled once, twice, and ended somehow with him on his back on the grass and Liz straddling him. Her hands moved to grip his wrists and force them to the ground.

'Don't move.'

Dark brown eyes blinked a few times. He made no attempt to struggle – if anything his body relaxed – which made her watch closely for signs he'd try to overpower her if she dropped her guard.

'You must be Liz.' The voice had an English accent. Posh English. 'I'm Hamish.'

SIX

Liz couldn't get off the man fast enough.

He lay there, smirking. 'Don't go.'

Meg, followed by Vince, were hurrying toward them.

Please don't have seen that. Please.

But it wouldn't have mattered because Pete was laughing his head off nearby and with his phone in his hand. Liz knew he'd done more than seen her attack a fellow Nobody member. He'd have taken a photo. She turned her back on him. He'd keep.

'*You're* Hamish.'

'At your service.'

Right hand outstretched to shake, the man still looked as if he had no intention of getting up. Liz walked a couple of steps away, pretending she'd not seen his hand as she brushed herself down.

'Why are you on the ground, mate?' Meg stopped where he'd been in the bushes. 'What's that sound?'

'Me laughing.' Pete's phone was away and he wouldn't look at Liz. 'You're just lucky she only flattened you.'

Vince was crawling between the bushes and Meg had a flashlight she'd pulled from the shoulder-bag which rarely left her if she was away from her workstation. She held it out for Pete.

'Now why would I follow Carter under a house? Do you know what's under there? Spiders. Rats. Cobwebs. *Vince.*'

Meg shoved the flashlight at him and he sighed dramatically.

'Shall I look after your phone?' Liz offered.

'Eyes only, Lizzie. Eyes only.'

With that, Pete slipped through the bushes a lot more easily than Vince.

Hamish finally stood and checked he had no grass or debris on his pants.

Meg reached out and flicked a daisy off his shoulder. 'Why are you here?'

'Because Liz and I decided to have a roll in the… grass.'

It wasn't taking long for Liz to form an opinion of the man.

'You don't have a gun yet, do you?' Meg addressed Liz. 'Nor a taser? Taser would've been the appropriate response in whatever situation you found yourself. Or at least, safer for you.'

'Probably is in any situation for some people.' Liz spoke directly to Hamish, her gaze finally back to the steady, controlled one she'd spent years perfecting.

He smiled broadly. Liz turned her attention to what was going on beneath Lyndall's house.

'Vince? What's happening?'

Liz turned on her phone's light and climbed in after them.

Vince was on his way back but Pete was a long way from him, the flashlight moving around. There wasn't room to stand but a person could move about carefully with the columns holding up the house and a maze of plumbing and wiring to contend with. Was Lyndall under here?

'Got… found…' Vince was almost out of breath. He wasn't the fit man he'd been in the force and Liz crawled to meet him. 'Mother cat.' He stopped and gestured at the top of his shirt. Whiskers and then a nose and eyes popped up. 'Must have been terrified and hid down here.'

When Melanie had first come to live with Vince, Lyndall had gifted her a kitten from a young litter. He was now a young adult named Robbie, and if his mother had a name, nobody knew. Lyndall always called her mama or mother cat and she was rarely far from Lyndall.

'Are you okay to get out with her? I'll help Pete.'

Vince didn't answer but started crawling again and as they passed, the cat disappeared again beneath his shirt. So much for Vince always claiming he wasn't a cat person.

Pete was sitting cross legged, his phone held above his face as he took photographs of the underside of the house. 'The panic room is above here. Look at the reinforcement, Liz. It'd take a week with some fancy tools to cut through it all.'

As an estimate, the inside of the panic room was about four by four metres. Down here, solid sheets of steel covered an area about a metre larger than that all around. They were riveted in, then criss-crossed with steel beams, all supported by solid uprights which looked as though they were dug deep into the soil.

'Reckon that above the sheets will be more layers of something difficult to get through. Possibly fire resistant as well although I dunno if the house itself is.' He finished taking photos and looked at Liz with the most serious expression she'd seen in a long time.

'What are you thinking?'

'Why would anyone build their house this way? I understand if you're head of a crime cartel or worth a billion dollars, but that isn't Lyndall. If I hadn't seen her shoot a man dead from a ridiculous distance, I'd think she was just a normal, if eccentric, human.'

'Whatever normal is. But I get your point. And it must have cost a lot to fit out so she was serious about her personal security.'

Pete flashed the light around but there was nothing to indicate recent activity other than the tracks Vince left behind.

'Couldn't believe my eyes seeing you knock that obnoxious twit on his back.'

Great. Now I'm keeping you entertained.

'And had I known he was with us I'd have refrained from doing so.'

'Much more fun that you didn't. Just watch him though. He likes himself too much.'

Liz started back. 'Just delete the damned photos.'

There was no response and she glanced back.

'Okay. If you insist.'

'What have you done?'

He shrugged and began to crawl out. 'Might have accidentally hit send.'

It was just as well Ben Rossi was making coffee when he clicked on Pete's message, the noise of the machine drowning out a chortle he had no chance of controlling.

Poor Liz. What a start to your new job.

He had no such sympathy for the man flat on the ground, arms pinned to either side, as a controlled, dangerous ex-detective with fire in her eyes held him down. Liz was a formidable operator and Hamish would do well to take note.

Of the team, Hamish was the only choice Ben second-guessed.

Not at the beginning. The man had every credential Ben needed for the team and was recommended by someone he trusted. But once Hamish settled in, which took all of a couple of days, he started getting on the nerves of most of the others. Particularly the women. Sooner or later, Ben would have to sort him out or maybe he'd give that job to Liz.

Ben had every intention of making Liz his 2IC once she'd had the chance to actually get a grip on what Nobody was about. He'd not thought through how quickly he needed her on board and fully functioning until today. What a way to join the team. Dealing with Candace's little entry tests, meeting her new team members, then having to go out on a case. She had no weapons yet, not even a proper talk about the reason for Nobody's existence.

I've let her down.

The coffee machine spluttered to a stop and he put the phone away and carried his cup into the main room.

Everyone was huddled around Annette's desk, looking at the photograph Pete had sent.

'I'd make a nice video of this for TikTok if we weren't covert.' Phoebe had a rare grin on her face.

'Don't let Hamish see this or he'll want a copy blown up,' Reuben said. 'He'll be proud of himself getting a woman to sit on him, even if she was planning on arresting him. Dipstick must have made himself look like an intruder.'

'Aw, I think it's kind of sweet.' This was Annette. 'In romance novels that is what's called a meet-cute.'

'Well, he isn't cute and I wouldn't want to meet Liz in a dark alley if I had bad intentions.' Reuben turned and when he saw Ben, rolled his eyes. 'Have you seen it, boss?'

The others dispersed other than Annette, who turned the phone face down on her workstation. Ben ignored it all. In his experience, intelligent adults were generally capable of sorting themselves out and he'd made it clear he had an open-door policy for any issues, no matter how small. He stopped at the central table.

'Updates please.'

Everyone gathered.

Reuben tapped the middle of the table and a full screen appeared. 'Satellite picked up Pete along the lower ridge past Lyndall's property. Should have some clear images of the ground between there and the main road within the hour.'

'Can it see into the bush?' Phoebe asked. 'I mean, if this lady is hiding or… something, could it find her?'

'Be lucky to spot her without having co-ordinates but I'm about to head up there with the drones. As long as that fits with you, Ben?'

'Yes, the minute we're done here. Phoebe?'

'Oh. Me. Okay. I'm working on the famous artist angle.' Her eyes darted around, nervous. 'I have some contacts in the art world… hope it was okay to carefully reach out. Thought I'd do a show on art thefts and scandals from the past and see what might show up in the way of anything unusual. Say, an internationally known artist suddenly dropping out of the limelight.'

The choice of Phoebe might have been a gamble but if this was the way she thought then it was one Ben was glad he'd taken. 'Good thinking, Phoebe. Once you have some plans in place talk to me and we'll go over what suits airing. But I like that approach.'

Her smile was small but she met his eyes for a minute and they showed her relief.

'Annette, I saw the boxes come in. Anything yet… I know I'm expecting a lot quickly.'

'Then it's a good thing I love nothing more than solving mysteries and can find my way around evidence boxes. There's really not a lot of information though and I'm halfway into writing a brief. Should have it done in under an hour. Unless Pete sends more photos.'

There was a ripple of laughter and Ben couldn't help smiling. 'I know it was amusing but whatever happened out there might have embarrassed both officers so let's move on. Okay?' He gazed around until each of them nodded. 'Thanks. And Candace.'

'Any chance I can meet with Vince Carter? One doesn't live next door to someone for what – twenty plus years, without picking up knowledge, even if much of it seems unimportant. Ideally, speaking with Melanie would be perfect but from past conversations with Liz, I feel she is the best person for that job. Maybe I can observe though.'

Candace had been a friend to Ben for years. Theirs was a trust there he shared on this team only with Liz, and Pete, at a pinch. The fact that she'd left her practice – a thriving practice – to join Operation Nobody was a gift.

Ben looked around the table and saw good people. Smart, innovative thinkers who also knew their crafts. Being their head was humbling. Today wasn't supposed to go like this but Liz would manage the best she could and then her training could begin. This new initiative was well underway.

SEVEN

Liz left Pete, Hamish, and Meg to continue their work at Lyndall's house and walked to the cottage with Vince. He still had the cat tucked in his shirt, which was funny when she occasionally meowed or peeked out over the buttons.

'How do I help? I already did a basic sweep of Lyndall's property but maybe the bushland... even up the back of my land.'

'If you can search your property that would help a lot. Just don't put yourself at risk because I know some of the land behind the orchard is pretty rocky.'

'It just feels like nothing's happening.' Vince stopped at a gate in the fence on his side of the driveway, gazing back at Lyndall's house. 'I know McNamara was running around along the ridge and Meg is doing her work but...'

Liz put her hand on his arm. 'Things *are* happening behind the scenes. Ben will get more people up here and if this looks like something too big for us then the regular police will become involved. One of our team is bringing drones right now and from what I've been told, these ones are better than anything even the military has.'

Nodding, Vince opened the gate and gestured for Liz to go

first. Always the gentleman. From the paddock, Apple nickered a welcome.

'She's looking good, Vince.'

'No idea how old she is, but Melanie has given her a new lease on life. Reckon she remembers going on rides with Susie all that time ago.'

Melanie has given you a new lease on life, my friend.

The arrival in his life of his eight-year-old grandchild, after the shocking death of both parents including his beloved Susie, had gradually changed him from a reclusive and bitter man into one who enjoyed his world again. At least more than before.

Once inside the cottage, Vince gently removed the cat from his shirt and she ran off, returning a minute later with Robbie. They chased each other for a minute then disappeared to another room while Vince put his kettle on. Liz went for a wander while it boiled. Last year, the old cottage which had stood here for decades was destroyed by fire and the replacement was not only larger, but well designed with modern touches like solar panels and proper heating. Previously, there'd been a fireplace in the lounge room and nothing else to keep the place warm during the notoriously cold winters.

There were lots of pictures on the walls and a bookcase filled with books, old and new. Colourful cushion were scattered on a comfy-looking sofa and the place felt both loved and lived-in.

Good for you, Vince. And Melanie.

Back in the kitchen, Vince had placed two cups of steaming coffee on the table and was transferring biscuits from a packet to a plate.

'Sit. Drink,' he said.

'Hanging out for coffee.' Liz pulled a chair out. 'Sorry about before. Hadn't meant to take off like that and startle everyone.'

Joining her at the table, Vince grinned. 'Meg and I might not have said anything but we both saw the two of you rolling down the hill with arms and legs flying and you ending up having full control of the situation. And that is one of your new team?'

'Apparently. The only one I didn't meet this morning and now I'm not sure if I've made an enemy or a...' It didn't bear thinking about.

Vince had no such reservations. 'From the way he watched you I reckon it's a matter of time before he wants to go on a date. A real one, without a hill and grass involved.'

'Hamish will be disappointed if he thinks I'm his type.'

He's definitely not mine.

Her old partner was staring at her a little too intently for her liking. He'd been a friend for so long now and was usually respectful of her private life – as she was of his, apart from times like this when someone close to him was at risk.

'You and Lyndall? Still just friends?'

Vince spluttered on a mouthful of coffee he'd just sipped and took a minute to collect some paper towel and pat his shirt dry.

'I am sorry to ask. We have to find Lyndall and surely its better me than Pete?'

'Oh, let's not get started on shithead.'

'Your choice.'

'Don't even try to use your reverse psychology crap on me, Elizabeth. Anyway, Lyndall is what matters so I'll answer the best I can and as far as that question? Yes and no.' Satisfied he'd dried his shirt, Vince scrunched the paper towel in a ball. 'We care for each other. She's a decent human. Loves Melanie. Accepts me. Does good where she can which is a lot more than most people.'

'Some happy marriages are built on far less.' Liz finally drank a mouthful of coffee, enjoying the heavy-handed way Vince made it.

'Not going to get married. Did that once. I won't risk being in the position to bury another wife. Besides, Lyndall would never agree to it. Far too much pain in her past.'

Liz leaned forward a little. 'From what.'

'I don't have details.'

'Then tell me what you do know.'

It took another couple of mouthfuls of coffee before Vince nodded. 'She once said she knew all about people with evil agendas. Understood what it was like to lose loved ones. And having to leave your life behind. That was last year and there's never been another word spoken about her past... well, only around the time of moving the weapons box.'

'Was that when she gave you the code to the room?'

'Yeah. We'd moved the box and secured it. Had someone in to set up the button because it wasn't working.' He frowned, deep lines creasing his forehead. 'Let me think this through... the button was always in the box and when she got her rifle the night she shot the man trying to kill Melanie, she remembers pressing it. But nobody from her security firm arrived and when she queried that, was told it hadn't alerted them.'

'Okay, so someone came and set it up in the panic room. From the security firm?'

He was concentrating on his coffee while he searched memories. Liz knew the look. Vince wasn't a big talker and preferred to get his facts lined up before saying much. She helped herself to a biscuit and nibbled on it.

'All that information will be in her filing cabinet in her study. Lyndall kept receipts and the like. I can describe the man but the name of the firm on his top escapes me, sorry. He was there for half an hour or so, and Lyndall didn't let him out of her sight. Did a test run of her pressing the button which resulted in her getting a phone call from the security firm within seconds.'

Liz's phone dinged a message and she glanced at it. Ben, wanting her to call.

'So that was working. And she gave you the code?'

'My own code, not hers. It bothered her she'd put Melanie in the panic room before coming to help find me. As the only person who had a code, if something happened to her it might have been a long time before we worked out where Mel was... who may have found out how to exit or not. I was her back up plan and a damned poor one I turned out to be.' He pushed himself to his feet and stood at the sink, both hands gripping the edge.

'Hey. That's a load of rubbish and I need you to help me instead of blaming yourself for this.' Liz took her coffee cup over and stood next to him. 'My first thoughts? This is someone from Lyndall's past. A highly trained professional who might have spent weeks or months planning to grab her – assuming she didn't go willingly.'

Vince's head shot around but he kept his mouth closed. They both knew she wouldn't have gone quietly.

Unless it was to protect you and Mel.

'Either way, they only wanted her. Not to have the complications of other people suddenly turning up.'

She'd said too much. His eyes narrowed and Liz was certain he'd be going back over any signs of trespassers or cars parked along the narrow road or anything to indicate surveillance might have gone on. If he thought of anything, that would help, but she didn't want him jumping at shadows either.

'Was there anything else she said? Even the tiniest comment which might make sense now?'

'Let me know think for a while, Liz. I'll write everything down and call you.'

'I'm going to find Lyndall, okay? We will all work to bring her home.'

Liz phoned Ben as she hiked up the driveway. The handful of cows in the front paddock gave her a hopeful look but quickly returned to grazing. Vince would care for them and the donkeys. And mother cat.

'All okay, Liz?' Ben sounded a bit cautious.

'Just going back to Lyndall's house after talking to Vince at his. Sorry I didn't respond sooner. Or answer… either time.'

'I see you met Hamish.'

'I'm going to cause Pete bodily harm, boss. Apologies in advance.'

The laugh at the end of the line assured Liz that Ben was on her side. Not that she'd actually harm Pete… well, not on purpose. Maybe.

'So everyone saw the photo?'

'They did.'

'Hamish looked suspicious. He was climbing under the house and I had no idea who he was, no weapon to back up me simply telling him to stand up, and—'

'And Liz, you are a superstar in the eyes of the team right about now, so stop explaining yourself. Does Vince know anything of value?'

Liz ran through the most important parts of what she'd learned. 'I'm about to go through the house and particularly any paperwork. Shall I bring it all back for Annette?'

'Good idea. Reuben should arrive there shortly. He and Hamish will likely manage the drone search so leave them to it. Just spoke to Pete and he has half a dozen things he's following up on.'

At the top of the driveway, Liz stopped for a moment and gazed back down to the road. Vince was walking along the front fence of his own land. Until Melanie was home in a few hours, he was best to stay busy and checking his own property would reassure him Lyndall hadn't hidden herself somewhere, perhaps hurt. There was no way she wouldn't have come out of hiding otherwise and the thought sent a shiver down Liz's spine.

Maybe I should help him look.

'Candace would like to talk to Vince. And Melanie.'

'Good luck with that. He'll talk to Candace if you tell him to but he has a strong aversion to what he calls shrinks.'

'We'll leave it for the minute then. And Liz?'

She began walking again.

'I wish your first day had been different.'

Me too, boss. Me too.

. . .

'Just letting you know that the next person to walk past the house is one of ours.' Hamish called from the back deck. Nobody other than Meg, Pete, and Liz were allowed inside for now. 'But I'm not worried because Reuben isn't nearly as good-looking or interesting as me and you wouldn't bother jumping his bones.'

Meg was closest and pulled the glass door across to shut him out with a stern, 'Do some work rather than act like a lovesick teenager.'

Liz managed not to laugh at the look of mock outrage, quickly replaced with a pout, on the man's face, but he turned and disappeared off the deck, presumably to meet up with Reuben. She wasn't about to jump anyone's bones and he needed to pull his head in.

She went back to transferring folders and large envelopes from Lyndall's filing cabinet into evidence boxes. Each one she opened and glanced over in the hope of finding some snippet of information about the woman's past. Almost everything were paid bills for the normal day to day running of a house and land. Stock feed. Machinery repairs and purchases. Receipts for donations to several animal sanctuaries. There were files on each of the donkeys as well as a more general one for the cows. Paid vet bills. Insurance. Nothing odd or out of the ordinary.

But in the bottom drawer at the very back was a file labelled 'old receipts'. Expecting it to be exactly those, Liz only gave them a cursory look then suddenly stood and carried the file to the kitchen counter. It was a thick folder holding sealed envelopes, none of which were marked up – at odds with the rest of the filing cabinet contents. What made her take a second look was a partly torn corner of an overfilled yellow envelope which revealed paper exactly like a photograph might be developed on.

Finding a sharp knife, she carefully ran it under the sealed flap to lift it.

They were photographs.

Lots of them in different sizes and across decades.

Liz gently placed them alongside each other. Images of a wedding and babies and children. Many of a smiling young man. Some with a young woman who looked like Lyndall. Houses and holiday snaps and photographs of artwork and galleries and mountains and boats. Many were clearly not taken in Australia with backdrops of European landmarks.

'Meg? When you have minute would you look at these?'

'I'm finished. What did you find?' Meg joined her. 'Oh... these are fantastic. Now I can really go in search of Lyndall.'

There were several images which Liz isolated. 'That's Lyndall for sure. She must have been in her twenties but those eyes are unmistakable. And this one? With the painting... surely that will help. And here.'

Meg nodded. 'This is going to make a difference, Liz. I might head back to base and take them if that's okay because I'll find her story out with these.'

EIGHT

The rocking of the boat woke Lyndall. Keeping her eyelids closed, she listened and used her other senses to take stock. There were hard boards beneath her body, her ankles were tied together and wrists bound in front of herself. She was on her right side, legs bent a bit, head on something marginally softer than the boards but stinking of fish. Covered with a blanket.

She'd been dosed with something. Her mind was foggy.

Marcus. In my house.

More than that. He'd been waiting for her inside her panic room.

If he wanted revenge then surely she'd be dead. This was a planned grab. Luring her out to her donkeys so he could get inside the house. Pity she hadn't stayed outside a bit longer and seen his thugs.

She opened her eyelids a little, and then completely. It wasn't night but she was in shadows. There was a motor humming and once her eyes focussed Lyndall worked out she was in the bottom of a boat. Near the end of her feet was a short flight of steps up. And she was alone.

Shuffling until she could get herself sitting upright, Lyndall looked around. Bare minimum for an overnight stay with a toilet through a door which kept opening and closing with the movement of the boat, a portable stove, and a couple of camping beds. It was probably headed for the scrap heap soon and would go unnoticed in most waters. Everyone looked at fancy yachts but not the shitty old ones.

Where are you taking me?

Last time she'd seen Marcus was more than thirty years back, through the telescopic sights of her rifle. But she'd recognised his voice and then his face. Ageing didn't change the substance of a person – not the kind of person he was. She'd been given the option of leaving with his men and no fuss, or being drugged then and there and carried. Maybe taking the second option would have been better. Made it hard for them. Potentially left someone's DNA behind if she'd managed to draw blood. But what if Vince was disturbed and came to investigate? She hadn't shot a man dead last year to protect Vince only to lose him now because of her terrible past.

She'd gone quietly. Marcus had put her spare phone into his pocket and replaced the rifle he'd helped himself to. She made a pretence of turning back in the doorway which gave her just long enough to prevent the door locking. Somehow it might alert Vince when he realised she wasn't attending to the animals. The earlier he got help, the better the chance she'd be found.

Except I won't be. Not with Marcus in charge.

It occurred to Lyndall this might well be a one-way trip on the boat. He had ample reasons to want her dead, but this wasn't his style. No, he was taking her somewhere quiet.

Footsteps thumped above her head then boots appeared on the steps.

All she had were her wits and knowledge stored from past involvement with him and his overlords. Because of them she'd lost everything and everyone she loved and the worst part was that she'd gone willingly into the fold of dangerous killers.

And now I'm going to find a way to avenge what they did.

NINE

Pete quickly tired of watching Reuben and Hamish debate over who would take on which role with the drones. It was obvious Reuben was the expert and by the time Pete walked away, had finally stepped up with some leadership.

He understood the inclusion of the ex-secret service operative in the team but was less convinced about Hamish. The man was a bit of a pest. A distraction with his stupid comments and as today's run-in with Liz demonstrated, he might not be able to handle himself physically. Yet Ben clearly saw something in him.

Deciding it wasn't a good use of his time to worry about it now, Pete went in search of Vince, who was somewhere on his own property doing a physical search. He had about thirty acres and apart from the flat area around the cottage and pony paddock, the rest was steep, rocky, and dangerous. Not that long ago he wouldn't have cared if the man fell off a cliff, but there'd been a subtle change after he'd saved Vince's life last year. After he and Lyndall saved his life.

And Lyndall is all that matters for now.

He found Vince in the orchard. He stood near a large fruit tree, one hand on the trunk and his eyes closed. This was close to where he'd been attacked by the man who'd killed many times over and had just set fire to Vince's cottage.

'That you, shithead?'

'Just another ghost from your past.'

'What? Haunting me.' Vince turned around. 'That night? I came here to draw that monster away from Melanie and give her a chance to get to Lyndall and safety. And I was done for. No weapons. Not fast enough these days to outrun him.'

Pete had heard this before, but it never got old.

'This orchard was neglected. Susie and I planted it when she was a kid and over the years I barely did a thing up here. She'd come and pick whatever fruit the birds and possums left and turn them into pies and jams and stuff.' Vince smiled to himself. 'Took after her mum in that regard. But that night I was done. Not a breath left in me. Until Susie spoke to me and told me to get going. Swore I could almost touch her then saw a branch sticking out and hung my jacket on it. Picked up a solid bit of wood as a weapon. She saved my life.'

'Lyndall did. I did. And you did, mate. Susie was there to remind you about skills you'd given up on. Yeah?'

'Maybe. I need to find Lyndall.'

'I doubt she's anywhere close by. But we'll search anyway.'

They both looked up as a shadow passed overhead. One of the drones hovered before tipping to one side and speeding away. Reuben letting him know they were active.

'Liz said there'd be drones. Good ones.'

'State of the art,' Pete said. 'Shall we walk?'

Between them they quickly checked the area, which was mostly fruit trees and overlooked the cottage. There was a narrow track leading up to a ridge.

'Susie used to ride Apple up here and all through the bush. Felt safe back then.' Vince was puffing and they hadn't gone far. 'Are those drones good enough to see through the vegetation?'

'They are. The operators are working on a grid with a drone

each and then will cross over and search again. Heat signatures will be the first to show. And movement.'

Vince stopped. 'I'm wasting both our time then.'

'So, who lived here first. You or Lyndall?'

They turned and headed in the direction of the driveway.

'Marion inherited this land from her auntie about the time Susie came along and we liked the idea of living out here. The cottage was already old and Lyndall's property was nothing but paddocks. A couple of years later the boundary fences went up almost overnight and there were diggers and noise and months of building. Once the house was done it sat empty for weeks and then Lyndall moved in with no fanfare. Doubt she'd have even come to say hello but Marion went up there with a lasagne and her friendly soul and they became friends.'

'Do you think Marion knew anything about Lyndall's past?'

'If she did, it was their secret.'

Marion had passed away many years ago, leaving Vince to raise their young daughter alone. And now he was repeating history with Susie's child. It was a sad history.

They were at the driveway. Vince gazed at the big house up on the hill. From here, nothing looked out of place.

'What now, McNamara?'

'Meg headed back to headquarters following a line of enquiry. Liz is finishing at the house and then we'll go back for another briefing. The two drone operators will stay as long as they need but Ben is sending private security up to keep the house protected. And he'll let them know you have right of access to feed the livestock and the like but maybe stay out of the house.'

'Just get her home.'

Alone in the house for the first time, Liz turned her attention to the things which might be overlooked during a preliminary investigation. Little touches a person gave to their home could reveal a lot about them. Including the artwork.

There was no studio and no sign of an easel and paints and brushes. So did Lyndall still paint?

Liz had seen many drawings done by Lyndall with Melanie, who often insisted they took turns with the same piece of paper. Cats, donkeys, cows, trees, flowers… even Vince. Mel had always loved drawing and her sketch pad was one of the few things which comforted her after losing her parents. Under Lyndall's guidance, the little girl was becoming more confident and structured with her sketches, while keeping the touch of wonder only a young child brings to art.

Liz started with the living areas and noted the lack of photographs. No family portraits or school photos. Nothing from a wedding or anniversary. Whatever ones Lyndall had were in the envelope in the folder Liz located.

What happened to your family?

There were a lot of paintings. In the sunken lounge room – which only had one wall, the rest being windows on the other sides of a walkway, and the space between it and the kitchen – there were three. All were different styles being a watercolour of the sea, an oil landscape, and a charcoal of a donkey. That one had to be Lyndall's work. But there was no obvious artist name on any.

The dining room and large sunroom were much the same. Three framed pieces of art in each and a similar mix to the lounge room and each charcoal either an animal or a recognisable part of the grounds.

Liz ventured into the bedrooms. Meg had been given the task of looking for evidence which she could use and unlike most searches Liz had attended in the police force, had left each room as she'd found it. Two bedrooms were made up for guests. Two were empty aside from a comfy chair and coffee table which were situated so someone using them could see the pretty views outside. And then there was Lyndall's.

Because this was a woman she knew was intensely private and proud, Liz hesitated at the door. But Lyndall had been forcibly taken from her secure home. Of this Liz had no doubt. Had she had a chance to leave any clues to her abductor? The fact the panic room was unlocked might be one and once back in the city, something to consider during the next briefing. For now she had to treat this like a crime scene rather than the intimate space of a woman who kept deep secrets.

The bedroom was around twice the size of the others with a large ensuite and walk-in-robe. In the latter were clothes which surprised Liz. Several evening dresses, even one with sequins, all in clear plastic clothes bags. A black dress was right at the end, again in plastic and accompanied by black shoes and a black hat with a veil. Mourning attire. Then a series of suits, pencil skirts, pants, and matching jackets in a range of subdued colours. If Liz didn't know better, she'd believe Lyndall was an executive of some kind or at the least, associated with one. Maybe Liz was assuming too much. What if Lyndall had had a whole different life before, or aside, from her art?

Lyndall's bed was king sized. There was no bedhead but on the wall was a huge oil painting. In fact there were three oil paintings in the room, each on a different wall, and Liz wondered if they were telling a story.

'Lizzie? I'm ready to head back.'

It sounded as though Pete was in the kitchen area.

'Two minutes. I'll meet you outside.'

After taking a series of photographs, Liz left the bedroom.

The panic room door was ajar by about fifteen centimetres and approaching from the bedroom, the door jam and door edge highlighted a long, narrow rectangle which framed a wall inside. It was the only part of the wall which wasn't filled with monitors or other devices.

Why it mattered, Liz had no idea, but she took several photos of what she could see from the hallway, then went into the panic room and took more. A close look at the wall showed nothing unusual and eventually she shook her head at herself. There'd been no signs of a struggle, nothing to indicate anyone was even in the room other than Lyndall unlocking it but being stopped before she could get inside. Liz was getting desperate for clues and it was pointless wasting time where none existed.

Before returning to the vehicle, Liz and Pete walked to the far side of the property where he'd found the tracks.

It was quiet up here other than the distant low hum of drones and occasional mooing of cattle. The air was clear with no breeze and not a cloud in the sky and from this vantage point, the view extended across Lyndall's paddocks to the road and then to the distant ridge on the opposite side.

'Do you think someone was over there watching her movements?' Liz pointed.

'There's a few places I've highlighted on the map app and that's one of them. Also the top of the hill behind Vince's orchard is a good spot and one which would be relatively safe for long-term surveillance. The drones are looking for potential hidey-holes as well as everything else.'

The tracks were deep enough to get decent tyre marks from, as were a couple of the footprints. Pete had taped around the gate and the tracks closest to it with poles and plastic ribbon. Instead of the police tape she was expecting, this read *DANGER STAY BACK* while being in the same blue and white.

'Not police tape,' she said.

Pete shot her a look. 'We are but we're not.'

'Well thanks. That makes perfect sense.'

Liz began to walk back and Pete caught up.

'Shitty day to start work, hey? No debriefing. No weapon. No vehicle training. But I did make you a decent cup of coffee.'

'You did.'

'And I'll make you another. Actually, we missed lunch and afternoon tea is overdue.'

'I don't need you making me afternoon tea, Pete.'

'Nah. We'll stop at Maccas.'

That made her laugh.

Reuben waved from the back of the house.

'Look, Liz? You need to talk to Ben to get an overview of how this unit works because I don't know about your contract, but mine went easy on some details while making me promise life-long servitude of any future grandkids if I broke confidential clauses. Thing is that I knew the basic structure before I agreed to come on board, and it is sound.'

Whereas I was too burned out and drifting after the crap my father pulled to really care.

'I'm here because I trust Ben and I trust you. And don't ever throw that last bit back at me,' she said.

He kept his mouth shut but was still grinning when they met up with Reuben.

'Security detail arrived. I've set them up and am going back to the drones.'

'Anything of interest yet?' Liz asked, already expecting a no.

'No sign of movement other than kangaroos and deer moving around. Same with heat signals. Might have located a couple of spots recently used for camping so once we're finished with the aerials, we'll go take a look.'

Liz and Pete left him to rejoin Hamish. After checking again that the house was locked, Liz took the keys to the vehicle. 'Got to drive it sooner or later.'

'Fine. I'll show you where the lights and sirens are.'

TEN

Liz finally had a few minutes to settle at her workstation and call Vince to arrange a time to see Melanie.

'I'd forgotten she has a dance class after school today. I pick her up at five but quite honestly, I don't know what to say to her.'

'About Lyndall?'

Poor kid. First her parents gone and now Lyndall missing.

'I don't want her afraid.'

'What if I meet you back at the cottage and bring a friend of mine? She's part of this team and is a psychologist and profiler. Very kind and gentle.'

'Dunno. Mel has a shrink she still sees sometimes.'

'Candace wouldn't be acting in an official capacity though. She has a way of asking questions which doesn't feel invasive or scary. Completely your call Vince, and if you prefer to handle this alone, just say so.'

He took a while to reply and Liz's eyes wandered around the room. There were changes since she'd arrived this morning. Rather than whiteboards, there were clear boards on wheels; two of them. One was behind Meg who periodically jumped up and added something to it. The other was in a space near the table. A table which had magically transformed into some kind of futuristic computer.

'Is six too late?'

'Not at all. Just me?'

'Bring your friend.'

That was good. Not that any of this was good, but Vince accepting help was something he was working on.

'Anything from the drones? Been hearing them non-stop.'

'All I know is they've identified a couple of spots which might have been used to watch from. So if you see anyone hiking up behind your place, please don't shoot them.'

Vince laughed. 'As long as it isn't shithead, they're safe. Anyway, no guns on my property.'

'See you later.'

Liz stood and turned, almost straight into Annette who was standing only a metre or so behind her chair. How had she not noticed her?

'Oh sorry, Liz! Just came over to see if you want a coffee.'

'In a bit, thanks. Just need a word with Candace.'

Candace looked up with a small smile as Liz approached. 'Would you like a coffee?'

I must be looking tired.

'Yes, but I came to ask if you'd come with me to Vince Carter's home at six. His granddaughter doesn't know about Lyndall's disappearance yet and he agrees that having you there might help.'

'Of course.'

'Liz? Got time for a quick chat?' Ben strode past, toward his office.

'Raincheck on the coffee?'

'Any time.'

Ben's office reminded her he used to run Missing Persons. Its walls were predominantly glass and he'd taped a photograph of Lyndall to it. Alongside were comments written in marker and notes, again taped up.

'Where did you get the photo?'

Lyndall stood with a donkey, her arm waving – but as if telling the photographer to go away. Not in a cross way but there was a touch of worry on her face.

'Did Melanie take this?'

'She did. Vince found it on his phone. Meg has a copy and is running a face recognition program. So far it is the only one we have of her in recent years, although Meg thinks she can use some of the ones you found in the filing cabinet.' He gestured for Liz to sit. 'We need a few minutes without interruption. Let's give it a go.'

'Boss?'

Both of them looked up as Annette stuck her head in.

'Sorry. Is it okay if I duck out for half an hour? I've got to sort something out for my kid, because I can see us being here late.'

'Go. Just let one of us know if you need longer so we can work out timing on briefs and the like.'

The minute Annette left, Ben leaned forward, his arms on the desk. 'Take two. Are you going back to Vince's?'

'Yes. With Candace.'

'Excellent. On the way, get her to talk you through the day to day running of the unit. Ask her anything and she'll say if she doesn't know. Once you are back, I want you speed-training with each member of the team. Reuben will need a bit more time than anyone else with you to cover the weapons, but by the end of today you'll have yours and know the routine.'

Thank goodness.

'If Meg gets a chance she can teach you how to use the app but otherwise Hamish will. And don't screw your face up. I know you had a less-than-ideal introduction, but he's as much a professional as you.'

'Why can't you do it?'

Ben leaned back, his expression serious. 'Time for me to speak with our bosses.'

'Who are?'

He half-smiled but said nothing.

Liz stared until his smile faded. She'd had enough of everyone keeping secrets.

'I'm on the back foot and I hate the feeling. I work at my best when I have good information but right now I'm investigating a potential abduction without the slightest clue of what I can and can't do.' She glanced at the main room but nobody was paying attention. 'My contract led me to believe I was accepting a job in law enforcement. I'm not qualified to be a private detective and I resigned as a member of the Victoria Police. So what exactly have I got myself into, Ben?'

'You're right and I'm sorry for making light of this, particularly with my plans for you in the future. Operation Nobody is privately funded but is overseen by a small committee in the police force. That's why I was able to make the decision to keep Lyndall's disappearance in-house for the moment.'

What plans for me in the future?

'Nothing has changed regarding being able to arrest a person, or procedures should anyone need to fire a weapon. There are still processes to follow and laws to obey but we are autonomous regarding choice of cases to investigate and have powers outside usual channels. Our team is one of two being trialled in different parts of Victoria.' Ben shook his head. 'This should have been our first conversation, even before you signed the contract and should you feel this isn't a good fit then I'll have you released from it.'

'But not everyone here is a police officer.'

'True. Some are employed as consultants – such as with Candace – or specialists. They still have to comply with the law and have been through appropriate training.'

'You said this is privately funded. Am I allowed to know who is behind it?'

With a lift of one eyebrow, Ben leaned forward. 'Are you leaving or staying?'

Liz might have responded that it depended upon his answer,

but she didn't play games. When he'd originally offered her a job in a new, dynamic, and covert squad she'd had little hesitation accepting because she trusted him and she still did.

'I'm staying.'

If it was relief which flashed into his eyes, Ben's voice didn't reflect it as he continued with the same firm tone. 'The funding is from the estate of a long-deceased police inspector. His parents, who were obscenely wealthy, were murdered in their home when he was in the force and even his position couldn't help him find the killers. He vowed to solve the crime but was forced to retire when his obsession ruffled too many feathers. Before he could do more than begin his search, he was diagnosed with untreatable cancer so created a trust.'

'I think I know who you're speaking about. Vince Carter would have served at the same time, I imagine.'

'Most likely. This has taken far too long to implement since his death but he had several distant relatives contest the will. Last year it was resolved and we've finally been able to get Nobody up and running.'

This was reassuring. Liz's mind had gone as far as wondering if there was political motivation behind the team, and it made sense that a wealthy benefactor with vision beyond his career would create such a trust.

'Still unsolved, his parents' murders. Is this something we're going to investigate?'

'It is. I wanted to take it out of cold cases when I headed up Missing Persons but there were some objections from on-high and that on its own means we need to find the killer. Killers, most likely. It might get nasty.'

Liz finally smiled. 'I think you have the perfect crew to stand up to anything a higher-up wants to hide. Cold cases matter. But Lyndall comes first.'

'She does.' Ben looked over her shoulder to the main room. 'Good. Looks like Meg is getting everyone around the table.'

. . .

"Everyone" was an overstatement. Annette was out and Hamish and Reuben were still mapping the region around Lyndall's property. Meg was at her workstation but paying attention to the conversation as she wrote notes on her board.

Liz started with a short overview of her findings and conversations with Vince.

'Just to get this straight for me, Vince Carter has known Lyndall for close to thirty years but has no actual information about her.' Phoebe gazed intently at Liz, her face serious. 'Only her name, that she is a crack shot and rescues animals, has a panic room, and lost some family members.'

'Perhaps that is all which appears relevant. On the surface.'

Pete butted in. 'See, Phoebe, you haven't met Carter. Keeps to himself. Wants other people to do the same. Mind you, he wasn't always like that, not back when he was in the force and liked to investigate perfectly good officers for no reason.'

If Pete had been closer, Liz would have kicked him under the table. Despite the apparent truce between the men, Pete obviously still had work to do getting over Vince's complaint against him years ago. It had amounted to nothing but bad blood for far too long.

'Point being,' Pete continued, keeping half an eye on Liz as though expecting her to reach over and smack the back of his head, 'Vince would have respected Lyndall's privacy.'

Phoebe didn't look convinced.

'Candace, has Annette provided you with anything of use?' Ben glanced at his watch.

'She sent you a brief and gave me a copy. Meg has also assisted with some background. Crux of it being that Lyndall Smith came into existence around twenty-eight years ago. There's nothing before then, not yet anyway. Her property was purchased outright. She hasn't worked in all those years… actually, she may have but there's no paper trail. No tax history. No Medicare card. She does have a driver's license. She also has insurance. And only one bank account found to date but access not yet obtained.'

'Have you formed any opinions?'

'Nothing worth mentioning. But Ben, what I will say is this isn't outside the realms of witness protection. A simple, low-key life. Lots of security measures. A house where she can see potential danger from a distance. And clearly, an identity change.'

Meg joined them. 'I've got everything I can think of, and can access. Running searches now. Facial recognition may be key to this but don't expect a result for hours, if days. Lyndall was fingerprinted after her rifle was taken into custody last year and they have vanished.' She raised an eyebrow.

Everyone's eyes were on her.

'Annette is going to follow that up once she's back but how do fingerprints disappear from a file, let alone a database?' Meg looked as if she had some suspicions. 'Ben, this might be something you need to weigh in on if I can't locate them using my methods.'

Ben looked deadly serious. 'There are processes to protect that kind of data. The rifle was returned and she was never charged with anything, but the prints should have stayed on her file. What else did you get from the house?'

Meg stretched. 'We all know I'm a forensic analyst, but today I took prints from a few key spots where it was most likely the thugs would have touched. But don't hold out any hope because they'd have worn gloves. At present I'm working through the folder Liz found. For those who don't know, it was in the filing cabinet at the house and contains a lot of old photographs as well as a whole lot of notebooks, letters, and the like. They'll keep me busy for a while, and Annette once she has some time.'

'Good, that's promising. Get help from the rest of the team as you need it. Phoebe?'

'Me? Oh, okay. I've written an outline of the potential podcast and just waiting for a trusted contact to fill in some blanks. They are more art world than me and will fix any terminology and stuff. That'll be back soon so I'll send you the revised outline.'

'I have a meeting,' Ben said. 'You're doing great. All of you. While I'm gone would you each spend time with Liz to bring her up to speed with the app and protocols and the like. And once Reuben is back he can cover weapons.'

The team dispersed and Ben was gone in a minute. Liz gazed around. The others were back at their workstations. Everyone here was calm and focused.

'So, who is going to babysit me first?' She asked the room.

ELEVEN

The minute Liz parked outside Vince's cottage, the front door burst open and Melanie ran out.

She stopped at the top of the steps when she saw Candace climb out of the passenger's side, suddenly shy.

Liz came around and together they walked to the steps, stopping at the bottom.

'Hi Melanie.'

'Hello, Liz.'

Melanie stretched out her right arm toward Candace with a solemn, 'My name is Melanie Weaver. Welcome to our home.'

Just as solemnly, Candace shook the small hand. 'Very nice to meet you. My name is Candace Carroll.'

Vince appeared in the doorway behind Melanie. He looked shocking. His face was worn and sad and his shoulders slumped. He leaned against the door frame and closed his eyes briefly. Liz's heart went out to him and when his eyes opened, they met hers and he sighed.

'Would you like to come inside?' Melanie was still being formal but her bottom lip quivered as she took back her hand and her eyes shot to Liz. 'You *have* to find Lyndall.' And then her brave face crumbled and she held out her arms. Liz hurried up the steps and picked her up, holding the child close while she sobbed. Vince had stepped forward but stopped to cover his own eyes with his hands.

In an instant, Candace was at his side. 'How about I make some tea? Are you a tea drinker?' She gently touched his arm. 'I'm Candace.'

He didn't speak and Liz, still carrying Melanie, walked straight past.

'Come on, Candace is right. Tea is a brilliant idea and I'd love a cup. And Melanie is going to help make it. Aren't you, love?' The last bit was whispered to Melanie, who sniffed and made what might have been a nodding action. 'Good stuff.'

She kept walking through the house to the kitchen, leaving Candace and Vince at the front. Two distressed people in the same headspace at the same time wasn't going to help anyone. 'Can I pop you down?' Another small nod. Liz lowered her and then turned on the kitchen light. 'Tissues? Or would you like to go and splash some water on your face?'

'I will go and carefully wash my face. Without splashing.'

Good girl.

As soon as Melanie left, Liz drew in a deep breath. Then, she began the process of making tea, working out where everything was kept by a process of logic and elimination. This new kitchen was lovely and much easier to navigate than its predecessor and she had the kettle boiling and a teapot ready before Melanie returned.

'I don't drink tea.'

'Ah, but you do drink hot chocolate and I found a cute mug which I think might belong to you?' Liz held up the thick mug with a kitten on the side. 'Looks a bit like Robbie used to.'

'He likes having his mummy visit. They're asleep in my bedroom. Why did a bad man take Lyndall?'

What on earth did Vince tell you?

'Did you know I'm in a special new team and all of us are looking for her? Every one of us and that includes Pete.'

'I like Pete.'

'He likes you too, Melly.' This was Vince, who came in with Candace behind him. His face was calmer. 'And Doctor Carroll is looking as well.'

'Please call me Candace. And if it's okay with you, Melanie, I'd love to see some of your artwork. Liz tells me you are talented and work hard at your drawings. Would that be okay?'

After a quick glance at Vince – who nodded – Melanie dashed out of the kitchen, calling over her shoulder, 'this way.'

Candace disappeared down the hallway.

Liz finished making the tea and hot chocolate and Vince found a tray for them and the tea cups.

'I had to tell her, Liz. As soon as we drove in she saw the drones and started asking questions and I won't lie to her. She was so brave about it and not a tear until out the front just then. Is there any news?'

'Not yet but there is so much going on. This team is smart and functional and everyone knows their role. The drones are down. We got a call a few minutes before arriving to say Reuben and Hamish are now doing a search on foot of a couple of spots identified as possible hidey-holes. They should be a couple of hours at most. The security patrol will rotate later tonight, so you might hear cars moving about.'

Looking like he was going to say something about not hearing Lyndall during the night... again, Vince snapped his mouth shut and picked up the tray.

Melanie and Candace sat on the floor of the living room with several sketchpads open. They both looked up with smiles as Vince set the tray down and he and Liz took seats. She poured tea, knowing already how Vince and Candace liked theirs. 'Mel? There's hot chocolate but it's pretty warm right now.'

'Thanks.' She was more intent on finding a particular page. 'Oh, here it is. Lyndall helped me a lot with this but I like it. See the pony? That's Apple.' Melanie pushed the sketchpad into Candace's hands.

'Apple is lovely. And what's really special is how you've made her eyes so soft and loving. Is she your pony?'

'Kinda. Well, she was my mummy's pony.' Melanie's eyes flickered toward Vince.

He leaned forward to pick up his tea. 'And now she's yours. Except I believe it is more accurate to say that *you* belong to *her*.'

'I love her.'

Liz remembered how terrified Melanie had been of the gentle pony at first. It took time and patience, but these days Mel did everything for the four-legged old lady who'd been part of the family for more than twenty years. Love and time fixed many ills.

'Did you always like drawing?' Candace asked.

'Oh yes! Mum and Dad let me do special art classes before… and now Lyndall is my teacher. She wants me to start learning about oil painting soon. Why aren't you and Liz looking for her right now?'

Vince went to speak and Liz quickly touched his arm to stop him. His emotions were too volatile and Candace was quite capable of formulating an answer. He kind of huffed beneath his breath but sat back and took a sip from his cup.

'There's lots of ways to search. You saw the drones flying around up the hill?'

Melanie nodded, her full attention on Candace.

'Reuben and Hamish are taking special images of the ground looking for clues about which way she went and once they have all the information, then Meg will run it through her special computer program. That is one way we are looking for her. Another is having conversations with people who know Lyndall. And it seems that you and Grandad know her best of all.'

'Do you think talking to me will help?' After picking up a different sketchpad, Melanie found another drawing. 'Lyndall did this one.'

Candace shot a look at Liz and took the offered sketchpad. 'Do you know who the people are?' She handed it to Liz.

It was a simple sketch of three people. Lyndall was one and she stood on a raft in the sea watching a man and a boy of about ten climbing a staircase which came out of the water. Both were looking back at her with their hands raised… a goodbye. It was haunting and when Liz noticed a tiny open gate at the top of the stairs she almost dropped the sketchpad. Tears filled her eyes and she blinked hard.

'Lyndall is watching her little boy and husband go to heaven.'

Vince drew in an audible breath and reached out to take the sketchpad.

Candace's voice was thick with emotion. 'What else can you tell me about the drawing, Mel?'

'She never said what happened. Only that there was an accident in a boat. Her son was called John-Paul and her husband was Alan. It happened a very long time ago but Lyndall still misses them terribly. And I miss her.' The last words were more of a sob.

Candace took Melanie's hands in hers and leaned closer, her gaze steady and reassuring. 'Of course you miss her. Knowing the names of her family is very helpful. You see, we think Lyndall used to have a different name and then she changed it.'

'It was a short name but I can't remember. She only told me once and said it was when she was an artist and used to have her paintings in the galleries in Europe.' Melanie's face was serious and screwed up in concentration. 'Have you been to visit the cemetery?'

'Melly? Do you mean the cemetery where your Mum and Dad and Gran are?' Vince asked.

She nodded.

'Is that where Lyndall's family are?' Candace's voice was encouraging. 'Have you visited them with Lyndall?'

'She doesn't like going there. But she did once.' Melanie looked at Vince. 'Remember? When you couldn't drive after the fire?'

'You have such a good memory, Mel. Yes, Lyndall drove us to the cemetery and she went for a walk while we visited with our family. But I remember seeing her with flowers so perhaps that is where her son and husband rest.'

Liz took the sketchpad back from Vince. 'Melanie, is it okay if we borrow this for a bit? Say if it isn't because I can take a photo. It just might help with more clues.'

'I don't mind. I'm going to go and see Robbie and mother cat.'

She was on her feet and out of the door in seconds.

Candace groaned as she got to her feet and stretched, and that made Vince grin in sympathy.

'This really helps,' Liz said. She closed the sketchpad. 'Vince, any recollection of where Lyndall was in the cemetery?'

'I wish. Only vaguely recall seeing her in the distance. Mel and I were at Marion's grave and Lyndall was in the direction of river, if that helps at all. Can't believe I don't know all of this but Mel does.'

'Sometimes talking to a child is easier than a peer, no matter how close.' Candace nodded toward the sketchpad. 'Powerful stuff, that sketch. I feel it will help.'

The desire to weep over a drawing was back and Liz quickly finished her tea. She had enough of her own sad past to take on someone else's. Not emotionally, anyway. But it was hard to ignore Lyndall's imagery of her loved ones saying goodbye on their way to heaven. Something told her their deaths were no accident and that raised the question of who was behind the tragedy and whether they were the ones who'd taken Lyndall.

Liz pulled up on the side of the road when she saw Reuben and Hamish driving down Lyndall's driveway, and all four climbed out to swap information.

'Not enough light to do a decent search,' Hamish said. 'We'll come back at dawn if we've not recovered the target earlier.'

'Lyndall. You mean Lyndall,' Liz said.

'I don't know her.' He shrugged. 'For now I want to talk to Meg about some of the footage we've sent her.'

'What about you two?' Reuben asked.

'Candace needs to get back and start building the profile, then I'll visit a cemetery thanks to a possible clue to Lyndall's past.'

'I'll come with you. Hamish can take Candace back.'

'Bossy,' Hamish said. 'But I prefer her company to yours any day.'

Although Candace gave Liz a look which made it clear she didn't feel the same about Hamish, she grabbed her bag from the car and swapped places with Reuben.

As they followed the other vehicle toward Melbourne, Reuben began going through the weapons training with Liz, skilfully describing what was in an armoury she was yet to visit and how a vehicle might be set up for different situations.

'Ben said you've done advanced training and can handle a range of weapons and have a decent martial arts background.'

Reuben was watching her as she drove. He'd not suggested he take the wheel and was relaxed in his seat. Unlike Hamish, this was a man who had a genuine confidence in himself and didn't put on a show. It made him far more interesting to be around.

'I've done a bit over the years. And I like kick boxing.'

'Me too. I run a lot.'

Liz grinned. 'Best form of stress management.'

'Almost the best.'

The cemetery entrance was closed so Liz parked along the street. After locking the vehicle, they let themselves through a narrow gate and Liz took a minute to work out the direction to start looking.

'Let's find Marion's grave. Vince's wife.'

Her resting place was almost on the furthest side of the sprawling cemetery.

'Last time I was in a cemetery after hours, someone filmed me and spread some interesting lies.'

Reuben chuckled. 'I saw that. Good old Teresa Scarcella loves nothing more than a scandal and if she can't find one, she'll engineer something. So why were you in Keilor Cemetery in the dead of night. No pun intended.'

'As it turns out I was wasting my time,' Liz said. She gestured for them to take a path. 'I thought I was visiting my father's grave. I'd just found out he was dead and was compelled to check for myself that a grave existed. And while it did, turns out a completely different man was buried in his place.'

There wasn't a response and Liz looked at Reuben.

'You knew that?'

'Oh, not why you were at the cemetery, but about Kyle Moorland, yes. I've read a lot about him and his history as part of getting an understanding of how we go about finding him. Ben is determined to catch him.'

For the first time in a long time, Liz had a sense of support around her. Leaving her beloved job in Homicide was hard and she'd second-guessed herself every day since then. But now there was a glimmer that her decision was a good one. She stopped near a grave with a simple headstone.

'This is Marion Carter's resting place.' She'd lowered her voice without meaning to. 'Vince remembers seeing Lyndall in that direction, so shall we start?'

TWELVE

Ben was back in his office and feeling pressure to get quick results. His meeting resulted in a veiled threat to take the case away and give to regular channels and only the personal connections to Lyndall guaranteed the team another twenty-four hours to make considerable progress.

What the heck is considerable progress?

Finding Lyndall was the goal. Alive. Unharmed.

With every hour which passed, the chance of that outcome reduced unless whoever had her wanted something which required proof of life. And not knowing much about the woman's history made it nigh on impossible to guess what. A money-motivated snatch seemed pointless with nobody close enough to Lyndall to fulfil a ransom demand. Surely Vince Carter wouldn't count and he was hardly in the position to pay a kidnapper.

Annette was back at her workstation. Everyone was busy. Hamish and Candace arrived together with the latter immediately going into the second room and closing the door, after making sure there was a wheeled board in there to use.

Meg waved and he stood, just as his phone rang. He nodded to acknowledge her and answered.

'Hey, sweetheart.'

Ellie's voice was welcome. 'Bad time?'

'Just super busy. Dealing with the abduction of someone known to the team.'

'Oh, that's horrible. Call me when you want. I'm taking Michael out for dinner.'

Michael was Ellie's older brother, sadly brain damaged from a tragic event but doing well since moving in with her and Ben.

'Sounds nice. Where?'

'Trying the new Greek place. Good to know what other restaurants have on offer and I like supporting local.'

Ellie had a thriving small restaurant of her own in the seaside town they called home.

'Have fun and tell Michael he has to try one of everything. Call me later?'

'You bet. Love you.'

'Love you too.'

He took a moment after the call finished. Missing Ellie was a constant, and Michael, who'd been his best friend before their worlds changed more than a decade ago. Ben had walked away from a glittering future in Victoria Police to be with them and never looked back. Not until this role came up. He went to see what Meg needed.

'Okay, so some progress, boss.' She swung her chair to look up at him. 'Lyndall has plenty of money in her account. Enough to live off the interest. She owns the property outright and has no debts I can find. Not that she's rich-rich. But very comfortable.'

'Any deposits into the account?'

'Very few. Annette is still going through her statements.'

'What else?'

'Liz messaged earlier with the names Alan and John-Paul as possibly being Lyndall's deceased family and Candace has sent me a photo from her phone. She has the original with her and

I'm not going to interrupt her voodoo to ask questions but take a look.' Meg turned back to her screens and tapped a key.

A sketch appeared. Three people. One on a raft in the sea. Two going up a staircase. He leaned closer.

'Are those gates?'

'Pretty sure they are pearly gates.' Meg zoomed in.

The detail was extraordinary, with ornate swirls and imagery on both of the gates. Behind, and barely visible, a hand was outstretched.

'Good grief. Just had a shiver down my spine.' Ben straightened. 'Do you think she's religious?'

'No idea. But this is a profound work of art. Deeply personal.'

'Wait… have you and Candace swapped bodies?'

'I'd love her insight into people. Thing is, the quality of the drawing is exceptional and will help identify her as an artist. And another thing. We can search for a double death in or around the water. A father and son. Presumably.'

'What do you need from me?'

She grinned, both eyebrows raised. 'Not a thing. Only asked you over to admire my handiwork.'

'Duly admired. Do you have the drone data?'

'Yes, but Hamish is capable of analysing it. Once he's created a proper grid then I can take a look. And Reuben can help when he and Liz return. Are we working through? I mean, I will but what about Annette and some of the others?'

Ben checked the time. It was after seven.

'Where's Pete?'

'Making himself useful by grabbing pizzas. He'll be back in twenty or so.'

'Good thinking. We might let everyone eat, have another brief, and set up shifts. Just a couple of us to keep working because I want people fresh for an early start. But Meg?'

'Boss?'

'What kind of pizza is he getting?'

. . .

Cemeteries were one of Liz's least favourite places. Some people found them comforting, but she was always overwhelmed with sorrow. Her own mum had died far too young and losing her profoundly affected Liz at the time. And then being stalked and videotaped at the grave allegedly belonging to her long-estranged father, and that video ending up on a late-night news show, left Liz wishing she never had to visit one again.

Yet here she was.

She'd spent a moment paying her respects to Marion before doing the same a little further along with Vince's daughter and son-in-law; Melanie's parents, Susie and David. She'd known all of them.

'Any idea what I'm looking for?'

Reuben had patiently waited for her at a discreet distance.

'I doubt Lyndall's real surname is Smith, but there's no harm looking for it. We believe her husband and son died at the same time. Melanie remembers their names as Alan and John-Paul. It may have been between twenty-eight and say thirty-two years ago but make some allowances. The son was only a child.'

'Crap. Poor woman.'

'Yeah.'

Before sadness could stop Liz from functioning, she gestured to one row. 'Do you want to start there? Vince and Melanie have a recollection of Lyndall being in this direction but a fair distance from Marion's grave.'

He glanced back, then in the direction she'd indicated. 'Let's stay in sight of each other.'

'Afraid of ghouls?'

'Afraid of getting lost in here.'

'Then let's both work on one row at a time, just on opposite sides.'

Do you think I'm scared and want to protect me?

Reuben had the air of someone who was used to being in

charge and being ready to step up at a second's notice. He'd not seen the incident with Hamish nor commented on it... not to Liz's knowledge, but should know she was able to handle herself.

Her phone beeped a message from Pete.

Pizza in half an hour. We need a catch up.

Hopefully we'll make it back in time to eat.

Phone back in her pocket, Liz followed Reuben's example of walking slowly along the 'feet' of the graves on one side of the path, checking the headstones for information, and moving on. She focused on finding male names, deceased around the three decades ago and trying to blur out the rest of the information. With evening falling she needed to concentrate because she'd rather find them tonight than have to return.

Reuben was ahead of her. He worked with precision, pausing at each grave, his lips moving in silence as he read the inscription on the headstone, then moving to the next.

This row yielded no results and they moved to the next which was parallel. Now they were heading back toward Marion's grave. After only three, Liz stopped and properly read a small headstone. The dates fitted.

Alain Dubois.

'Reuben?'

He joined her in seconds.

'Alain... close enough to Alan. No date of birth, just death. Seventh of March 1995.'

They moved to the next grave and again, Reuben read the headstone, which was the same size as the other.

'Jean-Paul Dubois. Seventh of March 1995. Our world.'

The lump in Liz's throat refused to budge and there was no chance of a coherent sentence leaving her mouth. Instead, she took several photographs, first of the child's grave, then the father's. Doing something helped but she was keenly aware of Reuben's eyes on her. When she finally looked at him, he offered a smile. A genuine, warm smile of shared understanding and she wasn't certain if it helped or made the emotions rise again.

'The flowers on the child's grave are quite fresh,' he commented. 'I know this is awful but I'd like to take them back with us. I doubt they've been there for more than a few hours.'

So observant.

'Of course.'

He removed gloves from a pocket and after slipping them on, carefully collected the flowers.

'They do look fresh. If Lyndall was taken during the night then she must have laid these yesterday. But they look fresher than that.' Liz didn't touch them but the sweet scent from the bouquet was strong. 'Perhaps she has them delivered by a florist.'

'Or another person left them here.'

'Let's get going. Apparently Pete is getting pizza for everyone.'

Reuben chuckled. 'He gets sent out a lot for food. Is he particularly talented in that regard or is it a way for other people to get some breathing space?'

I like you a lot.

'Bit of both. Pete is an acquired taste but he's the best partner I've ever had.'

They began to head back toward the exit, Reuben holding the flowers away from his body.

'Better than Vince Carter?'

'Different. I worked with Vince at the beginning of my career. In uniform. And he was a brilliant mentor and continues to be a close friend. Then there was a series of partners, mostly guys who were intent on climbing rank as fast as possible but not all willing to put in the hard yards.'

'And Pete?'

Liz grinned. 'Tough and rough as they come. Not much he won't do to get a perp. Sometimes he is close to crossing that line and he's had more than his share of reprimands as well as dealing with Vince's complaint a few years back. But he's a good cop and has a surprising ability to read a situation.'

'Might keep my judgement on that until I see his selection of pizza.'

Rather than the earlier communal morning tea around the conference table, almost everyone was eating at their workstations when Liz and Reuben arrived. The main room smelled like a pizza oven and Liz's stomach rumbled.

'Liz? Help yourself. I put a couple of slices of the ones with chilli in the far box for you.' Pete was on his way out of the kitchen, his plate piled high with pizza slices and a glass of cola somehow balanced on the edge.

Even the drink looked good and she wasn't a fan of soft drinks.

She found the slices Pete had kept for her and had to smile at his thoughtfulness. He remembered what she liked. There was a jug of filtered water in the fridge and she poured a glass, drank it quickly then refilled. She lifted the jug to put back as Reuben came in.

'Wouldn't mind some.'

He grabbed a glass and she poured, then put the jug away.

'I took the last two with extra chilli but can share?' Liz offered.

Reuben was opening then closing the lids of half a dozen boxes. 'Nah. Love chilli but imagine it's on a meat pizza?'

Liz peered at the slices. She hadn't even thought about it. 'Maybe some chicken or prawns. Lots of cheese.'

'Aha. Remind me to do something nice for McNamara.' He'd stopped at an almost-filled box and scooped several slices onto a plate. 'Decent of him. And these have chilli if you want another slice?' Reuben closed the lid and grinned. 'Vegan pizza.'

'You're vegan?'

'I am.'

'And Pete didn't give you a hard time?'

Reuben headed out of the kitchen. 'Not worth taking me on about it. I'd bore him with facts about health, let alone the animal side of things. Just think of me as the Peter Siddle of law enforcement.'

And every bit as good looking.

Before her mind could follow that odd train of thought – not only about Reuben but about the outstanding Australian cricketer – Liz helped herself to one of the vegan slices and made her way to her workstation. She had a keyboard, mouse, and two screens, pretty much the way almost everyone else did. The desk was long and curved and for the first time she noticed it was a standing desk, able to raise to a comfortable height should she want to be on her feet rather than her behind. For now, sitting was good.

Three slices of pizza later, all delicious including the vegan one, Liz wiped her fingers clean and opened the computer. However long it took, she was here to find Lyndall. No matter what she had to do. Despite any tiredness or future hunger or thirst. None of it mattered. All she could see were the two graves. Side by side. Father and son. And the engraving.

Our world.

THIRTEEN

The room was a quiet hum of activity. All the workstations were being used apart from Candace's and Phoebe's. The latter sat across from Ben in his office and they were intent on a printed document between them.

This is taking too long.

Despite every member of the team actively working on one aspect or another, Liz felt like they were spinning their wheels in mud. That made her think back to one of the first discoveries of the day and she went to Pete's workstation. As always, it was a mess. He had a way of turning any flat surface into chaos, which he claimed was organised and that he knew where everything was. At the moment there was a dozen or so photographs from the dried mud on the other side of the gate at the back of Lyndall's property on his screen.

'Narrowing the vehicle brand down, Liz.'

Pete didn't look up from his keyboard, which he was tapping on with two fingers. The photos showed clear tyre tracks, deep and wide and with a tread she didn't recognise – not that she was any kind of tyre expert. 'So not a Hi-lux or Ranger?'

'Nope but still pretty common. But if I can pin it down then maybe I can find the actual vehicle and we can go collect Lyndall.'

'If only it was so simple, Pete.'

He hit enter and sat back in his chair, eyes on Liz. 'If any of this was simple, none of us would be here. We'd be on a tropical beach with cocktails leaving this to the current members of Missing Persons. Or Homicide.'

The last word was said with such disdain that Liz grinned.

'Not a laughing matter, Liz. Andy Moorland is no Terry. That team will suffer, you mark my words.'

The smile left at the name of her old boss. 'Nobody can replace Terry, mate. And I miss him too. But someone had to step up and you and I were leaving so who should have got the job?'

He shrugged and glanced past Liz. 'Looks like the meeting is on.'

Ben and Phoebe stood at the table and within a few seconds, Candace emerged from the second room. She looked exhausted, yet determined and Liz wished there was time to sit with her and just talk this all through for a while. They'd worked together before on a time-sensitive case and the psychologist was a force to be reckoned with. And interesting.

Meg touched a few points on the top of the table and the black surface morphed. Liz caught her breath as a semi-clear screen rose from the middle. Nobody else was fazed so they'd seen it previously.

Ben gazed around the table. 'Thank you everyone for your incredible work today. This morning, all I expected was a day of easing Liz into the team. Yet here we are, almost nine at night, chasing a ghost. Or a series of ghosts. Whatever Lyndall's reasons for hiding her past and changing her identity, it's made our task more difficult. But someone found her and we are closing in on her history. Who'd like to start?'

Pete was brief, touching on the tyres and a few footprints which had been cast and sent to some lab Liz had never heard of.

Knowing they had access to a private forensics lab gave her new hope.

'Phoebe and I have had a chat about her podcast,' Ben said. 'Her approach is unique and I'd like everyone to hear her concept. Phoebes?'

Once again the young woman was shy about talking, her eyes on the table at first. 'Oh, sure. I've written a script for the podcast and if it sounds okay to you all then I'll record and release it tonight. I can send everyone a copy? Anyway, I want to start a conversation about scandals in the art world.' She finally looked up. 'My researchers found a couple which are pretty tame but will work to get things started, and one about an art theft a number of years ago which had an Australian connection. We already know who did that one but it might get people thinking. Now that we have more information about Lyndall, I've made a few changes to try and lead people to the right era and maybe countries.'

'But isn't your podcast more for... well, young people? Would this all be before their time?' Annette asked.

'You'd be surprised. True crime fascinates all ages and my demographic ranges from twenties to eighties. And this will go out worldwide. I'm not just focusing on Australia because Lyndall had strong ties to Europe.' She dropped her head again. 'That's the plan.'

'Thanks, Phoebe. Looking forward to hearing the podcast,' Ben said. 'Annette?'

'Everything I'm doing is going to Meg so rather than double up...'

'In that case, Meg?'

'Don't undersell yourself, Annette. You're picking up all the relevant stuff to save me time.' Meg touched the screen and it came to life with a list of sorts. 'This is what I'm working on. Well, not me but my programmes, plus some is outsourced, securely. This will update automatically as results come in. See the number beside face recognition? That's how many faces have been considered and discarded.'

The list was a living thing and Liz couldn't take her eyes off it. Under 'Faces' were the names 'Lyndall', 'Alain', and 'Jean-Paul' and next to each was a counter of sorts, rapidly ticking over. She finally moved on to the rest of the list.

- Flowers
- Bank account
- Drone data
- Background of family and their deaths
- Lyndall's weapons
- Builder of house
- Peripheral contacts

There were a few more which looked like reminders for Meg rather than actual parts of the list. Liz tuned back into the conversation.

'There's only so much my searches can do, boss,' Meg said to Ben. 'Some of this is old-style footwork during normal business hours.'

Hamish and Reuben spoke next, covering the early finding from the drones.

'Three possible spots where someone could wait for long periods of time and we're pretty confident Lyndall's house was in view.' This was Hamish. He'd barely spoken since Liz had arrived back but gave her the occasional smile. Perhaps he was conveying he harboured no hard feelings. 'I'll head up there again first light. Do we have access to tracking dogs?'

'We do. I'll contact someone and hook you up with them but only bring them in if you find evidence that there's been a watcher. Are you taking Reuben?'

Reuben nodded. 'Best we work together on it as we've spent the day narrowing down the areas and have the landscape in our heads now.'

Ben looked around the table, stopping at Liz. She expected him to ask her to speak but then he stepped back from the table.

'Our team has until this time tomorrow to make headway – actually, to be able to show solid progress in finding Lyndall or at the least, her abductor. We run the risk of this case being handed to Missing Persons and other major crimes units.'

Pete swore under his breath.

'We need to make the best use of the time we have. Phoebe, you go now and do your podcast. Sleep as soon as you can. Annette, go home. Hamish, Reuben, go home. Be up at Lyndall's property by first light. Pete—'

'Not leaving.'

'Thank you for getting pizzas.' Ben half-smiled.

'Yeah. No worries. Still not leaving.'

A ripple of laughter accompanied the movement of people away from the table as those heading out went to shut down their computers and pack up. Candace wandered into the kitchen and after a quick glance at Ben – who was talking to Meg – Liz followed. The other woman had the fridge open, staring in without moving.

'Tea? I saw some herbal ones earlier,' Liz said.

Candace slowly closed the door and turned to offer a small, tired smile. 'I was thinking of something a bit stronger. How are you doing, Liz?'

I'm confused and worried and exhausted. I barely know what I'm doing here.

'Okay. Everyone is great.'

'Even Hamish?'

'You saw Pete's photos?'

'I did. Thought it time someone put him in his place.'

Unsure how serious Candace was being, Liz changed the subject.

'How long have you been part of the team?'

'I helped Ben set it all up. Helped choose the right mix of people.'

On that surprising note, Candace returned to the main room.

Ben, Meg, Pete and Candace were with Liz at the round table in the second room. Two bottles of wine were open as well as beer and there'd been little talk for the first few minutes. Everyone else had left for the night. The calmness and quiet in here was welcome and Liz savoured her chilled white wine.

Candace leaned across to pull a laptop close then got up to wheel the board across. It was covered in her bold handwriting and there were several pages attached with magnets, including a blown-up photocopy of the artwork from Melanie's sketchbook.

'Am I able to sleep here tonight, Ben?' Candice asked. 'Most likely I'll draw more connections once I try to rest and would prefer quick access to the board.'

'Of course.' Ben opened his second beer. 'Liz and Pete, go back to your own beds tonight.'

Pete opened his mouth to argue but Ben continued.

'Meg needs the other room. No-one is staying up all night but three of us have to be here for any developments.'

Candace gestured at the board. 'I will brief the others first thing. I'm nowhere near profiling the abductor but by understanding the victim, I expect to lay the foundation to profile the criminal behind this.'

'Or criminals,' Pete said.

'We know there are at least four people involved from the video footage retrieved from the panic room. Three were there as muscle. One was known to Lyndall.'

'Known to her?' Liz hadn't expected that. 'Do you mean from her past?'

'Most likely.' Candace opened the laptop. 'I've studied this at length but perhaps not everyone has seen it?'

Pete and Liz shook their heads and Candace turned the screen to face them.

'This is just the footage taken inside the panic room. It

appears recording is activated by movement. Now from cross-checking against other cameras we know that Lyndall left the house at 12.57am. She returned at 1.08am and locked herself into the house. That's where things get a bit messy.'

Meg leaned forward. 'Someone tampered with the cameras and I think it was using an electronic device. I've sent everything from the time Vince and Melanie left until 3am to a trusted source to clear up whatever is possible. For some reason, it didn't affect the camera in the safe room. Probably the sheer amount of protective material in the floor and walls and ceiling.'

Candace tapped on the keyboard and the video began.

The door opened and a person stepped in, checking the door was again closed. They wasted no time opening the gun box and removing the rifle. And then they disappeared from the view of the camera. A few seconds later, Lyndall almost threw herself in, shutting the door in her wake. It was dark in the room until Lyndall turned on the panel of ten monitors, but even their light wasn't strong as the house itself was in darkness. What was scarily obvious were three shadowy figures outside the door.

Liz couldn't help a small gasp and Pete's hand pressed on her shoulder for a moment.

'Now, Lyndall would believe herself safe in there,' Candace continued. 'Nobody else knew how to access the door so all she had to do was phone for help.'

On the screen, a terrible scene played out. Lyndall opened the gun box which of course was empty. Her body language subtly changed, stiffened, but her hand kept moving in the cupboard, stopping for a second or two. Maybe to press the button for security. She started to tap on something. Something with a light. And then she froze. The muzzle of a rifle came into view until it was against Lyndall's head.

Candace paused the recording. 'See the light in the cupboard?'

'It has to a be phone,' Liz said. 'With the rifle missing,

Lyndall was trying to reach Vince or the police but we know he never got a message or alert of any kind.'

'Nor did the security company,' Meg said. 'In fact, they've been taking her monthly payments and never once done a check that the button works.'

'Hang on, Carter said he was there when it was all done last year.' Pete looked outraged. 'This was planned even back then?'

'Keep watching.'

The video resumed.

Lyndall slowly turned, hands up. Even in the semi-dark it was obvious she knew the person holding the rifle. She said a word. There was a brief discussion and then the abductor came into view, opening the door. The three men entered and Lyndall agreed to whatever she was being told. The first man put the rifle away and drew out a mobile phone before closing the cupboard. He slid it into a pocket, only the side of his face partly showing. Lyndall stopped at the door then was kind of pushed through and all five exited.

The recording ended.

Ben held his hand up as everyone started talking at once.

'Meg only got this isolated two or so hours ago and has already circulated the images of the first man and the others to her contacts.'

'And am working on facial recognition.'

'Yep. And I've started the process to identify the phone. I also rang Vince an hour ago and confirmed he didn't receive a call or text from Lyndall. He had no knowledge of this phone's existence and the phone which was next to her bed is the only one registered to her.' Ben looked grim. 'This is good though. What we're getting from this short recording.'

Going back to the board, Candace pointed to the sketch. 'Lyndall's loss was terrible. I believe whoever took her was responsible for the deaths of her son and husband. Or associated in some way. A negative way. She's been hiding for decades and preparing for an attack. We see that in her house. Her careful protection of her identity. But she was beginning to feel safe again and I put that down to her relationships with Vince and Melanie. Somewhere she's made a mistake and alerted whoever she ran from.'

'What would she be hiding from?' Meg yawned and quickly covered it. 'Sorry.'

Pete pushed his seat back but didn't stand. 'She's a crack shot. Reckon she's handled sniper weapons or similar and that's got to narrow down the options.'

This new side of Lyndall didn't add up. Liz knew her as an eccentric loner with a kind heart. A woman who'd rather be with her donkeys than humans. She was in her mid-sixties. A person of few words.

Now, Pete got to his feet. 'I'd be looking at government security forces or an elite military group. Legal or not. That's my best bet.' He began to collect the empty bottles.

Legal or *not*? Surely Lyndall's past life wasn't as a paid killer?

FOURTEEN

'Regretting your life choices yet?' The man sitting opposite Lyndall smiled as though they were old friends sharing a joke.

She didn't bother with a response. She'd barely spoken since being blindfolded and hauled out of the boat a few hours ago and forced up a dozen steps and into this building. Beneath her sock-clad feet, old floorboards creaked with the pull of the ocean. Lyndall had an idea of where she was, or at least the type of structure, and if she was right, then there was a chance she could get herself out. Once this monster left.

'I wouldn't bother, Nora. Quite apart from nobody being allowed within a hundred metres thanks to the seals which occasionally use it as a place to sunbathe, we're miles from shore. I have a boat patrolling at a distance. And there was a sighting of a shark as recently as yesterday.'

'I'm looking at one.'

'Ah. She does speak.'

Marcus had never been easily offended. Insults washed off him and he'd had his share in his line of work.

'Still killing people for a living?' she asked.

'Gave that away about thirty years ago. Around the time my superstar shooter vanished.' His face darkened. 'Never found a decent replacement so switched enterprises. Not that you need to know a thing about my new life.'

Lyndall forced a smile. 'Don't pretend you plan on letting me live. I know too much but surely if I've not said anything by now, it is unlikely I ever will.'

Getting to his feet, Marcus walked to one of the handful of windows lining the room. Each one looked out to the sea. And to the dark of the night. A door led to the other part of the structure but Lyndall had only seen the inside of a bathroom down a narrow hallway on the brief visit she'd been permitted.

He carried a phone and it rang, making Lyndall jump. He answered and muttered some words then turned back to her.

'I'm leaving. Wind is picking up and I've no intention of being stuck here overnight. But you get to stay and have the run of the place, Nora. There's a bedroom. A kitchen. Enough food for tonight. The door will stay locked and the windows are reinforced, so settle in.' He crossed the distance between them, keeping far enough that should she kick out, he'd stay safe. He'd know she no longer had the agility and speed to do other than have a token attempt.

He might believe that. He might be surprised.

'Why am I here, Marcus? If it was to silence me then I'd be in the ocean already.'

'True. We'll talk tomorrow. Take tonight to think about what information, including the location, you will provide me in order to retrieve The Tides.'

Lyndall's blood ran cold.

'You've gone quite pale, old lover.' The man nodded. 'As you might. Because by this time tomorrow it must be back in my hands.'

'I have no idea w—'

He moved fast, pinning her against the back of the chair, his face contorted in anger, his breath foul from cigarettes.

'You do. And you will ensure I find it.'

There was a tap on the door and he stepped back, straightening his jacket.

'It would be bad for you to ignore me. Bad for anyone you have made the mistake of loving. I wonder… will the second time around be even worse?'

Even as she scrambled to her feet he was gone, out of the door and his thug locked it, then peered in with a grotesque smirk.

She stood at the window until the boat was out of sight. There was only a lamp on in the room and she was able to see well enough if she pressed against the glass through cupped hands. In the far distance was a row of lights. A coastline with houses. Lyndall went to each window, searching for landmarks. The night was clear enough despite strong gusts of wind and through the final window she saw the distinctive skyline of Melbourne.

It made sense.

She was in one of the disused channel pile lights… structures from the 1800s functioning as lighthouses built upon pylons in the bay. There were several which had progressively been restored to a degree and moved to new locations purely for heritage reasons, as none were actively used for their original purpose. Not that she was aware of.

Daylight would give her a better idea of which shore was closest. Marcus might well be back before first light. These were patrolled by Parks boats to keep curious tourists off the structures. If she had any hope of getting off here and out of danger then she needed to come up with a plan.

One danger to another. I know which I prefer.

Lyndall was once a strong swimmer. But that was a long time ago and she'd not swum in years. Would her body cope with the difficulties of an ocean swim of an unknown distance? She only had to get near a boat to be found and then she'd borrow a phone and call Vince. He must be beside himself with worry.

And Melanie.

It wasn't fair for that sweet little girl to be put through the fear of what had happened to Lyndall. She'd had enough go wrong in her short life.

'It would be bad for you to ignore me. Bad for anyone you have made the mistake of loving. I wonder… will the second time around be even worse?'

Marcus' cruel words forced their way back and Lyndall gave in to tears.

But when she'd done weeping, she set herself a task. Find a way out of here. And as a backup plan… prepare for the worst and make a weapon.

FIFTEEN
~DAY TWO~

There was no chance Pete was leaving Hamish and Reuben –
particularly the former – to waste a lot of time tramping through
bushland. Not when he knew the area and could avoid much of
the more difficult terrain. He waited at the top of the driveway
after speaking to two of the security detail and assuring himself
nothing of interest had gone on overnight.

Daylight wasn't far away and the air was warm already.
Humid. Although the sky looked clear, storms were forecast for
later in the day and Pete had no intention of being caught out
here during one. He glanced at his watch. Two hours would be
enough to wrap this up.

One of two BearCat's assigned to Operation Nobody slowed
and turned into Lyndall's driveway. Similar to those used by
Critical Incident Response Team, these armoured vehicles
complimented several other modified SUVs and hatchbacks.
They weren't the most fun to drive, but better for rough terrain
and carrying not only personnel but larger equipment. And they
looked ready for anything.

Last night Pete had gone to the 24-hour gym he favoured,
pounding a boxing bag until his muscles ached. Finally
returning to his apartment, he'd messaged back and forth with

Liz for a bit. She'd been thrown into the team in the worst possible way and was making herself sick worrying about Lyndall.

So am I.

He'd grown fond of Lyndall over the past few months. She was decent, even if her past was shaping up to be shady. People didn't change. Not their personalities and Lyndall had a strong sense of right and wrong. Whatever she'd done more than three decades ago, there'd been good reasons and he only cared about what it was in order to track down the fool who'd taken her.

Fool, because when Pete found him he was going to kill him.

The BearCat parked behind his SUV and Hamish was out in a couple of seconds. 'Something wrong at the house?'

'All good here.'

'You just happened to drop by?'

Pete allowed a grin to widen. Hamish had been trying to annoy him since they'd met and hadn't managed to ruffle his feathers one bit. Pete had dealt with his kind plenty of times. Mostly when he was in deep cover as a detective and would spend months among the worst kind of people – the crime bosses who were tripping in their pride and presumption of superiority. And Pete didn't mind messing with their heads. Or Hamish's.

He pointed behind them where the first rays of the sun were making an appearance over the highest ridge. 'Nothing beats the sunrise up here. Thought I'd take some photos and then try my hand at painting one of them.'

Hamish's mouth dropped open.

Reuben was at the back of the vehicle. 'Morning, Pete. You coming with us?'

'Yeah, mate.' He joined Reuben and lifted out a drone box. 'I've done a lot of hiking up here and know how to avoid bush-land which gives way to sudden drops to painful deaths.'

'Handy skill. Just taking one drone in case we need to get more aerial images.'

'Two people is plenty. Aren't you better off back at base?' Hamish didn't look impressed.

'True. I'm indispensable but haven't mastered being in two places at once so seeing as I'm here, let's give this a whirl.'

Pete stared at Hamish until the other man shrugged and leaned past him to pull out a backpack. For the first time since meeting Hamish a few weeks ago, Pete felt uneasy. He'd judged him as a self-absorbed but capable man. One who needed a lesson in both humility and in how he spoke to women. Mostly, the latter. If Ben didn't jump on it soon, Pete would. And Hamish would like it a lot less than an uncomfortable conversation with the boss.

This feeling was different.

Almost a sense that there was more going on with the ex-military marksman. Pete shook it off and helped himself to a rifle.

Liz stepped inside the hub a bit before six in the morning, being as quiet as possible expecting those who'd stayed to be asleep. Her own night was restless and she'd already been up for two hours. A long run helped clear her head. Finding Lyndall was the only thing that mattered and if she needed to draw on every bit of her experience as a detective, then she was ready.

The smell of coffee welcomed her in and she followed her nose to the kitchen.

Candace was packing grounds into the coffee machine and without a word, collected a second cup.

'Anyone else up?' Liz asked.

'Heard a shower turn on just before you arrived.'

While Candace made the coffee, Liz dropped her bag onto her desk and booted her computer. There was a folder and inside was a report of sorts. Ben's doing by the look of it with an overview on the events of the previous day, a long list of clues – for want of a better word – and a prioritised workload. This was broken down by team member.

'Coffee.' Candace handed a cup over and perched on the edge of the desk. 'There's not a lot on there for your attention… well, apart from everything.' The lines around her eyes crinkled when she smiled. 'Ben needs time today to work his contacts and go back to his roots as a Missing Persons detective. Happy to step up and oversee the team?'

'Me? I'm not the best choice. Not when I barely know half of them or the procedures. I still don't have a weapon.'

'You'll have one within the hour. The rest of the team know the procedures. And you're a natural leader.'

Instead of insisting she wasn't, Liz tasted the coffee. 'My sweet lord, this is good.'

'Has to be or Ben would have a riot on his hands.'

'This place with its café quality coffee machine, wine fridge, sleeping quarters… what do the powers-that-be want in return? Do they have their own agenda for this unit? And what if we fail their expectations?'

Candace lifted her eyebrows. 'We won't fail anything. It might feel like we're being pressured right now but everything I've observed about the structure of Nobody assures me this is a long-term project. Not an experiment. And a lot of freedom. Probably the only agenda I'm aware of is solving the murder of the inspector's parents and there is no timeframe with that.'

Liz lifted the document again. 'Okay, so this is for me to use to oversee everyone's assignments? Are you not a better person for this?'

'I'm deep in profiling. After you and Pete left last night I spent a few hours with Meg and Ben. We've brainstormed some options. Need your input. But we're moving forward and that is a good thing. Another coffee? Breakfast?'

'Breakfast?'

'In the freezer are a dozen meal choices. Frozen yes. But not bad. If you want to actually cook something there's eggs and toast and who-knows-what in the fridge and cupboard. And yoghurt and fruit and seeds. Making me hungry talking about it all.' Candace gave a short laugh as she walked away. 'I hate cooking.'

Liz read through the document from Ben. The first pages were dedicated to today's plans with a note that any might change at short notice.

Each team member was allocated a series of responsibilities. For Annette it was to continue acting as Meg's main assistant but also follow up on important tasks such as locating the builder of Lyndall's house and possible source of the flowers found on the grave of Jean-Paul Dubois. Liz thought this was a good use of Annette's talents and felt confident of some early break-throughs.

Meg had full control over her own station and again, Liz would have suggested the same. She'd never worked with anyone more professional or self-motivated and it was a waste of time to micro-manage someone like her.

There were some notes about Phoebe.

- Podcast recorded and released at 11pm
- Copies sent to each member of the unit
- Phoebe to report any responses at first briefing of
  the day.

There was an email on the computer with a link and Liz made a note to listen later. Attached to the email was a copy of the script and she quickly read it, her admiration for the younger woman growing. It was cleverly written with an emphasis on encouraging the audience doing the research for her. Whether it would get any answers was yet to be seen, but bringing a social media influencer on board brought a whole new approach to the investigation.

As with Meg, Ben and Candace needed nothing from Liz, leaving just the three other men.

Actually, where was Pete?

He was only ever late if he was doing his own thing and now wasn't the time for him to run his own little side-trip. But it wasn't even half-past-six yet. She was worrying for nothing.

Half an hour later, Meg, Ben, and Annette were at their desks. But no Pete. Last night they'd texted for a couple of hours, tossing around ideas as well as talking more freely between themselves about their worries over Lyndall than they had around the rest of the team. If he'd slept a bit longer then she wasn't going to hassle him. Not yet.

Reuben and Hamish on the other hand should be at Lyndall's and the search well underway. They'd gone over the plan last night, intending to visit three spots which looked suspicious in the hope of finding anything left behind. Liz had seen the map and was convinced that one was the most likely. She didn't want to come over as intrusive but local knowledge could make a difference and save them time. Before ringing, she checked the app for their location.

Or tried to.

'Meg? Which bit will show me where someone is?'

She thrust the phone in the direction of Meg, who sighed with more drama than was required.

'We did complete the training on this, Liz.'

'Sorry, training? Was that the three minutes yesterday when your fingers went so fast over the screen than I was dazzled into believing this is some new game we're testing?'

Meg reached behind herself to where there was another chair and pulled it closer. 'Sit.' She handed the phone back. 'Okay, I might have forgotten not everyone is preternaturally connected to technology so I'll talk and you tap.'

Encouraging Liz to explore the different icons on the home screen, Meg guided her through the ones most useful today. It began to make sense. There was a logic to it which Liz quickly picked up and after one more practice, she followed the prompts to the location finder, specifically for Reuben. While it loaded, she gave Meg a grateful smile.

'Not so hard. Did you create this?'

'I did. And I should have written something up to help.'

'Nah. It is easy once the pieces fall into place. What the heck?' Liz's eyes had returned to the screen. 'Why is Pete with Reuben and Hamish?'

Ben hung up from his third phone call. Plus one from Ellie who'd wanted to check in with him before she headed to the produce markets. Hearing her voice gave him a sense of balance. He'd woken up dreaming of her and lay on his back, eyes on the ceiling, wishing she was there, and wondering – not for the first time – why he'd let himself be talked back into this kind of work. But the opportunity was too good to pass up, and if he was completely honest with himself, he had missed being a city detective. The reality of being back in this environment was far more difficult than he had anticipated because now he was missing her and Michael and the life they had.

Rather than pick up the phone and try yet another of his contacts and get the same negative response as the past three, Ben got to his feet and stood in front of the window, where he had been writing notes, intending to review his observations. Instead, he gazed through the window at the small group of people.

Meg was surrounded by computer screens and keyboards and dozens of piles of information that she could navigate more easily than anyone he'd ever met. He still couldn't believe she'd agreed to join this group but then again, why wouldn't she? After several years with Missing Persons, as well as helping with Homicide, she had still not received any official designation for her position – a position that was temporary from the beginning as an experiment. She once told him what she was being paid, and he'd been shocked that someone who was so instrumental in solving crimes, and in finding new ways to track criminals, was being so undervalued. That was one thing he could fix. Thanks to the very generous benefactor behind Operation Nobody, each member of the team had decent packages, sometimes far more than their previous position. And while he knew it wasn't all about the money for anyone, it certainly added a sweetener to the long hours and difficult work.

Liz was an exceptional cop and she'd taken on the role of managing the team for the next few hours without batting an eyelid. This gave him a small window to contribute to finding Lyndall. All his years in Missing Persons had to count for something and although the first few people he'd reached out to were unwavering in their refusal to assist, he wasn't about to stop trying.

At no time in his career was he more aware of making enemies within the force than right now. Perhaps he'd burned too many bridges by leaving the unit he'd headed for several years. More likely, he'd angered those whose incompetence or laziness he'd highlighted at different times.

Ben returned to his desk and dialled again.

'Hi, Andy. It's Ben.'

SIXTEEN

Back at her desk, Liz cast the navigation screen on the phone to one of her monitors, pleased with herself for managing that at least. Then, she took a better look at where the men were.

Similar to modern phone maps or share location apps, this one had options of map form or terrain and she switched between them to work out the location and direction. Each of the men was represented by a small diamond shape in a different colour, with a legend at the bottom of the map. Reuben was dark blue, Hamish was a pale green, and Pete was red. The three were close together and moving in a north-westerly direction from Lyndall's property, across to a high point behind Vince's.

Actually, it was on Vince's land. This was the second most likely spot and there was no way they'd already looked at the first. Perhaps the thinking was to deal with the most difficult place first and then move on.

Liz reached for her phone and stopped herself.

Whatever Pete was playing at, he had reasons and once she could speak to him privately, he'd explain. It might be as simple as putting his knowledge of the area to good use.

Or ensuring Hamish does his job.

Most people wrote Pete off quickly and it was his own fault.

He didn't care if his off-hand approach was a barrier to some. He preferred to sort out who was worth his time and based upon the arrest *and* prosecution success over his career, it worked for him.

Now that he and Vince got on for the most part, he might need the rush of having a new adversary in the form of a rather pompous man who was his opposite. Well spoken. Charming. Clean cut. And hungry for acknowledgement.

The map refreshed and the men had moved another hundred metres or so.

'You should be able to get actual visuals of them.'

Liz jumped when Annette spoke from over her shoulder.

'Are you a ninja?'

'Sorry,' Annette said. 'I used to be called that in uniform. Always quiet until I need to speak.'

My nervous system could do with more warning.

'How do I get visuals?'

'May I?' Annette knelt beside Liz holding a finger over the monitor.

'Please.'

'So if you touch this icon, the one with the camera? And hold. There you go. And to change back just repeat.'

The screen flickered then morphed from a flat terrain to something closer to Google Earth, except there were three tiny dots moving along a trail. She tapped on them and the images increased in size and the quality improved. Sure enough, there were three men hiking and carrying backpacks.

'How come there's three of them?'

'An excellent question and one I will ask once they return. Pete added himself to the search team and I imagine it is because he knows the area.'

'Pete does like to do his own investigations. Bit of a lone wolf.'

Liz kept silent. She wasn't about to talk about her old partner, good or bad.

'Do you need anything at the supermarket?' Annette got to her feet. 'We're out of the oat milk I use in my coffee and I thought I could run out quickly and get some. Darned lactose intolerance.'

Liz smiled. 'You have to be one of the few cops I know who won't drink black coffee.'

Annette grimaced. 'Gross without a splash of something.'

'If Meg can spare you, duck out now before the briefing. Nothing worse than missing a morning coffee.'

Returning to the screen, Liz refreshed again and the men were stationary. They'd reached the destination. Within a minute, they were on the move again. Her heart sank. If there was nothing to find there, then that was valuable time wasted. She should have called to suggest they prioritise the other site. With Pete tagging along, that was three people doing the job which possibly one might have managed. Or three people going to three destinations at the same time. Aware her shoulders were tensing, Liz stood and stretched. Being irritated at how other members of the team did their work wasn't helpful.

'Liz? Can I show you something?' Meg was at her wheeled board, attaching a series of photographs with magnets.

'Those are from Lyndall's house?'

'How did we miss this?'

There were four photographs. The first was a wedding photo with Lyndall and the man they had to assume was Alain Dubois. Then two photos of babies, not much older than newborns, in Lyndall's arms. Finally one with two children sitting together on a bench, grinning at the camera. A boy aged perhaps nine or ten and one of about two.

'I did see the last one and figured the toddler was someone known to the family. Perhaps a relative? He's not in any other photos.'

'Look closely at the pics with the babies.'

The poses were similar. Lyndall sitting on a sofa with a baby in her arms. In both, the baby was wrapped in a blanket, their head covered with a knitted cap. They might have been taken a minute apart. Except… Liz concentrated on Lyndall's face. 'No.'

'My opinion is yes.'

'Different babies. Lyndall looks older in the second image.'

'Correct. I'm going to run some tests on the photographs because there's no date stamps, but I think the second image shows a second baby, and then the one on the bench is of both boys.'

'Brothers?'

Meg returned to her seat. 'I'm going to add this to the search parameters.'

'If Lyndall has another child, where is he?' Liz was still at the board and touched a copy of the sketch from Melanie. 'There's not a hint that there's someone else. Surely she'd have included him had he also died?'

'What about the art in her house?'

'I've sent you all the photos I took of them but they're not great quality. I was a bit rushed.'

'Leave it with me.'

'Annette's just walked back in. Shall I get her to go over the photos?' Liz watched as Meg compiled a screen filled with every piece of artwork from Lyndall's house.

'No, I need her to follow up on the security firm.'

Liz's phone began ringing on her desk and she hurried to answer.

Once Ben finally emerged from his office, Liz wasted no time handing him back the reins. He and Candace went to the second room and Liz took a long overdue restroom break.

In a few minutes they'd have the first briefing for the day and Liz was already exhausted. Mentally and emotionally, this case was among the most difficult she'd ever worked. She washed her hands for longer than needed and pushed down anxiety which seemed to rise with every new piece of the puzzle.

Staying focused was all that mattered. Keeping her eyes on the end goal of safely recovering Lyndall. Steps beyond that, including catching the perp, weren't important at this point.

Reuben was in the kitchen, head in the fridge. Pete's voice filtered across from his desk.

'If you're after oat milk, Annette bought some earlier. Might be in the cupboard.'

He straightened with a sheepish grin. 'Food, actually. Starving. And there's two boxes of the milk in the fridge so no idea why she bought more.'

'Forward planning?'

'No. I mean this.' Reuben closed the door of the fridge and opened the pantry. 'There's six boxes already from last time we stocked up.'

Sure enough, six boxes of oat milk were in a neat column.

'Bit strange.'

'I don't mind. Might make a smoothie with some. Want one?'

Not even if it is the last drink on earth.

'Thanks, but no. I need to chat with Pete.'

Liz was certain Reuben chuckled softly as she made her escape and she found herself smiling. He was shaping up as one of those people who was good to be around. Not hard work and not pretentious.

'There you are, Lizzie-Beth. I wonder if we might have a quick moment? Away from the main room.' Hamish must have been waiting for her, so quick was his approach.

'Liz. Just Liz, thanks. What do you need to discuss?'

His eyes narrowed and then he glanced in the direction of Pete, who was sitting on the edge of his desk doing something on his phone. If he was planning on complaining about Pete then he was wasting his time. She'd tell him to take it up with Ben. Her phone beeped with a message.

'Sorry, just need to check in case it is Vince.'

Hamish waited.

It was Pete.

Don't believe a word he says. I saved his life.

Somehow keeping her face straight, she slid the phone away. 'That one will keep. Can you talk to me here? Rather not leave the hub so close to the briefing.'

Another glance, but this time around the room and then Hamish stepped a bit closer and lowered his voice. 'I'm a bit embarrassed, actually.'

'Is this about yesterday?'

'Gracious no. I thoroughly enjoyed meeting you the way I did.' He flashed a smile then sobered. 'Something happened earlier. Up at the property. Pete had suggested one path and I took another thinking it would be quicker and based on the topography from the drones it should have been. But there was a ruddy big crevice and I almost… well, suffice to say Pete came out of nowhere and grabbed me before I could fall. Never been saved before.'

While it was a relief to hear the man speak frankly, Liz had no idea where he was going with this. Ben and Candace were on their way from the conference table.

'Thing is, I don't know him well and suspect he doesn't like me. But he swooped in and didn't make a big deal of it and I want to say something about it but don't know where to begin.'

Liz looked hard to be certain Hamish was genuine. If he was leading into some kind of joke then she'd take a dim view. But his eyes were sincere.

'Begin by saying thanks, mate. Best way to avoid Pete ribbing you about it.'

'Shall we get started?' Ben was at the table.

'Appreciate the advice, Liz. Although Lizzie-Beth suits you.'

It wasn't worth answering.

'Thanks Liz for stepping up while I chased my tail all morning,' Ben said. He shook his head, his expression grim. 'Always considered myself a fairly nice bloke but apparently not enough to call in a favour.'

There was no ripple of laughter like there might have been, had he had a different look on his face. If Ben Rossi, ex-head of Missing Persons, wasn't able to garner support over an abduction, then where did that leave the team? Liz figured he was restricted with what information he'd have shared and asked for but even so, it worried her.

'Having had my complaint for the day, I'll give you the good news. Someone has agreed to do a quiet probe around for the missing fingerprints.'

'Oh, Lyndall's?' Annette asked. 'I've been following leads which are all stopping at dead ends, so thanks for that bit of hope.'

'Should have something today, if Andy can get anything.'

Pete snorted and all eyes moved to him. He shrugged.

If Ben was bothered by Pete's ongoing dislike and disrespect for Andy Montebello, he didn't show it. Andy worked for Ben back in Missing Persons before taking over the lead role at Homicide a month ago. They'd had a solid working relationship and Liz had got on well with them both… until Andy's involvement in her final case.

'Reuben, any joy on your bush walk?'

'Sorry, Ben. Nothing from the three potential places.'

'Then how were they watching Lyndall?' Candace asked.

'It's possible there's more cameras around her property. Well-hidden and put there by whoever was after her,' Hamish said with a glance at Reuben, who nodded. 'We discussed this on the way back and both Reuben and I have worked with surveillance equipment small enough to go unnoticed. Unless you are specifically looking.'

Meg tapped on the table to raise the screen. There was a 3D rendition of the outside of Lyndall's house, including the closest structures. 'I've identified a dozen potential sites for these and if we're careful, we might be able to retrieve one and bring back.'

'Just one?'

Up until now, Phoebe was as quiet as usual, but Liz had seen how she listened carefully to each speaker even if her eyes were often on the table or her hands.

'I'm worried that if we make it obvious we're onto them and possibly have a way of tracking them, it might escalate whatever plan they have for Lyndall. Ideally, we need one and if I can go take a look, Ben, I can do so in a way which won't alert them. Hopefully.'

'Then I should go with Meg.' This was Hamish. 'Used this type of tech before.'

Ben's eyes moved from Hamish to Meg. 'Your call.'

'I'd like to take Liz. Hear me out. We need to take a better look at the artwork in the house and quite honestly, if there's surveillance inside and its being monitored, isn't it better to make them think that is our motive for being there?'

There was a stillness for a moment. Phoebe's head was down and her fingers gripped each other. Candace had a familiar look as she slowly surveyed the people around the table. Always working them out.

'Liz, go with Meg. And both be careful, please.'

Hamish opened his mouth and closed it again. His hands, at his sides, were balled into fists.

SEVENTEEN

Phoebe gave a detailed account of the podcast and the results so far. She was a different person when she talked about her work, animated in a quiet way but clearly knowledgeable about her listeners' demographics and with a keen intellectual approach to offering entertainment with benefits.

'My PA is compiling a portfolio of the most positive leads. Several art thefts were mentioned as well as a scandal involving a three-way relationship between two male artists and a model who posed for them. Mainly a scandal because she stole from them both and managed to set them against each other at the same time.' With a rare smile, Phoebe continued. 'There are still comments coming in and we have a phone line where listeners can leave a voice message and talk for as long as they want. That does take a little more time for us to go through but I expect that by mid-afternoon I'll have a report.'

She stepped back a fraction as though to signal the end of her brief.

'Thanks for that. Who is left… Annette?'

'Sure. I have been chasing up on the security company responsible for Lyndall's house.' Annette referred to her tablet.

'Stone's Security based in Bacchus Marsh. They offer home and business surveillance, alarms, drive-by checks and the like. I've spoken to a member of staff who was unhelpful. She did speak to someone more senior who relayed that they will only discuss an individual client if we present a warrant.'

Ben and Pete looked at each other, the latter nodding. 'Leave it with me.'

'If you're going to visit them, then you need to know there is one thing they have said. They deny having received any alert from Lyndall and haven't attended her property in close to a year. The timing fits more with the incident with Vince Carter and the fire at his cottage.'

'Which doesn't match with the information at hand from Vince, nor the video where Lyndall appears to be pressing something inside the gun locker. I take it everyone has now viewed the footage of her abduction?' Ben gazed around. 'Pete, please pay Stone's Security a visit. I believe the builder of Lyndall's house is doing a video call in an hour. He's in the US at present so I'll take the call with him. Anything on the phone that the perp took with him, Meg?'

'It was purchased last year over the counter at a supermarket. I'm waiting for the phone number to come through to me. This is a big break. Once I have it, I'll have a shot at tracking it, assuming it is turned on.' Meg pulled the board over from her workstation. 'Liz and I believe there is a second child of Lyndall's. A brother to Jean-Paul.'

That caused a murmur of interest.

'Annette is following up the records of the family but so far this younger child isn't showing up anywhere. My guess is that he was about two years old, if that, when his dad and brother died.'

'So where is he?' Reuben asked. 'From the sketch I saw, there is one child. And there's one grave for a child at the cemetery. Did Lyndall hide him? Put him somewhere safe if she believed her family was under attack?'

'Good questions. Or did the killer take him?' Candace asked. She walked around to the board and pointed at the images of the two children on the bench. 'This isn't a photo taken by anyone expecting a tragedy. Two brothers at a park. Out in the open. Whatever Lyndall was involved with, she didn't imagine it would affect her family.'

Meg checked her phone. 'Okay, so we have some info on Alain Dubois. I'll go through it but to summarise, he was born in France and died in Australia in a boating accident during a long holiday here. No living relatives. Can't see the name of his wife or son yet but there's files dropping in fast. May I?' She glanced at Ben.

'Please. We're pretty much done here for now so everyone, great work so far.'

Liz's chest hurt from tension. She was good with fast-moving cases. Meticulous with details and pretty efficient at sniffing out a liar. More and more though, the emotional toll of working on cases which were close to her was draining.

I need to move. I need to be doing something.

Candace was watching her. Somehow, they had a connection and the psychiatrist always picked up Liz's moods… at least, when she was stressed. Their eyes met across the table and immediately a sense of calm lowered Liz's rising anxiety. She knew she had to put some time aside to work with Candace. To learn some new techniques to deal with very difficult situations.

'Meg, sorry…' Ben had turned to walk to his office but spun back. 'Do you want Liz to go up to Lyndall's on her own and let you go through the files?'

'Um. Let me just see how much there is.'

'Or I could go with Liz.' Hamish hadn't moved from the table.

'No need, I can read on the way.' Meg was on her feet and tossing things into her shoulder-bag. 'But if you're free Hamish, can you cast your eye over the aerial map I've generated from the drone footage? Just use the vertical screen if you want and make a note of anything I've missed or doesn't look right. Please and thanks.'

Before he had a chance to respond, Meg was at the table touching the buttons to raise the screen. Then with a grin at Liz, she grabbed her bag as well as her laptop case and disappeared in the direction of the lift.

'The best way to handle Hamish is to keep him busy,' Meg said. 'And I really did need someone to check the map but anyone could do it.'

Liz was driving and they'd elected to take a hatchback rather than one of the larger vehicles. It might appear less threatening or official to anyone still observing, assuming that was the case. She was happy to be doing something. Anything, rather than what felt like endless discussions and computer work. All important. But not for her state of mind.

'Do you want me to read bits of interest?' Meg asked. She had her laptop open and was using the scroll pad to flick around.

'Yes. Is there anything about the wedding? Alain's wife?'

'Still not. And it is getting stranger by the minute because based on this, one would think he was single and child-free.'

'Hang on, how? Where is this information coming from?'

'Several sources which have come via a colleague from the past. He's brilliant at finding facts which are otherwise buried and if he can't find something, it may not exist. But even so… for example, Alain's documents for him arriving in Australia include a three-month holiday visa, a copy of his passport – the pages which matter – and an itinerary. Oh, this is interesting.'

Meg's face moved closer to the screen and she adjusted her glasses to better see.

'The itinerary is for a tour of several art galleries.'

'Go on.'

'Not the ones most of us think. Apart from the National

Gallery of Victoria the rest are smaller and include three private galleries.'

'Private? Who even has those in Australia?'

'Liz, Liz, Liz. Do you not hang out with the mega-rich? The indecently wealthy?'

'Actually, no. Purely by choice of course.'

They both laughed, then Liz turned onto the last road before Lyndall's.

'Two of these galleries, the private ones, are owned by old money. Discreet families of great wealth and both are major contributors to the arts, so I should be nicer about them. The third is also from wealth but apparently self-made and the owner is an art dealer.'

'Why would Alain be going to private galleries? I imagine they either own Lyndall's work or were going to buy some. Would he and Lyndall have been guests at events? Or was he something like an agent for her?'

'Excellent thoughts. I've sent my friend a few questions and asked him to obtain a list of who else was on this exclusive tour. I'll just email Annette and get her to find any events at those places during those dates.'

Liz stopped the car at the bottom of the driveway, waiting for Meg to stop tapping her keyboard. The cows were in the bottom paddock where the grass was long and lush. Somehow the property was always green other than in the middle of summer and it was something of an oasis among the heavy bushland and some land in the area which tended to look dry more often. But Lyndall only had her rescue donkeys and cows and frequently rotated them between paddocks.

'I'm done. Remember there may be listening devices as well. Let's keep our conversation about the paintings and so on rather than clueing them in on our other mission.'

'If I see something suspicious?' Liz began to drive again.

'Take the photos and send them to me and add a note or highlight the spot. I'll take a sneaky look. And don't be shy about close ups if anything looks interesting. No matter how small or weird.'

A security guard spoke to them before they went in. He reported nothing of interest other than Vince checking the animals several times including a late-night visit to lock the donkeys into the paddock with the big shed. Apparently the donkeys protested for a while until one of the security guards took them a heap of carrots he'd pulled up from the vegetable garden. Liz wasn't sure that Lyndall would appreciate her garden being touched, but it was probably a nice gesture to reassure the creatures.

They kept the lights off inside, doing a silent walk-through which they'd discussed earlier. At the panic room, Liz guided Meg to the exact spot where the slightly opened door framed the wall. Only there for a second or two, Meg nodded slightly and they kept going.

'I'm sorry we have to do the photographs again, Liz,' Meg announced when they reached the living room. 'The original ones were just not clear enough. Shall I do in here?'

'Okay. I'll start in the end bedroom.'

It was pure speculation that cameras were operating within the house, placed by whoever was responsible for taking Lyndall. Finding evidence was all Liz cared about and she was careful to take photos with her phone which would show anything planted within a painting or its frame. She took plenty of time in the hallway, mostly to allow her to get a lot of images of the panic room from different vantage points, always careful to appear to be photographing paintings. More than ever she was convinced she needed to take a much closer look at the wall inside the room but it would take planning to do so. She sent them to Meg with a question.

Any idea how we check the wall?

Not yet. We'll talk outside soon.

Meg was finishing up when Liz joined her.

'Just one in the kitchen and one in the dining room left. I'll do the dining room.'

Since when was there a painting in the kitchen? Liz spent a minute gazing around before noticing the sketch on the fridge. It was one of Melanie's drawings and quite sweet, with Vince sitting on an armchair while Lyndall and Mel did sketches – which were both little pictures of their own.

Liz took a few photographs and when she looked back through them, something jumped out at her. A fridge magnet held the paper in place. It was square and covered with square, artificial gemstones. Except one of them was round.

She sent the image to Meg, adding a little arrow to highlight the round one. Then she opened the fridge, removed a container of milk, made a show of sniffing it, checking the date, and then poured the contents down the sink. If anyone was watching then staying in the kitchen wouldn't seem suspicious. Nobody wanted to come home to spoiled milk.

'Ready, Liz?' Meg had her gear packed and typically slung over her shoulders. 'Oh my goodness, is that one of Melanie's drawings? Gosh, she's getting good.' She pulled it away from the fridge as though to take a closer look and as the magnet dropped to the ground, put her foot on it until there was a slight 'crunch'. 'Uh oh. I hope that wasn't a favourite magnet. Darn.'

'Looks cheap. I'll throw it away.'

The magnet was partly crushed and when Liz picked it up, Meg discretely took it and slid it into one of her bags. Liz made a show of opening the cupboard with the bin inside.

After locking up and letting security know they were done,

Liz and Meg put their bags into the car then walked a distance away, out of everyone's earshot.

'Good pick up, Liz. Definitely surveillance. I think I killed it. But we might have a quiet trip back, just in case.'

This was a breakthrough. Liz didn't mind not saying a word for the next half hour because this had to be a step toward finding the abductor... and locating Lyndall.

EIGHTEEN

If there was one thing which Pete hated during a case, it was the slow times. No different from most cops and he knew Liz was struggling with it but that only made it worse.

It couldn't all be action and a fast results.

Pity.

Police work was about asking questions and research and comparing reports and finding gaps in information. That took time and was crucial to connecting the dots and making a solid case. No point catching the perp and seeing them walk on a technicality.

Pete knew this was where they were right now and it didn't help that the new team had teething issues. Not a lot, but there was too much hand-holding while everyone found their groove and got to know each other's strengths. Give it some time and experience and Operation Nobody had the makings of the best squad he'd ever been involved with. Just not yet. Not on one of the most important cases he'd ever worked.

He drove past the office of the security firm and parked.

Bacchus Marsh was a rapidly growing town just outside the suburban sprawl of Melbourne and although it still had the country feel, it was busier every time he drove through. Loved for the fresh produce grown and sold along Bacchus Marsh Road, it was a hub for a lot of outlying homesteads. Such as Lyndall's. The security firm was one of several warehouse-style units behind a big fence and as Pete walked down from the road he had a good look through an open roller door.

Half a dozen small vans were marked up with the business logo. There was shelving and uniforms hanging along a wall. Not a person in sight. For a minute Pete stood just inside the doorway, waiting for someone to come and ask why he was there. But nothing.

He pushed the door open into the office and a young woman, perhaps twenty, looked up from a mobile phone as if he'd interrupted something important.

'Quiet day?' he asked.

On the reception desk was a monitor with a split screen from surveillance, including where he'd stood, unnoticed.

'Can I help you?'

'A friend recommended this company. They used it to set up a lot of cameras and an alarm in their house and there are patrols and stuff. Thought I might do similar to my place.'

The receptionist gathered some brochures and offered them to Pete. 'All of our services are in these. Pricing depends on what you want and how difficult the installation is.'

'Thanks. So, how do you monitor a house?'

She picked up a phone and pressed a line. 'Someone here asking about monitoring.' Just as quickly she hung up. 'Please wait.'

It was close to ten minutes before a man wearing a suit opened a door at the back and gestured. 'Come through.'

Pete extended his hand when he was close enough. 'Pete. And you are?'

The man shook his. 'Aiden Strong, the owner. Let me show you our monitoring station. He led the way up a flight of stairs and around several corners, stopping outside a heavy door with a keypad on the wall. 'Are you a local?'

'Seem to spend most of my life up here,' Pete said. 'Noticed you have quite the fleet of security cars. Booming business?'

After tapping on the keypad, the door clicked and Aiden Strong went through. He held it for Pete. 'Plenty of business. Not enough staff. Like everyone else, I guess. Not that it interferes with our day to day of course, but we've all learned to do jobs we normally don't. Like my daughter on reception. She'd rather be anywhere rather than working with her dad.'

Pete laughed. 'Kids, eh?'

This little chat seemed to relax the other man who looked Pete up and down. 'Don't suppose security work interests you?'

'Nah. I'm a pushover. Bit like the proverbial labrador helping the burglars out with the silver, which is why I reckon getting some cameras in my place is the go. So what happens in here?'

They'd stopped at a room made of glass on three sides and a concrete wall. Inside were a half-dozen long tables in a semi-circle, pushed against each other and each had a wall of monitors, a large panel with buttons and lights, and a couple of phones. There was one person in there although several chairs were stacked against the wall.

'Impressive set up, Aiden. And one person can manage it?'

For a minute Aiden seemed uncomfortable, put on the spot, but then he hastily nodded. 'Sure, for a short time. Other two are at lunch. At night we have three on. Four sometimes.'

Time to stop messing around.

'Never missed an alarm? Failed to get to someone's home when they relied on you.'

Aiden began to direct them back the way they'd come. 'Absolutely not. We have expensive and responsive equipment. Our installers are second to none. Our staff are beyond reproach.'

'Yeah, I'm sure, but mistakes can happen.'

'Not from our end. If someone doesn't regularly check their equipment is working as set up, then it is out of our hands.'

'And how often would one need to check it?'

They'd reached the reception area and stopped not far from

the desk, Aiden's daughter barely giving them a glance. 'We recommend annual check-ups. They can do so following our instructions or we offer a service. Now, would you like me to begin a quote and get your own security experience underway?'

Security *experience*? Pete felt a smile creep onto his face. Not the one he used to be nice.

'My friend's alarm wasn't responded to by your security team. She pressed the button installed by one of your people but nothing happened. And it was—'

'What do you mean!' Aiden's face was a deep shade of red. 'Which friend? We've attended every alarm. When did we install it?'

'Last winter. And your installer checked it in front of her and another person.'

'And it worked?'

'She got a call within a few seconds from your firm.'

'Well if her alarm isn't working, why hasn't she contacted me? I think you have the wrong security company.'

Pete took a small step toward the man, who backed up. 'Thing is, she pressed that alarm button but nothing happened. No call to check on her. No guard driving up to make sure that four thugs hadn't abducted her.'

Aiden laughed shortly. 'Four is very specific for an example.'

Another step forward and this time, Aiden was trapped between him and the desk.

'Let me show you something.' Pete had already cued part of the footage from the safe room and held his phone up. 'This is what happened in the early hours of yesterday.'

Aiden and his daughter watched, their eyes widening. She held a hand to her mouth, shocked.

'This lady is Lyndall Smith. She's one of your customers and nobody responded the one time she needed you. Now I can wait for a warrant and help tear this place apart, or you can tell me precisely what happened to her alarm.'

. . .

Liz had her phone on speaker in Ben's office so he could hear Pete, who'd called minutes after she and Meg returned.

'After some stonewalling, our Mr Strong eventually realised I wasn't going away anytime soon and he looked up the history. I've got it printed out because he refused to share digital files without a warrant.'

'Anything of value?' Ben leaned his elbows on the desk. He looked bone-tired.

'Some. Seems they go through staff fast. One blow-in was there for a week, keen to show off his skills and volunteering for all the installations. He set things up at Lyndall's house then that same evening did a night shift. Probably in case she ran another test. Next day he quit and disappeared without bothering to say a word or return his uniform.'

Ben's eyes met Liz's. 'Do we have a name? Details?'

'Took pics and sent to Meg.'

'She's a bit busy.'

'Hang on a sec then, I'll send to you both. But yeah, a name and a contact address but I expect it to be fake.'

Both phones dinged at the same time and Ben read his. 'Fancy dropping by his place, Pete?'

'Thought you'd never ask. I'll be going past so who'd like to share the fun?'

Although Ben's eyes had lit up, he nodded at Liz. 'Go on. You two do your stuff.'

'Be there in twenty to get you, Liz. Bring your good cop attitude because I've used all of mine up today.'

Meg stopped for a moment to read the message from Pete. There was an attachment of photos he'd taken of several printed pages. Information about Lyndall's account with Strong Security including the details of both installations over the years. She put it aside to return to.

She was in a room at the opposite end of the building from the team. A room designed for multiple purposes including handling sensitive materials and devices. It was soundproof and would prevent or at least, heavily reduce, any kind of surveillance being sent or received and according to tests run by Reuben, made anyone inside invisible to heat sensing from outside.

The message from Pete had arrived before she'd locked herself in and responding was pointless until she left the room.

As it was, she could safely take the bug – so cleverly hidden in the fridge magnet – to show the team. Her calculated crushing of it had resulted in a loss of signal capacity but she'd not known for sure until dismantling it, the minute camera kept covered to mimic being inside a household rubbish bin. While she recognised the components, Meg needed Reuben and Hamish to take a closer look. Sliding the pieces beneath the magnifier, she quickly captured dozens of images, using long, fine tweezers to turn an element or hold a wire up. A couple of years ago such detailed photographs would be impossible to consider. Certainly not in the police force, not even here in Australia where forensics was often at the forefront of international advances.

Operation Nobody was the best thing to happen to Meg.

Ever.

Working in forensics for Victoria Police was her dream come true, the goal she'd had since the age of twelve when a forensic scientist had done a school talk. Because she excelled at everything computer and digital, she was steered toward the analysis side and ended up not with a double degree, but a triple one. And then the calls started.

Her application was already in with Victoria Police and suddenly she had offers from seven different private companies. Only one was in Australia and she had zero interest in working overseas. She didn't even go overseas for holidays. Meg was offered four times the starting salary by the local private company over what the police force would pay yet she chose to follow her dreams.

It wasn't what she expected.

Although she loved the work and her team, Meg was bored silly and frustrated by the lack of funding which necessitated blow-outs in the time to turn around evidence, including analysis. She had no help. She pushed through and was proud of the little steps which would help not only find but then nail a killer. Over the course of a decade she grew a reputation and developed a network, mostly outside the force. And when she was seconded for a brief trial by Missing Persons, Meg jumped at the opportunity.

The images all taken, she saved everything to an encrypted speed stick and returned the fridge magnet and all its pieces to an evidence bag.

Missing Persons gave her a taste of field investigation because Ben Rossi saw her as more than the analyst-on-loan. When he left, she stayed, working with Homicide for a while but then the world and the team she was an integral part of fell apart. Her boss was murdered by a child abductor. Her position was under scrutiny and Meg was caught between being returned to her original position or facing a life in private enterprise.

Then Ben had called.

Meg checked she'd turned all the equipment off.

She stood at the door looking at the small room. This new team came calling at a pivotal moment in her life and she would never let it down.

NINETEEN

Nobody was coming for her. Not unless she could count on the seagulls to band together and break her out. Even the seals which normally visited the structure were absent.

Lyndall rubbed her wrists, wincing at the pain. They'd bound since early morning. She'd been careless. Stupid. Shown her hand almost the minute Marcus returned instead of biding her time and waiting for the right moment.

Finding no way to escape the structure overnight, she'd fashioned a weapon from hours of scraping the end of a loose floorboard until it was sharp. Over and over she'd thought through how to best use the makeshift weapon.

Marcus had arrived hours into the day and the boat had moved away to stop within sight, not far from the larger boat dressed up as a Parks Victoria vessel which had hung around all day. He brought food. Bottled water in a six-pack. A smirk which didn't leave his face even as he'd grappled with Lyndall for control of the timber stake. Later, she'd realised he'd set her up. Pushed her buttons. Probably for the sole purpose of exposing her intentions after a long night on her own.

The food was croissants and not just crappy supermarket

ones. These came in a box from a French bakery. Traditionally made, so it said.

She'd reacted out of sheer anger, fuelled from hours of remembering her distant past and the grief it refreshed, along with exhaustion, and lack of nutrients. The sharp end destined for his stomach ended up in the sea. He'd laughed at her then tied her hands together and forced her to sit at the small table.

'So much fire in your eyes and your heart. But not the speed or strength of your younger years. Nor the beautiful body which I remember with such—'

'No wonder bears in forests have become so popular.'

His face had gone blank. He had no idea what Lyndall meant and that was completely expected. Marcus believed to his core that women fawned over him. The sad truth was that for a while, she *had* adored him. The young him. The one who had elevated her reputation in the art world and stepped back, with grace, when she chose Alain as her husband.

She wasn't ready to revisit how it all began. Or why. Let alone how it ended. Not yet.

'Perhaps it is the lack of coffee which makes your tone so sharp. What a shame to be only a couple of kilometres from excellent cafés, yet have no way to reach them.'

'I could borrow your speedboat.'

Marcus threw his head back and laughed. Had her hands not been tied and her weapon not been floating in the sea, Lyndall might have used that instant, with his throat exposed, to stab his jugular. Stupid waste of opportunity.

'Eat, Nora. You're no good to me if you can't think clearly.' He pushed the box of croissants closer. 'I'll be your companion for the next two hours. By the time I leave, I expect you to have made the right decision about The Tides.'

She had no intention of helping him. Not yet.

Her hands were tied with the palms against each other, the rope tight and movement difficult. But she picked up the corner of a croissant and manoeuvred it to her lips. It was buttery and delicious but might have been poison, so much did she hate biting into it. This was one of Alain's favourite treats and there'd been a time she would make them for him, rising extra early to have them ready for the oven when he woke.

This was purely a power play from Marcus. A reminder of what he'd taken from her and all it did was harden her resolve to kill him.

He watched her eat the entire croissant, the indulgent smile on his face at odds with the cruelty in his eyes.

She drank from an open water bottle, just enough to help force down the last of the food. Then she leaned back in her seat. 'How did you get into my safe room?'

'I know the code.'

Her mind flicked over the hallway at home. There was no direct line of sight through any of windows or doors.

'You bugged my house.'

'Bug is such a coarse term, but yes, I have eyes all over it.'

'Then you've left a trail of evidence behind.'

Another laugh and he got to his feet. 'Not where anyone is looking, Nora. They're more interested in whether your artwork offers up any clues of your background and as recently as one hour ago, the women searching your home were clueless.' He came around the table and leaned in. 'Don't expect the cavalry anytime soon.'

When he'd finally left, not with the outcome he wanted, he'd cut the ropes from her wrists with an angry hiss. 'Next time is your final chance. I *will* bring those you love into this if you fail to give me what I want.'

If he meant Vince and Melanie, then she would hand over The Tides. She wasn't going to lose another family to the evil which was Marcus Bonner.

TWENTY

Liz and Pete were in his car a bit up and over the road from the address he'd found. She'd finished reading the information from the security company and reached the same conclusion – that Tony Shaw was involved in the abduction. He'd gained employment for the sole purpose of setting up a fake alarm system in Lyndall's house. How he knew she would need it was a whole other question.

Annette was running a background check on him from the little they knew and had confirmed the man did indeed live at this address.

'Has Aiden Strong sent over an image yet?' Liz asked. 'I can't believe they don't have a headshot in his file. Not for security work.'

'Nothing yet. He said he needed to go back over the shifts Shaw worked and would send the clearest one he could find of him in the building. Hang on, this is him now.' He opened the message and swore. Twice. 'Wiped.'

'What?'

'Little shit must have used the night shift he did to delete every bit of footage when he was at work.'

'Did he at least give a description?'

'Two secs.' Pete dialled.

Liz followed suit, calling Vince and stepping out of the car to talk.

'Any news?' There was hope in his voice.

'Some, but not enough. Sorry.'

'Saw you go up to the house earlier.'

'Meg and I had a hunch to follow and then had to get back. We're trying to gather intel on the person who installed the panic alarm last year. You said you were there.'

From the car, Pete's voice was raised enough to make out a few words, mostly uncomplimentary.

'There was nothing that stood out about him. Quiet. Friendly enough. Late thirties or a bit older. Lean build. Brown hair. One-eighty centimetres.'

'Do you know how Lyndall came to choose that firm?'

'Far as I'm aware she's used them for a decade or more.'

'That helps, thank you.'

'You think he put in a dud. This had to have been planned for a long time, Liz.'

'Yes. And yes. Vince we're getting some leads and once Pete gets off the phone, will go and speak to one. Can I catch you up on things later?'

'Yeah. Go follow the lead. Stay safe.'

When Liz slid back into the car, Pete was just hanging up and he looked pleased with himself. 'Got a description.'

'Brown hair, lean build, one-eighty centimetres, thirties or early forties?'

'Impressive. And yes. Plus, his daughter walked in on Shaw changing into the uniform, poor kid. Had his shirt off and she remembered a tattoo on his back.' Pete's eyebrows raised as a message dinged. 'This would be her artist's impression of it.'

There were times Liz admired Pete a lot. Annette had got nowhere with Strong Security despite having a track record of getting results with difficult people. Pete had swanned in there as if he was a new client and then thrown in the plot twist of knowing a whole lot more about their failings than they did. And now they had a decent clue.

The image was rough but sent a chill down Liz's spine.

She'd seen similar.

'Am I imagining it, Lizzie?'

She shook her head and opened the door, pausing to look at Pete. 'I think there's three tattoos and perhaps the only one we should focus on is the anchor. But my father had something eerily similar to the multi-headed serpent. We need this young woman to spend time with an artist to get more detail.'

Pete sent the last couple of messages to Ben. 'I'll arrange that. Let's go have a chat.'

As he climbed out, Liz's phone rang and they faced each other over the roof of the car as she answered. It was Ben and again, Liz got back in the car to speak privately, putting the call on speaker for Pete.

'We're at Tony Shaw's residence,' she said. 'About to cross over the road.'

'Sit tight. Meg has worked on the camera inside the fridge magnet. It was dead, thanks to her well-placed foot, and is a gift which keeps giving.'

Pete and Liz exchanged a glance.

'Reuben recognised the device and further to that, is aware of a theft just over six months ago which included dozens of them along with other high-tech toys. And he says they are very high-tech.'

'And you think Shaw is involved?'

'Reuben's gone to have a conversation about it with an old contact. Are you in sight of the residence?'

'Fifty metres away. Down the road.'

'Can't risk it. Come back for now.'

'Yes, boss.' Liz ended the call, somehow able to keep the frustration from her voice. 'Who do they think this man is if we can't even sit here for a bit?'

Pete pulled onto the road before answering. 'High-tech

surveillance equipment and other items stolen, but from where? Nothing which has come through VicPol. Maybe in another state. But if Reuben knows about it then how?'

'Through his previous employment,' Liz said.

'And if so, then is it of national security interest? Why can't we keep an eye on Tony Shaw?'

'Either someone else is watching him or no-one is because they don't know where he is. We might have found a person already under scrutiny and have to take very careful steps not to interfere,' Liz said. 'Or they might take this away from us.'

'We're not going to let anyone stop us finding Lyndall.'

'Agree, but is she involved? Pete, what if Lyndall's hidden past is criminal in nature and is catching up with her?'

Candace had papers strewn across the round table and she had one knee on a chair and supported her body with a hand on the table as she reached to the middle. Liz had no idea why she kept working in here rather than at her station, but with all the space she was currently using it did make some sense.

'Can you pass me the two pages closest to you?'

They were images printed from the photos Liz and Meg took earlier in the day. A hundred or so in A3 size. Some were from a distance, including the entire painting or sketch and its frame, while others were parts of one. The pieces Liz handed over the table were the latter.

'These are from the painting nearest Lyndall's door in her bedroom,' Liz said. 'It is a bit different from anything else in the house.'

Candace sorted pieces like an oversized jigsaw puzzle. 'Tell me how it is different.'

'I actually came in to offer you coffee. Or some lunch because Pete's in the kitchen making a giant communal salad or his version of it. But I'll try to explain what I mean first.' Liz wandered around the table, eyes on the plethora of parts.

'Almost everything on the walls of the house is either an oil painting or a charcoal sketch. The subject matter is all about Lyndall's life… her current life. Donkeys, cows, cats. Landscapes which are recognisable as views from around her property. Flowers, again ones she's grows. But the one near her bedroom door is from somewhere else. I don't know where but it is a sad painting.'

Now, Candace straightened and looked directly at Liz. 'Go on.'

'So, it is raining. There's a path through a forest but not like we have here. More an English forest or at least how I imagine one.'

'You've never been there?'

'I never have.'

Candace's face changed. A longing for something. Just for an instant. She must have a connection to England.

'The colours are vibrant but in a different way than the other oil paintings. I don't know much about art but there's a glow about it. And just one person. A young woman walking along the path.'

'In what direction. On the wall, I mean?'

'Toward the door. Oh.'

'Oh, indeed. And what do you make of that revelation?'

Liz found the image on her phone and enlarging it, moved it across the screen to scrutinise the parts. 'The girl is walking toward a kind of doorway or a portal? Perhaps Lyndall is into science fantasy and portals but look how narrow it is compared to the path.' The pieces fell into place. 'I'm probably seeing things which don't exist but…'

'But?'

'I believe, and so does Meg, that there's something inside the wall of the safe room. Hidden behind plaster and important enough that Lyndall left the door ajar at the risk of angering her captors. But the portal in the painting and shapes through open doors being similar is just me seeing things, right?'

'She's left the only clue she could by keeping the door open and it would be in the hope against hope of smart minds connecting it to her disappearance. That and the photos of her family which was terribly risky if she's been hiding from this danger for all of these years. Lyndall knew Vince would raise the alarm and find you.' Candace began to clear the table, piling the paper up. 'And I would love something to eat, thank you. And Pete.'

Over a bowl of salad which included about ten types of vegetables, nuts, cheese, and seeds, and was accompanied by bread rolls, Liz dug around on the team network for information about the tattoos. Annette was doing an official search but Liz couldn't shake the feeling that the smaller of the three was connected to a past case. Not only a past case, but a deeply personal one.

Ben had told her that the first case he'd planned for the team was to find her father. Kyle Moorland. Also known as Garry Ford, the unfortunate man whose identity Kyle stole after killing him decades ago. Last seen, Kyle was in a boat off Williamstown which exploded. The police couldn't locate his remains because there were none. Kyle was a sociopath who could weasel himself out of anything, including death. Twice.

All the files were loaded in anticipation of their investigation.

Liz took another bite, impressed with the results of Pete's scattergun approach to meal making. There wasn't much time to find what she wanted. Ben had asked her and Candace to meet with him in twenty minutes and she knew he needed answers. The powers-that-be were waiting like vultures to remove Lyndall's case from the fledgling team and like the rest of Nobody, Liz was determined it would not come to that.

Rather than open each file, she did a search of 'tattoo' and 'supremacist'. The latter being one of the ugliest parts of her father.

Sure enough, there was a report based on interviews with her niece who was one of the few people who knew him after he switched identities. She had described a number of tattoos and scars and with an artist, reproduced them as close to the original as possible. One of these was eerily similar to the image drawn by Strong's daughter.

No longer hungry, Liz pushed the bowl to one side and stared at the two images, which she'd put side by side. They were too alike to discount some kind of connection but was it through a mutual belief system or something far more troubling. Was there any chance that Tony Shaw knew Kyle?

TWENTY-ONE

Ben had made copious notes as well as recording the video call with the builder of Lyndall's house and for the first time today, he felt a corner had been turned. Liz arrived first, worry creasing her forehead.

'What's wrong?'

'I asked Candace earlier if I was seeing things which don't exist and now I'm thinking the same about a different issue.'

'What did Candace say?'

'She says that Liz has a sharp mind and great instincts and is on track with her investigation. May I join you both?' Candace was at the open door.

Ben waved her in and Liz offered a small smile as the other woman sat next to her.

'I've got interesting information about Lyndall's house. The builder now lives in the States and it took a letter from our legal department before he'd discuss Lyndall.'

'We have a legal department?' Liz asked. 'It wasn't a threatening letter?'

That made Ben chuckle. 'Nothing of the kind. We needed to prove we were a legitimate agency with Lyndall's best interests at heart.'

The fact the man had put up so much resistance was testament to his loyalty to a past client, but once he was aware Lyndall had been abducted, he was quick to assist.

'Lyndall worked closely with our builder on the plans, especially regarding the visibility from so many rooms and the panic room. She approached the latter with her own list of must-haves and he refined them to make it viable. The under-floor beams and metal plates are replicated in the walls and ceiling but only for that room.'

Candace shuffled in her seat. 'Lyndall wanted to know who was approaching the house. I imagine her cameras are trained on the areas the eye couldn't see.'

'Meg can confirm that. There's something more though. Something which fits in with the theories I'm hearing about the panic room. Lyndall insisted a system be installed which only she knew of and was infallible. The door employs a mechanism responding to a hidden button. Pressed twice, it prevents the door from being relocked until that is repeated. Further, it opens the door after a set period but only for fifteen centimetres, and even if then closed or opened wider, will return to its position after a few minutes.'

Liz and Candace glanced at each other.

'Share, please'

'It ties in with our speculation that there's something hidden in the room. Meg and I were careful at her house not to alert whoever is watching, but there were clues to that effect.' Liz opened the gallery on the phone and turned it for Ben to see. 'This painting is in the hallway between Lyndall's bedroom and the panic room. Candace and I feel it represents someone walking toward a portal of sorts, see, narrow, like a doorway?'

'This is a clever painting,' Candace said. 'because there's nothing else like it in the house and it is positioned to direct the eye to that door. She's made it almost impossible for the average person to connect her careful dots.'

'She's made it almost impossible for the people who want to

rescue her!' Ben couldn't believe the lengths Lyndall had gone to. 'We'll see what the team has to offer about a way to look behind the piece of wall.' He sat back. 'Andy called. Lyndall's fingerprints are gone.'

'Sorry, what?'

'I know, Liz. Fingerprints don't disappear from data bases yet hers have. Or been misfiled. He's looking into it.'

'Is Annette certain she doesn't have a hard copy? What if I go over it with her. Second set of eyes.' Liz looked ready to jump up and find Annette. 'There's so much pressure on us all that she might have simply missed them.'

Ben shook his head. 'We're narrowing down Lyndall's identity in other ways so let's keep on top of the priorities. There's only a few hours until I go back into a meeting and fight to keep this case with us. I'll call a team meeting shortly but I need you both to tell me where you think we are. Where we need to be. Candace?'

'We need to open up that wall.'

Liz nodded, and Ben agreed. It was more a case of how they could.

'Lyndall has gone to incredible lengths to hide something yet she's also made it possible – barely – to draw attention to it under the right circumstances. This is more than a person hiding from a bad past. I feel there's a contingency plan here, a way to negotiate her way to safety should she be found.' Candace frowned. 'Or to barter for another person's life.'

'Do you mean Vince and Melanie?' Ben asked.

Liz answered. 'She didn't know Vince when she built the house and Mel's only been in her life for a year or so. If we're right and Lyndall has another son…'

'Exactly. He may be unaware she is alive,' Candace said.

'But she knows he is.'

'Maybe, Ben. When her husband and son died, Lyndall may have found a way to protect the younger child or it may be more sinister. Whoever she's hidden from for all these years may know where he is.'

'Candace, would you work on finding this child, well, adult? If we can ensure his safety then perhaps these monsters lose their leverage. Annette may have something already but I'd appreciate your involvement. We need to find a way into that wall and I'll raise that at our meeting. Liz, where do we need to focus?'

For a moment he wondered if she'd heard because her attention was on her phone again, but then she turned it to show the drawing of the tattoos by the person who'd seen Tony Shaw dressing. She'd zoomed it in to focus on one in particular and seeing it isolated, Ben was sure it was familiar.

'Annette is searching the tattoos. Why this one?' He asked.

'Am I seeing connections which couldn't exist? Look at this second one which is also a drawing.' She slid the frame across to a similar image. 'This is from Kyle's file.'

Ben took the phone and switched back and forth between the two, his heart sinking. He'd long suspected Liz's father had a much wider network than they'd uncovered and had half-expected the criminal to assert his power over his daughter – all in his mind, of course – and flaunt being alive. He had no proof the man still lived but if he had to put money on it, he would.

'Crap.'

'Sure is.'

How can you sound so calm, Lizzie?

'Anything else?'

She gave him a look of 'isn't that enough for one day?' but took her phone back. 'Tony Shaw. Why can't we talk to him or at least watch him?'

'We'll revisit that once Reuben returns.'

'Then how about Pete and I start visiting the private art galleries where Alain Dubois had meetings?'

He must have taken too long to respond because Liz crossed her arms, her mouth in a straight line. She would do whatever he asked but he was disappointing her and there was little he could do to avoid it right now. His phone beeped a message from Reuben.

Back in twenty. Good intel.

'Reuben has something. Liz, would you set up a team meeting in twenty-five minutes? Everyone there if at all possible. And see where Annette is on the tattoos and double check the fingerprints.'

Liz rose and headed for the door.

'And me?' Candace asked.

'Stay a minute. Liz, can you close the door on your way?'

Waiting until Liz was not only out of earshot but sight, Ben considered his words. Talking about her behind her back wasn't comfortable.

'She's fine, Ben,' Candace said with a small smile. 'The best thing for her is finding her father and putting him behind bars, but she's exceptionally patient and resilient.'

He nodded, relieved. 'Thanks. This is a curve ball, the tattoos.'

'One which may be irrelevant. Or might be the connection we need to find Lyndall. Tony Shaw needs eyes on him, Ben.'

'We'll hear what Reuben has to say and I'll make some decisions then.'

'And you're fine. The team is happy with you as leader. Anything else?'

After she left, Ben gazed at the computer screen where he had an email confirming his meeting in just a few hours. Time was running out for them to keep this case. He hoped time wasn't running out for Lyndall.

'This is our last chance to speak face to face before I go back to the city to plead our case and I want enough positives to take with me. Who'd like to start?' Ben gazed around the table. Everyone was present and they all looked drawn. It was only going to get worse until the team was removed from the case or found Lyndall.

'May I?' Phoebe half-raised a hand.

Ben had only received a brief from her minutes ago and barely glanced at it. 'Please, go ahead.'

The young woman took a quick sip of whatever was in her keep cup, then began talking without making eye contact with anyone.

'My team has done a good job of collating and cross-referencing several of the more believable accounts we received following the podcast. We had close to one thousand responses and it took a while to narrow them down to fit the parameters from Meg regarding when and where.' She shot a look at Meg, who smiled encouragement. 'A pattern emerged. Over a two-year period there were three assassinations and a likely failed attempt across France, Italy, and Spain. And the failed one was also in France.'

'Assassinations?' Hamish asked.

'Figures.'

That was Pete, whose face was unreadable. Liz had her eyes on him and he gave her the slightest nod. There was always something between them which was unspoken. Ben was certain it wasn't anything physical but a synchronicity of thinking and knowing each other for so long.

'Yes, assassinations. All very bad people who ran drugs or guns or people.'

'What is the connection to the art world, Pheebsie?'

'My name is Phoebe.' She raised her head and stared at Hamish until he mouthed 'sorry'. 'The connection is that each victim was shot from a great distance as they entered an art gallery.'

The hush around the table was palpable.

Then Pete muttered, 'Knew it.'

'Knew what?' Phoebe asked. 'Lyndall's reputation as an excellent shot is based upon the one incident anyone knows about, but what I've uncovered has no evidence she was involved.'

'Not yet.' Meg grinned broadly. 'You are a legend, Phoebe. And your team. If you can send me the brief, I'll find those connections.'

Phoebe nodded and tapped on her phone. 'That's all from me.'

'Terrific work. Annette, seeing as you were working on the private art gallery angle relating to Alain Dubois' visit, do you have anything to add?'

'Ah, yes. Well, no.' Annette frowned as she picked up a notebook. 'Okay, nothing about assassinations as far as I know but I do have complete contact details for the curators of each gallery. Or at least, who was the curator in the year of Dubois's planned visit. Shall I follow up with each of them with a personal visit or phone call?' She looked at Ben.

'Let Meg have the list first so she can start a deep search and also a copy to Liz, please.'

'Of course. But I'm happy to go and talk to people as well.'

She must be getting frustrated being stuck here.

'Let's see what the outcome is of my meeting first. What you're doing is valuable here. Any news on the tattoos?'

'Still chasing those. And Tony Shaw is an enigma. Can't find much about him other than confirming his address.'

Reuben, who'd not spoken since returning a few minutes ago, cleared his throat. 'I can help with him.'

Ben and Liz's eyes met. There was finally a bit of fire back in hers. The briefing was giving them all a lot to work on and he anticipated she'd want to be on the road soon.

'The surveillance camera retrieved so capably by Meg and Liz belongs to a model which was trialled by certain covert groups in Australia. A batch of around five hundred disappeared from a secure facility a few months ago and the serial number matches records for those stolen. This is the first located.' Reuben's face was the most serious Ben had ever seen. 'As for Tony Shaw... he is a closed book. I guarantee he is ex-covert of some description and my guess is toward para-military. Sanctioned, most likely from the security surrounding him.'

'Yet he's waltzing around getting jobs, going into people's homes, and apparently untouchable!' Liz waved her arms around. 'Pete and I were right there at his house.'

'Give me a little time and I'll make it possible for you to bring him in,' Reuben spoke directly to Liz. 'An hour or two. Leave it with me?'

She seemed to relax and nodded. Pete raised both eyebrows but for once, stayed quiet.

Through all the conversations, Hamish had tapped his fingers on the table, only stopping a couple of times when Meg shot him stern glances. Ben didn't think he was being deliberately rude, but rather, had his own news to tell and was struggling to keep it in.

'Hamish, do you have—'

'Yes! Yes, I have found out where Lyndall was taken. I think. Or at least, in the general direction.'

'Good grief, Hamish, could you not have spoken up sooner?' Meg shook her head at him. 'Nobody would mind you jumping in with decent intel.'

'I see. Sorry. Anyway, you… Meg that is, wanted me to cross-check all the aerial data. Drone footage, satellite video and images, everything. Most of it is useless. At least for this mission. The land around Lyndall's property is difficult terrain and—'

'Hamish! Get to the point please.' Meg was getting impatient.

'Can I show rather than tell?' He tapped on the table and the horizontal screen appeared. It was a drone's eye view of Lyndall's property. 'Right. Now here, where the gate is at the top of the ridge, Pete found tyre tracks and footprints. All helpful, by the way.'

Pete's grunt gave nothing away, but like everyone else, his eyes were fixed on the screen.

Hamish touched the screen with both hands, using his fingers to expand the view. 'I found a neat little setting on our app which allowed me to kind of grab those tyre tracks and follow them and I have no idea how it works but please do not sell the tech to any governments.' One finger traced a route and he kept expanding the view. 'We are going to assume the vehicles, or one of them, carried Lyndall away. All the way along here, this long ridge, and then a turn through an empty paddock almost a kilometre away. See how it leads to this dirt road and then back to the main one.'

Even Ben had no idea Meg's app had features so advanced. She had a faint smile on her face as she leaned forward to observe.

'Things get tricky after that but I applied data from the satellite imagery at around that time and came up with this. It is a bit messy but anyway, take a look.'

The screen changed to a night time view of greater Melbourne. In the top left corner, a red circle indicated the tracking of the vehicles. It was all set to go at a much higher speed than real time and the red circle weaved past the outskirts of the western suburbs, ending up along an area Ben knew all too well.

Liz's father had led everyone to the same dock near Williamstown.

It was where he'd murdered a decent police officer and attempted to steal a child. And only a short distance off that dock, as he had fled arrest, his boat had blown up.

TWENTY-TWO

Pete drove and Liz fumed. In the backseat, Hamish had the sense to concentrate on his tablet. If he said anything annoying then she'd throw him out of the vehicle and might not even get Pete to stop first.

Her mind was a mess and she needed every quiet moment to get it back under control. Being frantic or reactive wasn't going to find Lyndall. Or her father.

What was the connection between Kyle and whoever took Lyndall?

If it was her father's appalling white supremacist views, then was there an underground organisation to uncover? Annette had just sent through a third image of the tattoo, this time from a prison inmate who had Neo-Nazi leanings. Apart from these three, it wasn't in the databases the team had searched to date. But Kyle was a loner who'd been removed from extremist groups because he was too… extreme.

My own damned father. What the hell does that say about me?

Liz had never been in a position to have children and in the past year she'd come to appreciate that. Passing on the kind of genes from such evil was terrifying. Yet her sister, Anna, had a beautiful daughter who Kyle raised, yet had none of his disgusting traits. If anything, she was the complete opposite.

'What are you expecting, Lizzie?' Pete spoke quietly enough for only Liz to hear. 'No one is waiting at the end of the pier to take us to Lyndall.'

She turned to look at him. 'I'm expecting us to do our job and find who left that dock with her whether by car or boat. Anything less and we're not fit for this work. Or her friendship.'

Pete's face was set. He agreed, she had no doubt. But there was something between him and Lyndall he wasn't disclosing, and it worried her. She'd thought through so many possibilities and ruled them all out. He had spent time at her home. He also brushed off any questions about their relationship which served to make Liz worry more.

'There's some parking a street back from the pier,' Hamish said. 'Keep things low key.'

Rather than tell Hamish that she and Pete both knew where to park and why, Liz looked back at him. 'Is there a way of seeing where Lyndall went after here? Where the vehicle she was in went next?'

'Reuben and I are working on it and Meg is hustling to add something to her software which might assist. So the answer is maybe.' He offered a hopeful smile. 'Lots happening out of sight.'

Pete pulled into a supermarket carpark and took two spots with his crap parking skills and general lack of care about what anyone thought. The BearCat was unmarked, but conspicuous by its size, dark tinting, and add-ons. He didn't need to bring it to anyone's attention further.

They waited to cross the road, Hamish still tapping on his tablet to the point of Liz wondering if she'd need to guide him over, like a kid. But he abruptly slid it into a shoulder satchel.

The wide grassed zone between the road and sea was busy with lots of children and teens, some using play equipment and others just chilling. A few older people walked their dogs and it was a typical afternoon in late summer along this popular strip. The pier was quiet. Most people used the much larger one a few hundred metres away down the beach. This one was purely for the dozen or so vessels berthed.

I don't want to be here.

Stomach churning, Liz forced her legs to keep walking when all she wanted was to run to the public loo and throw up. It might make her feel better for a minute but wouldn't help find Lyndall and nor would it bring Terry back.

'We won't be here long, Liz.' Pete's words were for her ears only.

He always knew. And he'd been here that awful day.

She nodded and led the way down the middle of the pier, past the boat she'd hidden behind holding the child she'd rescued from her father. Past the spot where Terry stepped into the line of fire to give her the chance to get to safety. And to the place where her father's boat had been tied up, filled with explosives as a contingency plan. He'd almost got away with the child.

But we saved her. She's with her mother again.

Liz stared out at where his boat exploded, sending timber and metal flying into the sky. Somehow he'd survived, of this she was certain. But what did he have to do with Tony Shaw or Lyndall?

Hamish was back on his tablet, slowly wandering along the pier before stopping beside Liz and Pete. 'I'm certain she was put onto a boat.'

'Go on,' Pete said, giving Hamish his full attention.

Liz kept her eyes on the water.

'Meg has requested more satellite footage from several companies and its beginning to filter through. We know the time the vehicle arrived here, so as long as Lyndall was still inside, it is a case of finding images which show the number of boats before and after.'

'How long?'

'Liz, there's no way of telling—'

'Then why even mention it? Get the information and then share it!' Liz spun around. One look at Hamish's fallen face and the anger evaporated. 'Sorry. Hamish, I am sorry. This place gives me nightmares but that's no excuse to snap at you.'

Pete was grinning and when Liz whacked his arm he acted like he was mortally wounded, which lightened the atmosphere. But Liz was kicking herself. This wasn't her at all and Hamish was being honest. She needed to use her energy for good.

'Let's talk to anyone we can find about that night.'

After they'd worked their way from the boat closest to the road to the last two at the end of the pier, Hamish took a phone call, walking quickly to the park to answer after glancing at the caller ID.

'Fine, we'll do it alone, Liz, like always.' Pete opened a bottle of water. 'He's probably a double agent reporting in.'

Liz stared at him. 'Seriously, Pete.'

'No, really. Look at how he acts. He's disruptive. Plays down his intelligence. Goes out of his way to be obnoxious so no one gets close to him. Disappears at odd times. Reckon if you tried to be his best pal he'd show his true colours.'

'You're being ridiculous but please, you go and be his best pal and test your theory.'

'Me? Nah, he'd be too suspicious. Do you want the boat on the left or the right?' He took a long drink of water, eyes never leaving Liz.

'Left. Have you told Ben you feel like this?'

Pete shrugged and drank more.

Liz headed to the last boat on the left of the pier but she glanced over to where Hamish was in animated conversation on his phone. Pete had good instincts about people and everything he'd observed was true, but it was more likely the ex-soldier with a clouded history was just a prat who was unaware of how annoying he could be than a double-agent. Or whatever Pete wanted to call him.

The boat was a decent sized cruiser with a locked side hatch. Liz called out a few times then peered over the side. Everything was locked. But there was a security system on board with two cameras pointing back at the pier. Liz tapped a message on her phone with her name and a request to call urgently on a police matter, then held it in front of the closest camera for a full minute. She sent the boat's name and registration to Meg.

Pete was chatting to a man at the other boat so Liz walked back to the park. They'd already noted other security cameras and got Meg onto it, so it was a matter of time to get footage, whether from cameras or satellites.

'Sorry to run off, Liz.' Hamish was puffing after jogging across the grass to meet her. 'Reuben is bringing in Tony Shaw.'

'What? Oh that is brilliant.'

This was the best news of the day.

'Looking forward to seeing him in action.'

'Reuben?'

'He has a reputation for getting what he wants.' Hamish smirked. 'At least when it comes to criminals.'

And there you go again with your double meanings.

'I barely know him. Or you.'

'I'd like to change that.'

Some things were best deliberately misunderstood. 'Yes, I really should spend some time getting to know Reuben.'

'He isn't what you think.'

Liz's phone rang and she held it up to show Hamish it was Reuben calling. His face went blank and he wandered off in the direction of the pier.

'Are you going to pick up Tony Shaw?' Liz asked without a greeting.

Reuben chuckled. 'News does move fast.'

'Hamish told me.'

'How does he know? Anyway, yes, I'm almost at his house

and will politely request he accompanies me for a pleasant chat about missing surveillance equipment.'

'And if he doesn't want to? Are you able to arrest him?'

'Doubt if I need to do more than ask. I've got a bit on him and he's been around long enough to know how the world works. I rang to ask if you'd like to observe the interview.'

'Yes. Yes, thank you. We're almost finished at the pier so won't be far behind you.'

Liz went to find Pete, who was on his way to her with Hamish.

'Owner of the boat had it out the other night. All night, taking a group for a tour around the bay,' Pete said. 'Probably a bit of illegal activity as well.'

'So they saw nothing?'

'I didn't say that. He reckons when he was chugging his way out that he noticed another boat take his berth. Didn't think anything of it because there's room there and he figured it was someone stopping for supplies. But when he returned in the early hours it was gone.'

This fitted with the belief that Lyndall was put onto a boat.

'Hamish? Can you extend the timing parameters to when Pete's new friend left and returned?'

'Of course.'

'Are you going to observe the interview with Tony Shaw?' Liz asked, watching Hamish closely.

'Huh?' That was Pete.

'Um… nah. I think I'm needed elsewhere, sadly.'

'So Reuben didn't ask you?'

Hamish fussed over his tablet. 'Hm? Oh, yeah he did. That's why he called me.'

Liz's heart dropped. Who had Hamish been speaking to? It wasn't Reuben.

'Hello. Anyone? What interview with Tony Shaw?'

Nobody answered and Pete threw his hands in the air.

· · ·

Tony Shaw was exactly how Liz imagined. What she was unprepared for was the interview room and observation area which weren't remotely like any she'd ever seen. It was on a different floor from the central operations hub and through a carpeted reception room, although with no friendly face to greet you.

She sat on what might be considered a gamers chair – high-backed with arms and headrest and the ability to adjust into a dozen positions, and incredibly comfortable. It swivelled, so she could simply turn to speak to anyone else observing if she chose. And there were three levels with three chairs on each. Liz half-expected an arm to appear from below with a tray of food and wine. It truly was gold class.

In front of her was the normal one-way glass but it filled an entire wall.

Beyond was a room which defied the norms of interview or interrogation rooms. There was a table. But on it was a coffee machine and cups. And a water cooler and glasses. A bar fridge was tucked beneath. The seating was comfortable. Tub chairs by three around a coffee table. A sofa which looked like a pull-out bed. And in one corner, two straight-backed chairs upside down on a smaller, rectangular wood table.

Tony Shaw leaned his back against a wall, eyes closed. He was an uninteresting man, physically. Average height and build. Cropped brown hair. Lean face. He'd pass for a doctor if in a white jacket or a teacher or a taxi driver. Useful for someone who liked to steal and misrepresent themselves. Was he contemplating his future? Planning his answers? Or dozing?

Reuben entered the room through a door on the opposite side of the room and his eyes flicked to the mirror, so clear through the glass Liz smiled as if he could see her.

The other man straightened, blinking rapidly.

'Please take a seat, Tony. Wherever you want.'

Reuben waited until Shaw sat on one of the tub chairs, running both palms over the material. Then he sat opposite.

'Nice chairs. Nice room. Might settle in here for a while.' Shaw folded his arms.

'No need. I have a few questions then won't hold you up further.'

Shaw threw his head back and laughed.

Reuben waited, impassive.

Pete would love to see this.

But Pete was busy chasing intel from the pier with Hamish. For once though he hadn't moaned about it and Liz was certain he was watching Hamish closely. Her long-time partner often jumped to conclusions but was correct more than wrong. But this was a serious accusation he'd made because Ben and Candace chose the team and neither of them were easily fooled.

'You've never had jail time,' Reuben said. He'd waited until Shaw stopped laughing. 'I'm guessing you have plenty of friends or associates who know what a prison is really like so it makes me wonder why you'd want to be the recipient of a life sentence. And at the worst prison we could find for you.'

'What do you mean.'

'About the prison? Think of ninety percent of each day in solitary. Think of eating the same food every single day for decades and it will be the foods you hate the most. No contact with anyone, not even guards because you'll be in a wing where no contact is possible. A door will open once every twenty-four hours for exactly one hour. Outside the room is a garden… did I say garden? I meant a ten-by-ten space which is bricked higher than anyone could ever see over and covered with electrified mesh. Sure, you can see the sky but it will be at night. And whether it is bucketing rain or as hot as an oven you stay there for one hour while your cell is cleaned. That cell is the same size and has a loo and a mattress and nothing else. Not a thing. Sound inviting?'

Another laugh but this one was nervous and short.

'Why would you think I'm not serious, mate?'

'We don't do that to inmates in Australia. Mate.'

'Yeah. We do actually but only for the most stupid criminals. The ones who think they fly under our radar and then make a stupid mistake. Like stealing surveillance equipment from the government and then being caught installing it in a civilian's house.'

Reuben had barely moved and his voice remained steady to the point of being almost relaxed. He let the words do their work, his body language open. This confused Shaw, who tightened his arms and shifted a bit so his legs weren't directly facing Reuben.

'You saying I'm stupid isn't going to make me answer questions.'

'Did I say it was you I described?'

Behind Liz, the door opened and Candace took the next seat.

'Meg has some news for you. I'll stay and observe.'

'Reuben's good at this.'

Candice smiled, her attention on the window. 'Shaw doesn't have a chance.'

TWENTY-THREE

Meg's fingers were flying over a keyboard and she didn't look up when Liz approached. 'Two secs. Grab a seat.'

Liz pulled up a wheeled chair and sat close enough to admire how fast Meg was – and admit how little she understood of what was on one of the screens. Lines of code moved rapidly as Meg added even more. Another screen had two facial recognition programs running based on photos of Alain and one of Jean-Paul. The third screen was blank.

'Has Shaw cracked yet?' Meg lifted her hands from the keyboard.

'No, but I like how Reuben is handling him.'

'Matter of when, not if. Okay, I have some news.' She clicked something and the third screen faded in, showing a receipt. 'Flowers from the florist at the cemetery. I traced the credit card used but please don't mention that to anyone at this point as I may have taken liberties with due process.' Another click. 'Belongs to this man.'

There was a professional head shot of a man, maybe late fifties, jet black hair combed back. He had sharp features which were attractive in a television mafia-boss way.

'Marcus Bonner. German-born Australian citizen. Has lived here for close to forty years. International art collector and dealer. Travels through Europe each year to attend showings and auctions. He owns Bonner Art Gallery.'

'Please tell me this was on the list for Alain?'

'It was on the list.'

'So am I going to go say hello?'

'You are.' This was Ben, who'd wandered across from speaking with Annette. 'Take someone.'

'Everyone is busy, boss. And I'm less of a threat alone.'

'I can come. I really want to do more than I am.' Annette had followed Ben. 'All I'm doing is waiting for people to come back to me and I can manage any new info on the road.'

Liz looked at Ben, who nodded. It would be good for Annette to get out of the building. She'd been a beat cop for a long time before moving into managing interviews and interrogations and it would give them a chance to talk. While she'd known Annette for years, she'd barely caught up since arriving at the building.

'Can you be ready in ten minutes?'

'Sure thing.' Annette grinned and hurried to the back rooms.

Meg glanced at Ben. 'We are confident the surveillance cameras planted at Lyndall's have no sound attached and I am as certain as I can be there's nothing other than those inside. All we need is to confirm Lyndall's abductor wants something from her, rather than a third party. There's been no ransom request.'

'And then we can go and find whatever she's hidden and offer it as bait,' Ben said. 'Reuben might get some results which point us in the right direction. And Marcus Bonner. But be careful with him, Liz. His reason for leaving flowers may be innocent.'

'Or not. I know and we'll be cautious.'

Liz tracked down Pete before leaving. He was in front of the wheeled board Candace used in the second room, deep in thought. She didn't want to disturb him and backed away.

'I know you're there. Come in.'

'Annette and I are heading out to speak to the person who left flowers in the cemetery.'

He turned around. 'Should I come?'

'No. But you need to know the man owns one of the art galleries on Alain's itinerary.'

'Wait, he might actually have known Alain? I should come with you.'

Maybe you should.

'You're busy, dude.'

Pete ran a hand through his hair. 'I need to finish this. Candace and I are working on finding the second child, although she's conveniently racked off to watch the interrogation.'

'She might pick stuff up we wouldn't.'

'Yeah, I know. Go talk to this art person but if you think he's involved, call me.'

'Yes, Mum.'

'Lizzie…'

'I'm teasing you. Stop being so protective and find that kid. Adult. And I will call.'

Once inside the vehicle, Annette hardly stopped talking. Through the Burnley Tunnel, along the Monash Freeway, onto Eastlink and finally Peninsula Link, she chatted about everything other than the case. If she was trying to make up for not seeing Liz in so long then it was working.

'You need this exit,' Annette said.

'For Mount Martha? No, the next.'

'Quicker this way.'

Liz took the exit and the navigation complained, going on about rerouting.

'I went to high school near the art gallery. Well, not close but the same area. We had an excursion there once.'

'But you haven't mentioned it to anyone.'

'Sure I did. I told Hamish once I saw it on the list of galleries.'

And there's that name again.

'So what was it like? I believe it is private.'

'We weren't allowed through all of it. Um… it is an older building. Heritage listed I think. Behind big gates. The art was too weird for me. I like landscapes and portraits but this was mostly abstract.'

'Do you remember Marcus Bonner?'

'No. I was only there because I was going through a phase of thinking art was cool and anyone could do it. That I could do it.' She laughed shortly. 'I was terrible. I tried abstract after the excursion and never bothered again. Moved my course selections for the next semester to follow my other dream.'

'The police force?' Liz glanced across.

'Would you believe I wanted to be an historian? I loved religious studies and had visions of myself wandering around dusty old tomes in some European church but somehow that turned into dusty old boxes in a police station.'

Somehow it fitted that Annette, who was a superstar records cop, had longed for a quieter and slower life. She'd been great on the beat but never had ambition.

'Take the next left then a sharp right. From memory the road climbs for a while.'

Again, Liz ignored the navigation program and in a few minutes had parked outside a long, high wall in a quiet road. From so high up she could see glimpses of Port Phillip Bay despite being on the wrong side of the highway to expect views.

Impressive wrought-iron gates were closed and Liz pressed a button on a security panel marked 'visitors'.

'How may I help?' A deep, male voice responded.

'Good afternoon. Detective Sergeant Liz Moorland and Detective Constable Annette Benski here. We'd appreciate a few minutes of your time. Specifically of Marcus Bonner's time.'

The gates opened enough for them to go through and then immediately closed behind. Liz glanced around for alternative exits, should it come to that. She had no reason to view Bonner as a suspect but this meeting might change that.

'I do remember this place!' Annette pointed to where the driveway went around the building and disappeared. 'We all came in a mini bus and the gates were open and we drove all the way around the back.'

'What's around there?'

'Probably it was originally the servants entrance and quarters. Because this isn't a residence as it would have been in the eighteen hundreds, I imagine it is where they get deliveries. I recall we followed a long and narrow corridor with lots of rooms off it. We passed a kitchen and I got a look inside and it was huge.'

Liz had researched the property quickly before leaving headquarters.

'This has been a private gallery for more than fifty years. There are occasional fundraisers held here for a different charities plus regular balls for the patrons.'

'Who even has this kind of money?'

Annette looked star struck. If she'd wanted to become an artist, she'd understand how difficult it was to rise to the top. Few did. Even fewer Australians.

So what made Lyndall different?'

'Welcome to Bonner Gallery.'

Marcus Bonner was a man who looked after his body and wore a suit tailored to make the most of his efforts. His presence was commanding and Annette went very quiet and turned her eyes to the ground. He stood on the top step with a disarming smile.

'Please, come inside.'

Liz immediately took the steps, offering a hand to shake. Bonner was a head taller and close up, the signs of ageing were more obvious.

'Good afternoon. I'm Liz and this is Annette.'

Best to keep things casual.

Annette had joined Liz and nodded rather than extending her hand. Bonner didn't seem to notice, turning with an arm gesture for them to follow. He strode to a side door.

'Are you alright?' Liz whispered.

'Bad feeling about him.'

'He's just a man. You observe everything we see and I'll talk, if that helps?'

There was a slight nod and Liz took that as a yes.

They stepped through the side door, into a tiny, glassed foyer.

'I have a wonderful curator who insists no outside air comes in without filtration. Better for the artworks, particularly the older ones.' Bonner locked the side door. 'Only a few seconds then the internal doors open.'

They did. A silent parting of double doors.

Bonner headed through a grand foyer, complete with sweeping stairway to a mezzanine level, then into one of many rooms.

The room was the size of a small house with no windows, and all walls displayed a dozen paintings each. In the centre of the room were cushioned chairs, each facing a wall.

'Please, take a seat so we can talk.'

I'd rather look around.

Liz made herself comfortable while Annette perched on the edge of her chair, gazing around with wide eyes. Bonner moved another seat so he could face them, which he did with an expectant expression.

'Thank you for seeing us, Mr Bonner—'

'Marcus.'

'Marcus. We're investigating a missing person case and your name has come up as a possible past contact. If you don't mind answering a few questions, it might be helpful to us.'

'Certainly, although I'm not aware of anyone I'm close to being missing.'

'The questions are more around someone close to the person in question. Alain Dubois. And his son, Jean-Paul.'

Liz watched Bonner's face like a hawk. His eyes narrowed for a split second.

'Alain? He passed away many years ago. As did his young child, A tragic boating accident in Port Phillip Bay. He was a fellow art dealer and visited this gallery just days before his death.' Bonner's shoulders slumped. 'A terrible thing.'

'Was his visit here the only time you met?'

'Not at all. My work takes me to Europe often and our paths crossed a dozen times. He was a fine man.'

'Is that why you left flowers on his grave?'

He sat back, eyebrows raised. 'That is how you have connected me to him? I am confused how you would discover this but no matter... how is Alain relevant to your missing person?'

'We're investigating the disappearance of his wife.'

Bonner got to his feet and walked halfway down the room to gaze at a painting.

Annette's attention was on the rest of the gallery as she slowly turned her head as far as possible to stare at any artworks in her line of view. Then she turned the other way, abruptly dropping her eyes again when Bonner stalked back.

He didn't sit, putting his hands on the back of the chair and staring intently at Liz.

'Why would you be looking for Nora Egan?'

A name at last.

'Alain's wife. Jean-Paul's mother.'

'Well, yes, unless he'd married someone else earlier in his life. Nora left Alain, taking their other child and neither were ever seen again. She's hardly a missing person after what... thirty years or more?'

'Left him when?'

Straightening, Bonner shrugged. 'I was hardly in their inner circle of friends, I'm afraid. But it was not long before his visit here. He was sad. When I heard he and the child had fallen from a boat it was obvious it was by his hand. Some men don't do well with loss and he'd been devoted to her.'

'You knew Nora. Personally?'

He returned the seat to its earlier spot. 'I met her once or twice. She was a great talent but clearly a poor human. Most artists lack the ability to return the love so eagerly bestowed on them by lesser mortals.'

Liz stood and wandered to one of the paintings close to the doorway, Bonner on her heels. In her peripheral vision she saw Annette go the other way.

'I'm afraid I have a video conference scheduled shortly, so unless you have anything else?'

'This is beautiful painting. Do you buy art from all over the world?'

'Well, yes. The collection is renowned internationally for its quality and we have hosted some of the world's most important art critics and collectors. Are you collector?' Bonner was uncomfortably close to Liz but she merely smiled.

'Not at all but I am impressed by anyone who can create such a gallery. I read that you've been its driving force for many years. Without trying to sound rude, was it your own work or an inheritance?'

He stiffened slightly.

'My father, if you'd call him that, was a drunk Irishman who loved gambling and my beautiful mother spent much of her hard-earned income bailing him out of his messes. My work ethic is from her as she ran an inn in Germany, where I grew up, once we got away from him. But no inheritance. Just hard work. I really do have to go.'

'Thanks for your assistance.' Annette was back at Liz's side and nodded at him. 'We won't take up any more of your time.'

A moment later they were in the sunshine and the door at the top of the steps clicked shut behind them. Neither spoke until they were back in the car on the other side of the gates. Liz locked them in, then shook her head at herself. They were quite safe out here.

'I got a photo,' Annette said. 'The painting he walked off to look at when you asked about Alain's wife.'

'Oh, that was risky.'

'But I think worth it.' Annette handed the phone over. 'If you enlarge the bottom left, the name of the artist is quite clear.'

It was Nora Egan.

TWENTY-FOUR

Having put as many queries out as he could about Lyndall's second child, Pete joined Candace to watch the interview. She was engrossed, making notes while keeping her eyes on the window, and didn't even glance at him.

He dropped onto the seat beside her.

Tony Shaw sat without a word as Reuben made them both coffee.

'Shaw was just about to say for the twentieth time that he doesn't know a thing about Lyndall or bugging her house. Reuben got up and began making coffee so his words fell flat. He's an excellent interrogator.'

'Wish I was in there.'

'We do need Shaw alive, Pete.'

'Oh, he would be. For long enough.'

Candace chuckled then made a note on the tablet on her lap. 'Shaw's crumbling. With Reuben's back to him, look at his demeanour. His neck is stiff. Arms straining against nothing but the pressure of his hands pushing down on the table.'

'He's pouring sweat.'

'Good observation.'

Reuben returned to the table with two coffees, placing one

near Shaw before taking his seat again. He didn't touch his cup but Shaw took a gulp then pulled a face.

'What? Too hot? Can't be the taste because I chose the beans myself.'

With a glare, Shaw took the lid off a bottle of water and drank.

'Imagine a world without coffee. I peg you as a coffee connoisseur. Someone who has an expensive coffee machine and takes his time savouring the first of the day. But in solitary confinement, there's no coffee. You don't get to line up with the other inmates to drink your ration of watered-down java. I can see it now.' Reuben leaned back in his chair and put an ankle onto a knee. 'Those long days and longer nights? You'll be remember what it feels like to make your own coffee. Go to the cafés of your choosing. Sit in the sun with a croissant and juice.'

'Don't like croissants. Not even the authentic French ones from the Peninsula.'

'I'm new to Melbourne and I do like pastries. Where's best on the Peninsula?'

'What's in it for me?'

'Might not throw my steaming hot cup at your face.' Reuben hadn't changed from his relaxed, conversational tone. 'And I won't add croissants to your daily rations.'

Shaw threw his head back and laughed.

'All an act. He's about to crack.'

Candace's voice was excited and Pete looked at her with surprise. She was the trickiest person in the team to get a read on because she masked everything. Not now though.

The laughter stopped.

Shaw pushed his cup away. 'What do you want from me? I'll talk but I need immunity.'

Reuben picked up his cup for the first time and took a sip.

. . .

Candace and Pete headed back to the hub. Reuben had called a break and was moving Shaw into a room without anything other than a loo, sink, and bed cut into the concrete wall topped with a thin mattress.

'This second child of Lyndall's?' Candace asked.

They were following a series of passages.

'Without her real name this is difficult. Alain Dubois doesn't show up as the father of any child apart from the mention on the headstone. And while I remember, I've asked Meg to look for whoever paid for the burials.'

'Now *that* is good thinking.'

'I agree.' Pete grinned. 'Underestimated as always.'

'Rubbish. Every one of us is here for our unique talents.'

'Even Hamish?'

Candace stopped dead and Pete backtracked to face her. 'Well, other than playing the drones and being a sharp shooter, what is it he does, exactly?'

'Not that Ben needs to explain his choices, but Hamish has skills the team needed. We all know his way of interacting is a bit different but he has a decent track record of results. Other than his obvious admiration for Liz, what actual concerns do you have about Hamish?'

Pete gave it some thought. All he had was speculation. No hard evidence that Hamish wasn't playing by the rules or worse, working against the team. He wasn't about to be considered a whinger.

'Maybe I'm just used to being the one who pushes boundaries.'

She wasn't convinced. Not by the way she tilted her head slightly and kept her lips straight.

'I'll give him a break, okay?'

They began walking again.

'You know, Pete, you can tell me anything. If it isn't for the team's ears then let me know. And if anyone – not just Hamish, arouses your suspicions as opposed to poking at your ego, then you can trust me.'

'Yeah, I know.'

'So, the child?'

'I've left a crap-load of messages for contacts from my… past life. People who know stuff about deliberate disappearances and don't mind asking difficult questions. One may or may not have access to records concerning witness protection and may or may not take a quiet look.'

'May or may not?'

He shrugged. 'Best we don't know too much. Also have someone following up French connections. It is a slow-moving machine trying to get facts about Alain Dubois.'

Pete's phone rang. 'It's Liz.' He tapped 'accept'. 'I'm with Candace on speaker.'

'Oh good. Annette's listening in here. We've had a meeting with Marcus Bonner which was… interesting. He is very suave and slick and charming until pressed. He knew Alain Dubois as an art dealer who he met on a number of occasions but only once at his gallery. He referred to him as a fine man.'

Annette spoke. 'He has the opinion that Alain is responsible for the tragedy which took his life and Jean-Paul's.'

'As in, deliberate?' Pete asked.

'Yes. He knew Lyndall and has a low opinion of her. Get this. He says not long before the visit to the gallery by Alain, Lyndall took the second child and left the marriage and the older son behind. And we finally have a name. He called her Nora Egan.'

Candace stopped and opened her tablet, tapping the name into the search bar. 'Liz, Annette… I'm doing a quick search and there's several pages just using her name. Public information.'

'I've already spoken to Meg who is keen to get us all together. We're half an hour away. Annette sent her a photo she sneakily took of a painting in the exhibition room we were in. It has Nora Egan as the artist and it definitely reminds me of some of

Lyndall's work. I keep going back to him saying she left with the second child.'

'We're on our way up to Meg now,' Pete said. 'And I'll give Reuben the name of Nora Egan to add more weight to his interrogation.'

'Okay. See you soon.'

'If you like, I'll tell Reuben,' Candace said. 'Go and see Meg.'

She turned without waiting for a reply and Pete carried on to the hub. This was a major step forward.

Meg needed more fingers and monitors. Cloning herself would be an even better solution. She left a couple of searches running and went to the table, tapping instructions for a few minutes before raising the vertical screen.

Having Lyndall's real name changed everything. Instead of searching based upon a range of clues – some of a dubious nature – and then attempting to cross-reference the results, she now had a place to look. She set the screen up, using a finger to hold, then move, images and text until satisfied.

Reuben let himself in and headed for the kitchen. Candace was close behind. Pete had already returned from watching the interrogation and was in one of the back rooms after a brief discussion with Meg.

Nobody else was here.

This would have to do for now and she could brief the others as they arrived.

She checked her desk and made a couple of adjustments to one of the searches, then gulped down some water.

I know we're close. So darned close now.

'Has Ben left?' Pete glanced at Ben's office as if to confirm it.

'Only a few minutes ago. He has the meeting in the city.'

Pete circled the table, his eyes missing nothing.

When Candace and Reuben joined them, Meg touched the screen. 'Meet Nora Egan. Lyndall in another time and place.' The image enlarged. 'She is aged twenty in this photo. So far this is the oldest I've found.'

Everyone stared. Young Lyndall had long dark hair flowing over her shoulders and she wore jeans and a blouse which showed off a good figure. Her smile was broad as she posed behind an easel. She was outdoors, holding a palette and brush, her eyes directly on the camera. And her eyes gave away it was definitely Lyndall.

Meg began to scroll through more images, each enlarging for a few seconds then returning to its original size as the next pushed it away.

'I'm still building a profile but what I can tell you is that Lyndall is Aussie by birth. Her connection to Europe began through her art and then she moved to France to marry Alain, an art dealer. She travelled a fair bit for exhibitions and the like and this photo tells me she was a popular guest at those, and exclusive dinner parties. I'll know more soon and once Phoebe is back, she can help me cross-reference the assassination information.'

Reuben looked grim. 'Are you trying to link Lyndall to murders?'

'No way,' Pete said. 'She isn't a killer.'

'Of course she is and as recently as a year ago.' Hamish wandered in.

'She was saving her neighbour's life, not assassinating a mafia boss.'

Meg was impressed with how measured Pete kept his voice but his hands were pressed against the side of his legs. How interesting. Was that because of his soft spot for Lyndall, or his unease with Hamish?

'Do we know with certainty the man she shot recently was not part of organised crime?'

'Mate, this is a waste of—'

'No, we don't.' Meg didn't have the time or bandwidth for their... whatever it was. 'But right now what matters is connecting enough dots to lead us to Lyndall.' She hoped her expression was enough to make them pull their heads in. 'Hamish have you got any further with the imagery around the dock?'

'Some news. May I?'

He looked at Meg for permission to touch the screen.

'I'll lower this one so go ahead and use the horizontal.' One tap and the vertical screen disappeared. This way she wouldn't lose the way it was set up for later.

Hamish wasted no time in turning the entire table into a nighttime map of Greater Melbourne. 'If you look closely, this is a recording of a combination of live images all merged to create a fairly decent overview of the night Lyndall disappeared. Nora Egan, that is.'

Pete shot Hamish a look, his eyes narrowed, but his mouth stayed shut.

'We can more or less follow the path from her house to the dock... at least the vehicle which carried her there. I've been back down there and found a shop on the opposite side of the street which had a camera pointing in the right direction for us.' He used his phone to send something to the screen. 'Hope this works.'

A dark image appeared. Grainy. It was night and there was no sign of anyone around. The park was just visible and beyond it, masts of yachts.

'I've tried to improve the quality but here,' Hamish pointed. 'there's the outline of what I think is a Pajero or Land Cruiser. Its lights are off but there's a door open.'

Meg adjusted the focus and the contrast. 'Not much improvement but yes, I agree with what you are seeing.'

'The tyre tread we found along the back of her place would match those 4WDs.' Pete leaned in to stare at the image. 'So are they moving her onto a boat, or into another vehicle? Has there been no other results from cameras? The dock had some. One of the boats did.' He straightened, eyes on Meg.

'I'll chase those up again, soon as I get some help on other things.'

'I can go back and speak to boat owners again,' Hamish offered.

Meg checked the time. 'No. Let's keep things central until the boss returns.'

Reuben spoke for the first time. 'This will help me with Shaw.' He gestured to the table. 'Having Lyndall's real name as well. There's something he said though which made no sense.'

'About the croissants?' Pete asked.

'Yes. He dislikes them, even what he called the 'authentic French ones.' From the Peninsula.'

'Which Peninsula? Can we push him on it?' Meg pointed to the map. 'From the dock, a boat has relatively easy access to either Mornington or Bellarine Peninsulas. Both have hundreds of places to moor. But Liz and Annette went to Mount Martha so it links to the former.'

The others turned to her.

'I'm going to need some help. We need to find everything on Marcus Bonner.'

TWENTY-FIVE

'Is Annette with you?' Meg met Liz at the inner door, looking past her.

'No but she's only a few minutes behind. She wanted to smoke.'

'She smokes?'

'First I knew that she did. Poor thing got frazzled by meeting Marcus Bonner and she said something about the stress of this week getting to her.'

She'd dropped Annette on the corner. Liz wanted coffee and a loo break but the expression on Meg's face was compelling.

'What's happened?'

'There may – emphasis on *may* – be a connection with Marcus Bonner beyond his past relationship with Alain Dubois. Tony Shaw made a throwaway comment to Reuben about croissants on the Peninsula.'

'What exactly?'

'I didn't hear the conversation but Shaw expressed a dislike for croissants, even the authentic French ones from on the Peninsula. Reuben, Pete, and Candace confirm he said that, so I need Annette to search for bakeries and the like to find who makes ones which fall into that category.'

'Or at least his understanding of it.' Liz followed Meg to her desk. 'Assuming he means the Mornington Peninsula. France. Art. Each man having a different kind of contact with Lyndall. This is pointing toward Bonner.'

'Sure is. Ben better get the approval of us to continue. I sent through a brief a few minutes ago in case he is still in the meeting. For now, Reuben is working on Shaw. Would you talk to Vince please? I'll send a few images of Nora to you and I'd like his opinion. See if there's anything new which comes to mind.'

After a dash to the restroom and collecting a diet cola instead of a coffee, Liz rang Vince from her desk.

'Liz? Please tell me something good.'

The worry in his voice was distressing. She pushed away an urge to apologise for not staying more in touch because, when? Her time was fully occupied and she was doing her best.

'We're getting closer. Are you at home?'

'Yeah. Just dropped Melanie at a friend's house for the night. Birthday party sleep over and she wanted to go something bad.'

'Best thing for her. It can't be fun having security patrols up and down the driveway and knowing Lyndall isn't home yet. Vince, have you ever heard the name Nora Egan?'

Annette arrived, hurrying to the back rooms.

'Yes. Yes, I have. Doesn't Lyndall have one of her paintings?'

'Which one?'

'Give me a min. It isn't signed, I know that much.'

Liz began writing notes by hand. She'd checked every piece of artwork for signatures and many had none. Not one had Nora Egan's name.

'After we moved the gun box into the panic room, she told me… damn, why didn't I think of this earlier?'

'Take your time.'

Vince's tone was gruff. He was annoyed with himself. 'She stood next to a painting and said it was painted by Nora Egan. It meant nothing to me but she made me repeat it. I asked why and she gave me one of those intense stares and said I'd know if I ever needed to tell anyone it existed.'

There was a sound. A thump.

'I should have remembered, Liz.'

'Keep it together, Vince. Her disappearance was stressful and she hasn't helped herself by being so vague all the time. Which painting?'

I know which painting.

'In the hall between her bedroom and the door to the panic room.'

Liz closed her eyes. She'd been right to pay it attention. It meant something important. Critical. And Lyndall had carefully planned for just such a worst-case-scenario. Clever.

'Vince, we're smart enough to work this out. Candace and I have already discussed the significance of that painting without knowing Lyndall painted it.'

'Wait. Lyndall is Nora Egan?'

'She is.' Eyes open, Liz scribbled words in a haphazard fashion, her thoughts mingling with what Vince revealed. 'You're alone all night, tonight?'

'Mel's not back until tomorrow afternoon. Why? What do you want me to do?'

'I have an idea forming. Can you leave it with me? And be ready if I need help?'

'Not going anywhere, Liz. Other than feeding the animals.'

'Do they need feeding right now, or can they wait an hour or two?'

'Any longer and there'll be a donkey rebellion.'

Ben called a meeting the minute he returned and everyone met at the round table which Candace had cleared. The wheeled board was to one side. Phoebe – who had been sleeping in one of the units after being up most of the night – still looked exhausted, but she sipped iced water and quietly watched as the others sat.

'Thank you all for being here,' Ben said. 'Particularly you, Phoebe, for letting us disturb your much-needed sleep.'

Ben had given nothing away since striding through the main door fifteen minutes ago. He'd shut himself in his office to make phone calls after asking Liz to gather the team.

'Thanks to your efforts around strong leads in respect of Tony Shaw and Marcus Bonner, we have been granted another forty-eight hours without interference.'

There was a collective sigh around the table.

'We're going to find Lyndall well before that deadline. The new information about Lyndall's real identity is incredibly useful and I'm about to pay Shaw a visit.'

Pete grinned. 'Never seen you get into a dust-up.'

'And you never will. Reuben?'

Reuben was also grinning, presumably at the thought of the always-calm and well-dressed Ben Rossi getting physical with a perp. Liz knew better. Ben had stopped killers before now but he wasn't as down-and-dirty as Pete or presumably, Reuben.

'Right. Our visitor in the interrogation room is primed to assist us in our enquiries but maintains it won't be until he gets immunity from prosecution,' Reuben said.

'Which we can't offer. Can we?' Annette asked.

'We've all seen cop shows where the perp's demands are met on the spot and we all know how ridiculous that is. I think even the perps believe it.' Ben shook his head. 'My intention is to see Shaw prosecuted for his part in this and whatever else we can dig up on him, but for Lyndall's sake, I have the authority to assure him that our recommendations to the powers-that-be will be directly affected by the level of his cooperation.'

Word it right and he'll believe he's getting a good deal.

Liz only had one goal. Find Lyndall alive. Everything else was a different problem for a different time. Until recently she'd been strictly by the rules. Never crossed any lines and couldn't imagine doing so. That was before a child was kidnapped… a second child under eerily similar circumstances to one close to Liz. Crossing lines was what found the child and brought Liz to Operation Nobody, so she didn't care if Ben lied outright to the piece of dirt in the holding cell.

'Boss?'

Everyone turned to Liz.

'I just spoke to Vince Carter whose memory was jogged by the name Nora Egan. I have an idea about how to get into the panic room.'

Pete was in the chair beside Liz and suddenly kicked her ankle, not hard enough to hurt but he'd got her attention and when she glanced at him, his expression was easy to read. He was warning her to stop talking.

'Go ahead, Liz,' Ben said.

Hamish leaned forward, expectant. Liz hadn't bonded with him in any way and if anything, didn't entirely trust the man. And she knew Pete didn't. Perhaps it was a case of their history but Liz wanted to know why this was an issue for her old partner before saying too much more.

'Still thinking it through. Do you mind if Pete and I brainstorm it first?'

Ben nodded. At his side, Candace narrowed her eyes.

For a few more minutes, Ben allocated tasks, helped by Meg who was overwhelmed by the sheer volume of enquiries she was running. She took Annette, Phoebe, and Hamish to assist. Reuben headed back to get Shaw out of the cell. When they'd left, Ben looked at Liz, waiting.

'I have an idea which includes getting Vince to go into Lyndall's house. He hasn't been up to feed the livestock yet so his presence there won't be questioned. There's no reason he can't let himself into the house and go to the panic room.'

'Other than the risk of there being further surveillance we aren't aware of,' Candace said. 'Do you want him to explore that narrow piece of wall?'

'Even break it open. I'm sure it is simply plaster.'

Ben got to his feet. 'We can clear it with the security team at the house for him to gain access but I think it'll look too suspicious for him to just walk in and smash up a wall.'

'What if he staggers in?' Pete stood and began to weave around the room. 'Had a long afternoon of drinking and was feeling sad that his lady friend is still missing. Finds himself in the panic room and in his drunken haze he trips and lands against the wall.' He pretended to do exactly that, stopping short of touching the bricks.

With a grin, Ben was leaving. 'Why don't I see what Shaw has to offer first?'

'Okay, but can I prep Vince in case you say to go ahead?'

Liz caught up with Ben as he walked into the main room, the others following. 'What Pete suggested might sound stupid but it is believable and might even just get us a glimpse.'

'Boss? Can I show you both something?' Meg waved both hands in the air.

There was a receipt on one of her monitors for two funerals.

'This was paid by Bonner Art Gallery. Did he happen to mention his involvement with that, Liz?'

'No. And he wasn't happy we knew about the flowers.'

'Marcus Bonner is alerted already, Ben,' Pete said. 'Get Vince to do his part before the bad guys make another run at Lyndall's house.'

Meg nodded in agreement. 'I can talk him through the best approach.'

'Yes, work with Liz and Pete on it. And I want you both close by when he goes in so get going soon.' Ben glanced around. All eyes were again on him. 'Hamish, I'll tell Reuben to meet you in the garage. Go and get Marcus Bonner.'

Liz ended up in the lift with Hamish after Pete went back for something, saying he'd be down in a minute.

'He doesn't like me.'

'Mate, at this point in time I'm not interested in school yard politics. My only concern is Lyndall.'

His face fell but then he nodded. 'I do sound a bit pathetic. Sorry. Once we find her… maybe a trip to the local pub will help us find some common ground. With you as well.'

'Pete will rarely say no to a drink.'

'And you?'

'Sure. I think the whole team will deserve a few drinks once Lyndall is safe.'

The doors opened and they followed a couple of hallways to the garage. Neither Reuben nor Pete were there yet.

'What should I expect from Marcus Bonner? Anything at all to give me an idea of him.' There was a new intensity about Hamish, as if he'd switched gears.

'Don't underestimate him based on his age. His physique is powerful and he looked agile. If he's the man who was on screen in the safe room with the rifle, we know he's smart and stealthy.'

'And if he was once Nora Egan's handler, he'll be prepared for just about anything.'

Liz crossed her arms. 'Handler? What do you know that I don't?'

'I'm joining dots, Liz. Assassinations of high-profile crime figures at or around art galleries in Europe at the same time Nora apparently lived in France. Bonner was a regular visitor there and knew them both. Liked Alain but not her. Nora's husband and one child drown in Australia and you know where? Boating in Port Phillip Bay. Her other child disappears and so does she, only to emerge as Lyndall Smith, donkey rescuer.'

Careful not to sound accusing, Liz dropped her arms. 'How do you know about Bonner's relationship with Alain and Nora, and his opinion of them? And Lyndall's real name.'

'Annette told me.'

The stairwell door banged shut as Pete and Reuben emerged, deep in conversation and heading their way.

'Hamish... do you remember Annette telling you she'd visited Bonner Gallery when she was still at school?'

His face was blank and he shook his head.

'Are you certain? It was before we identified Marcus Bonner as the person responsible for the flowers on the graves.'

'I'd remember. But she and I have barely had time to talk until she was smoking earlier and I joined her. Never touch them unless someone is alone puffing away and offers me one. Social thing, really.'

'Ready, Hamish?' Reuben called from one of the larger vehicles.

'Is it a problem?' Hamish lowered his voice as Pete approached.

'Not at all. Stay safe and get the creep.'

TWENTY-SIX

Another hour and all light would be gone. Already Melbourne was a distant beacon. Closer, brilliant late sunlight reflected from the windows of some of Victoria's most expensive homes along the Peninsula's coast. Huge houses with beachfront access, or high upon cliffs.

Lyndall had worked out she was just over three kilometres from Rye Beach. There'd been times today she'd seen boats leave its pier and head in her direction, only to be warned off by one of Marcus' people dressed up as a Parks Victoria ranger in the boat which never strayed far from her sight. He'd gone to a lot of trouble to keep her from discovery.

At times during the long day, alone apart from the occasional seal and many seabirds, Lyndall's spirits had flagged.

She'd been close to giving in to his demands.

To hand over The Tides would solve some of the problems. Vince and Melanie would no longer be under threat, nor the one person she grieved for daily. Nobody who Marcus dangled as a threat. Thinking too hard about the monster and his ability to destroy lives was soul-destroying.

But it was her only insurance policy.

Once he had The Tides, she was expendable. Everyone was.

And he'd have control of dangerous information he'd sought for decades.

Instead of feeling sorry for herself, Lyndall dug deep for the resilience which had seen her through the worst of times. She took stock of the situation, wandering around the small internal space of the old building as it creaked and groaned with every movement of the sea. Ideally she would have broken a window or found another way out but the glass was built for the ocean conditions and proved impossible without a proper tool. Her attempt to smash her way out with a chair was quickly noticed by Marcus' men and the threat of being tied up again was enough to deter her.

She'd outsmarted Marcus more than once and could do so again.

He'd be here soon and he'd want to know where The Tides was. If Vince had picked up any of her hints and shared them with Liz, then there must be an investigation underway. Surely the cameras in her house would have picked up her own abduction and hopefully seen her turn the phone on. By now she'd worked out whoever had installed the new alarm was one of Marcus' crowd but she had to believe the other measures she'd put in place would lead to her rescue.

Speculating on what the police might be thinking was a waste of time, but there was one thing she had to try. Marcus had her second phone. If he turned it on here, surely Liz would have a track on it. All Lyndall needed was a way to make him do it.

TWENTY-SEVEN

'We can't come within sight of the cottage nor Lyndall's house, Vince. Not until you've been in the panic room.'

'But the security guards know to leave me to my own devices?'

Through the phone, Vince sounded like a man reborn. His old self, back in the days of being the best street cop Liz ever met. With Pete, they'd talked at length about how the next half hour would play out and Vince was about to begin what he called phase one. Feeding the animals as normal.

'Yes. The one who normally hangs around the house will go down the driveway to have a casual chat with the other one. Apparently that happens a few times a shift so in the unlikely event that the property is being watched, nothing will seem out of place.'

'Except you'll be carrying an open beer as you go past them,' Pete added. 'Maybe slosh some over yourself to make it realistic.'

'Nah, I'll leave that for you to do. Seems more in character.'

'Always happy to pour beer over you.'

Liz let them blow off some nervous steam.

Pete turned onto the road which led to Vince's.

'We're almost there, so please head up to Lyndall's. Leave your phone in your top pocket recording and we'll keep an eye on you remotely.'

'I'll talk to you soon. And Liz, thanks for this.' Vince disconnected the call.

'He'll be fine, Liz.'

'If anyone can pull this off, its him. Where are we stopping?'

'When I was traipsing around the countryside supervising Hamish I came across a track we can park along. Can't see it from Lyndall's but if we get out and walk a bit, we'll be able to see her house.'

Liz concentrated on her phone, setting up the link to the live feed from Lyndall's security system. Meg had worked her own brand of magic to make it accessible through the app and by the time Pete parked, it was displaying on one of the vehicle's two screens.

'We're good to watch now.' Liz glanced around. They were in bushland on a rough dirt track and couldn't see the road they'd left. 'And you found this when?'

'Don't you ever listen to me?'

'Only if forced to.'

Pete climbed out. 'Shall we get a bit higher?'

Grumbling under her breath that she'd just set up the live feed, Liz collected a tablet and joined him, tapping madly until she had the inside of Lyndall's house on something bigger than her phone. She followed him up a steep incline with no idea where he was leading her.

Even Pete looked a bit lost but after a couple of false starts, disappeared between some bushes. 'Through here.'

'Through where?'

He reappeared and she kept him in sight along his somewhat dodgy path. But there was a tiny clearing and that was pure gold with Lyndall's house across the valley. Pete handed her binoculars.

'Vince seems to have put feed out in the bottom paddock for the cows and is walking up the driveway.'

The binoculars were exceptional and Vince might have been a hundred metres away instead of a kilometre or more. Halfway up Lyndall's long driveway he passed the two security guards, lifting his beer bottle in greeting.

The guards were from impeccable backgrounds, as were their entire team which had protected the property since hours after Lyndall was taken. Ex-police, all good people with solid reputations and being paid well in excess of the standard. Liz handed the binoculars back.

'Is this one of the places looked at by the drone? As a potential watch-site?'

'It is. At least Hamish didn't almost fall off the edge here.' Pete clearly had a bee in his bonnet. 'What was he saying which was so interesting in the garage before?'

'He asked for my take on Marcus Bonner and what to look out for.'

'Right. Like he's going to suddenly care enough to do his job.'

'Dude, enough alright? Cut him some slack.'

Pete's eyebrows rose. 'Best pals now?'

'Hardly. But he's got a sharp mind and has a strong theory about Lyndall and what is happening.'

'He knew her real name walking into the meeting where the rest of us found out.'

'Annette and he had a smoke outside and she filled him in. Where's Vince now?'

Pete moved the binoculars around. 'Got him. Well at least I can see the donkeys all trotting toward the paddock where he's been feeding them.'

Nerves hit Liz's stomach and she forced herself to breathe deeply and slowly. This was risky. If she and Pete were able to watch the house, there was no reason to believe they were on their own. Probably not out in the bush like this, but around or inside the house with cameras she and Meg hadn't found last time.

'There's no drones, are there? Strange ones?'

'Nah, I've been checking and the security team are well aware to watch for them. Best we can hope for is an easy extraction of whatever is hidden in the wall.' Pete lowered the binoculars to look at Liz. 'And a quick capture of Bonner. Reuben is looking forward to adding him to the cells.'

Liz checked the app. 'He's about to go in. Are you listening to him?'

Pete held up his phone. 'I am. So is Meg. I'll put it on speaker but he can't hear us.'

Go safely, Vince.

As the donkeys, and Apple, who trailed behind but still managed to snaffle the lion's share of feed, settled into chewing on their biscuits of hay, Vince ducked inside the large shelter and turned the video on his phone. He couldn't see a way to safely record the images without knowing if some carefully hidden camera would spot it, so slid the phone inside the top pocket in his shirt and trusted that the audio would be enough. He didn't trust technology, but he did have complete faith in Liz and her new team. In his right hand he hid a small but thick screwdriver.

He took the path to the house, not really staggering but certainly doing an Oscar winning job of representing understated inebriation.

At the deck he stood for a minute, swaying a bit, taking a swig from the bottle which had earlier been emptied into a tall glass and refilled with cold tea. In all his years as a police officer, he'd never wanted to be a detective. Today, he did.

Like Liz.

Not like shithead.

He couldn't help a grin thinking about how this would irritate Pete, although to his credit, the detective had been nothing but helpful running through how to make this all happen.

Vince had plenty of anger to draw upon. Lyndall meant the world to Melanie. To him. He'd lost a wife and a daughter and through it all, Lyndall was a constant, quiet support.

He lifted the bottle and shouted at the almost-night sky.

'Hey you! I want her back!'

From a pocket he pulled a set of keys and made a show of finding the right one to open the sliding door. All of this might be for nothing. If no-one was watching then it was wasted time. But from what Liz had said, the mongrels who'd taken Lyndall were savvy with surveillance and her life was at risk should the wrong move be made.

Vince slid the door open and stepped inside.

His heart thudded. The house was cold, bereft of the natural warmth of its owner. Lyndall had a kindness often hidden beneath a practical and brusque persona, but since Melanie came to live with him, he'd seen the real Lyndall more often than not.

Except now I have to find out who you really are.

Reading between the lines, this team of Liz's saw Lyndall as someone with a dark past. Possibly a criminal past. If that was true then she'd been coerced or forced into that life because he knew she had no evil in her soul. He just needed her safely home. Anything else would be dealt with and he'd be at her side.

'Lyndall? I keep hoping this is a bad dream.' He made his words slow and heavy. In the kitchen he put the bottle on the counter. 'Are you back yet?'

He wandered into the hallway, leaning against the wall for a minute, his eyes on the painting he now knew was Lyndall's own work. Nora Egan. She'd had a family. A glittering career. An entire life which was destroyed by the loss of her husband and son – perhaps by the man who'd taken her.

Vince used the rising distress to his advantage. He covered his face with one hand and staggered from one side of the hallway to the other where the door of the safe room was slightly open, shoving it wide and almost tripping over his feet.

He kept the momentum going, arms now outstretched and body swaying as he cried out some guttural sound. His hands hit the wall hard and together, both gripping the handle of the screwdriver and forcing it into the plaster. All he could hope was that his bulk hid the tool from any cameras.

'Dammit, now look what I did. Gotta fix it.'

Vince made the small tear larger then slipped the screwdriver into a pocket and used his fingers.

'Now there's a hole in Lyndall's panic room. So clumsy. Sorry, Lyndall.'

He couldn't believe his eyes.

There was a black cylinder taped against a timber upright. This had to be what Liz had speculated was hidden by Lyndall. Vince unbuttoned his shirt partway, still shielding the damaged area.

'Gonna need some new plaster.'

As he spoke, he tore the tape and carefully extracted the cylinder. It was rigid but fortunately small enough to fit against his torso. Vince redid the buttons and folded his arms. 'Might take more than plaster. Need a builder. Nah. I need a vodka.'

'That's the phrase. He found something!' Liz and Pete had been watching Vince through the live feed. 'We have to go.'

Getting back to the car only took a couple of minutes and all the time, Vince was talking. At first it was more loud and fake self-recrimination for the damage, then finding the right key to lock the house, and then once he was walking, it was directed to them.

'I got it, Liz. Going to go all the way down Lyndall's driveway to meet you.'

'You were right. You and Candace and Meg. All right to

believe something was hidden behind the wall.' Pete was grinning as he drove. 'Unbelievable police work.'

'Vince was brilliant. We didn't see one glimpse of whatever he's found.'

'Yeah… he did okay.' But Pete was still ecstatic and gave a small fist pump.

Meg phoned, her voice just as excited. 'Do you know what he's found?'

'No. He's being cautious with what he says.'

'Call me the minute you leave.'

'We're just turning into the road now. Vince is almost at the end of the driveway,' Liz said. 'Call you back.'

'Tell him he did great.'

Pete drove past the two driveways and did a U-turn, then pulled up on the road as Vince caught up. Liz had her window down and Vince got as close to the car as possible, carefully sliding a black cylinder from under his shirt.

'This is going to help find her. Isn't it?' He leaned down to peer into the car. 'Could anyone have seen what I found?'

'Doubt it. We were watching the live feed and nothing showed on Lyndall's cameras.'

'Remind me not to annoy you,' Pete said.

'Too late, mate.'

'Are you okay to stay at the cottage? I can arrange somewhere for the night or until we catch these people.'

'No, but thanks, Liz. Just in case she comes back. Or something.' Vince stepped back. 'I'll keep an eye on things.'

Pete leaned across Liz. 'Meg said you did an adequate job.'

Liz pushed him away. 'She said you did great. And yes, we think this will help find Lyndall.'

'Go.'

Vince raised a hand as Pete drove away.

TWENTY-EIGHT

'Annette, anything on the croissants?' Meg called from her desk, too tired and far too busy to walk to the other woman's desk.

'She's gone onto the roof for a minute.' Phoebe hurried over, holding a notebook. 'I've been chasing it up and found three which might fit the criteria.'

Pushing down annoyance that Annette had left Phoebe to do her work when Phoebe had enough on her plate already, Meg lifted her hands from a keyboard. 'Go on.'

'There's one on the Bellarine Peninsula, near Wallington which is kind of in the middle. Another in Langwarrin, and the third in Rye. Langwarrin isn't technically part of the Mornington Peninsula so with the other connection to Mount Martha…'

'Gotcha. And the one in Rye is considered the real deal with their pastries?'

'Owned by a French baker who trained in Paris. Probably as close as you'd get here. I checked and Rye is a little under thirty kilometres from Bonner Art Gallery.'

An email came up on one of the monitors and Meg immediately opened it, her eyes scanning the brief message. 'Oh, thank goodness. That's the information I've been chasing about Lyndall's other phone.'

Now I can find whoever has it.

She turned back to Phoebe, who was close enough to have read the email. 'Can we keep this between us for now, please? Just until Ben has cleared the details being shared.'

'Of course. What about the Rye French Bakery though?'

'You and Annette please work together to find the owner.' Meg glanced at her watch. 'They'll be long closed for the day but Annette should have a way to get home numbers so I'd like someone who works there to take a look at images of Shaw and Bonner. Do you know where Candace is?'

'Conference table.'

'Ta. And thanks for getting the bakery info. Good work.'

Dropping her eyes, Phoebe nodded and returned to her desk, her colour high. Meg liked her enormously and totally got her. The younger woman had a brilliant mind competing against social anxiety and still managed to run a successful business and now, help this team.

Meg sent a message to Candace, giving her the number she'd just received and asking her to keep this quiet. When Ben was back, he could make that call but he'd want Candace to know.

She gazed at her screens for a moment. There were so many programs running already but she needed one more. One to alert her the second Lyndall's other phone turned on and also to track when it was last live. By now the damned thing might be out of battery life or destroyed, but it was a wildcard she had to ensure did not slip past her.

In a few minutes, Liz and Pete would bring the single most important part of the puzzle... if they were all understanding Lyndall's cryptic clues.

The sun was setting.

I don't want you out there another night, Lyndall. Find a way to let me know your location.

. . .

Pete insisted that Liz go with him a different way in the building. It was yet another wing separate from the team head-quarters and as soon she went inside, knew Meg was responsible for creating it.

He turned on lights. 'She can't be far away.'

'I thought we'd be using the second room.'

'Too sensitive. And we actually don't know what's inside the cylinder you are clutching so tightly. Could be some air-borne poison we're about to release.'

'Aren't you the cheery one.'

But Liz placed the cylinder on a stainless-steel bench and stepped away. Just in case.

'There's still nothing from Reuben and Hamish?'

Pete checked his phone, the way she'd just checked hers. 'Forgot there's no signal in here. Should be on their way with Bonner.' He ran a hand through his hair. 'I want to eat. Drink a coffee without it going cold. Have a beer.'

'I know. Oh, I should have mentioned that Hamish wants to buy you a beer once this is over.'

'Yeah well right now the devil himself is welcome to buy me one and I won't refuse. And Liz? I'll keep my mind open about him, okay?'

'Sorry, guys. One million things happening all at once.' Meg breezed in. 'This is smaller than I expected.'

The cylinder was about forty centimetres in length.

'Pete, there's masks and gloves in the drawer near your left. For us all please.'

'See, I told you there's probably some biological weapon inside.'

'Stop being ridiculous,' Meg frowned. 'This will be a painting and I don't want you breathing all over it or touching it.'

They began donning the protective wear.

'Meg, any news from Reuben? Or Ben?' Liz adjusted her mask.

'Ben has paperwork arriving from his higher-ups for Shaw to

sign. The man is stupid enough to be caught but smart enough to ensure he gets something in writing. And nothing from the two guys yet.'

Something was wrong. Liz knew how long the drive was to the gallery and even had they needed to climb over the wall to access the grounds, then force their way in, there should be news by now.

After setting up a camera to record her actions, Meg carefully opened the cylinder. What she slid out was sealed in a slightly shiny material.

'Waterproof. And I imagine airtight.'

Once this covering was removed, Meg slowly unrolled a canvas. The work was a seascape. A long stretch of beach at night with waves rolling in and moonlight streaming across the surface of the water. It was a beautiful painting with such deli-cate brushstrokes that the waves were translucent in parts and a lone footstep remained in the wet sand.

'Nora Egan's signature,' Meg said. 'The Tides. I think that's the name?'

Everyone peered at the words above the signature and agreed.

'Well, this is gorgeous, but what makes it so important that Lyndall not only hid it inside a custom-built safe room, but left cryptic clues to find it? Is the painting worth a great deal or is it another clue?'

'Hope not. My brain isn't wired for these puzzles,' Pete said. 'Could it be one of those paintings with another beneath it?'

'One way to find out,' Meg said. 'but I need a scanner. I'm going to borrow one. I just shouldn't be leaving right now.'

'Then get Annette to go,' Pete suggested.

'No. No, I need her close by so can you, Pete? I'll phone ahead and you'll just need to collect it at the door. Its portable.'

Meg placed the canvas inside a safe and as soon as they were out of the room, made a phone call.

Liz began to search for Nora Egan paintings called The Tide.

'Nothing, Pete. Not under her name or its title. So what makes it so important?'

Her phone and his beeped at the same time with messages.

'Oh, from Reuben.' Liz's heart sank. 'They haven't caught Bonner.'

The hub was almost deathly quiet when Liz returned. Pete had just left to collect the scanner and Meg was right behind her, still on a phone call. Phoebe didn't look up from her computer and Annette barely smiled as Liz headed straight for the second room.

Ben was leaning against the wall, rubbing his eyes.

Slumped at the table, Candace looked just as defeated.

For the first time since Lyndall disappeared, Liz didn't know what to do or say. The team couldn't fall apart over a setback. But each of them was exhausted and most probably hungry. She wasn't about to turn into the team mother, but Liz wasn't ready to give up.

'We all need to stop for a few minutes,' she said. 'The three of us will go and make coffee or whatever for the team and find some fruit or who knows what and we'll get the others in here to take a break. Reuben and Hamish are only a few minutes away, so come on.'

'Liz, that's a nice thought but—'

'She's right, Ben.' Candace pushed herself to her feet. 'Spirits are flagging and we can turn that around.'

'If you need to rest we can manage.'

Ben straightened. 'We all need rest and we will, once Lyndall is safe.'

He led the way to the kitchen.

While he made an assortment of hot drinks, Candace threw some frozen chips into the large air fryer and Liz sliced fruit and cheese and added crackers to a large board. Doing something so simple felt productive and when they carried their respective wares past everyone, they got plenty of attention.

'Phoebe, Annette, Meg? Fifteen-minute mandatory break.'

The first two jumped up and followed after Ben's announcement but Meg didn't move from her desk. Liz put her board on the table and went back.

'Too much to do, Liz. Sorry.'

Meg hadn't even lifted her head to look at Liz. She had one hand on a keyboard and the other on a mouse and was working two screens while a third showed a map of Victoria.

'What's the map for?'

'I got the phone number for Lyndall's other phone and I just need it to turn on. Just for a second.'

Meg's voice wavered and Liz squatted beside her.

'It will alert you remotely, yes?'

'Yes.'

'And the other programs?'

'Yes. Yes, Liz, they'll all alert me but how can I walk away when Lyndall's life might depend upon my searches?'

'I hear you. But a few minutes might recharge you a bit and the guys will be here shortly and we're going to need our energy and wits to deal with what comes. Do you need to bring a laptop with you?'

With a sigh, Meg shook her head and rose. 'Phone will do.'

As they entered the conference room she sniffed the air. 'Pete will be annoyed to miss hot chips.'

The food was almost demolished when Reuben and Hamish arrived. Liz had just made more coffees and gestured for them to help themselves.

'We'd expected a debrief but not one with cheese and grapes,' Reuben dropped into a seat near Liz. 'Where's Pete?'

'Picking up a special scanner for me to see if Lyndall hid

anything inside the painting we've retrieved from the panic room. And I'll bring you both up to speed shortly but we're all a bit desperate to know about Bonner Gallery.' Meg took the last chip.

Hamish looked grimmer than Liz had ever seen him. 'There was no response to our requests to enter the premises so we found a way in. The gallery was locked up with nobody home.'

'However, whoever had been there left fast,' Reuben added. 'A door at the back was unlocked and the alarms weren't set so we got inside readily enough. There's a whole suite set up for surveillance and not just their own grounds.' He turned his phone. 'Screenshot of three cameras still activated at Lyndall's.'

Liz couldn't believe her eyes. The footage showed Vince. First heading for the sliding door, then in the hallway, and worse – in the panic room.

'I can't believe... damn,' Meg said. 'Did you watch Vince? Did you see anything he did?'

'Fell against a wall. He did a good job of hiding whatever he found but he did find something. You said a painting.'

At least they don't know what we have.

Ben took the phone for a better look. 'You saw this live?'

'Yes. But no way to tell if they have remote access and realistically, they will,' Hamish stopped eating long enough to speak. 'This ties Lyndall's disappearance to Bonner with no doubts and I feel we missed him by minutes. It is as though he knew we were coming.'

He gazed around the table, eyes stopping on Annette. She returned his stare, unblinking. It gave Liz the strangest sensation that something was wrong but was it a conflict between them or something far more sinister?

Handing the phone back, Ben stood. 'Where did you leave things?'

Reuben also got to his feet. 'Have a couple of trusted people near enough to report any activity. Didn't want to put anyone on the grounds. I'd like to get a forensics team in there to go right through the place, as well as do a proper search.'

'Soon as we have some free resources we will. I'm going to see where that document is for Shaw so hang around, Reuben. Everyone else, keep doing what you were. We're getting closer.'

As Ben began to leave, Meg's phone beeped.

'Pete's downstairs so I'll get him to help scan this artwork. Liz, I can't get a signal in that room.'

'I'll take care of monitoring. You go.'

Meg took off and as the others began clearing the table or leaving the room, Candace took Liz aside and waited until they were alone.

'You observed that moment between Hamish and Annette?'

Liz nodded. 'I thought they got on pretty well but that left me feeling the opposite.'

'Once we find Lyndall and everyone has had a proper rest, I'll speak to them. We need a coherent team and while there's always little personality differences, we can't afford major ones. You did well to pull Ben and I out of our moods.'

'We're all a team who look out for each other. And speaking of that, I need to get to Meg's station.'

TWENTY-NINE

Half an hour of sitting at Meg's desk saw no changes to any of the programs running. Liz wasn't game to touch a thing and had her own laptop on a spare part of the workstation, checking the monitors every few minutes. Pete and Meg were still working on the painting and Ben and Reuben were back with Shaw after the paperwork came through.

'Liz? Phoebe and I have some intel from the bakery.' Annette was excited, her eyes wide. 'Can we get the vertical screen going?'

'Um… yes? Can you make it work?'

Annette laughed. 'That's what I was like the first few days but I can work it. Just takes practice and Meg says it can't be broken.'

'Not going to test that theory right now. Go ahead.'

From the table, Meg's workstation was in easy view and Liz put herself where she had a direct line of sight while Annette set up video footage. Phoebe and Hamish joined them.

Phoebe spoke first. 'Annette did a great job of tracking down the owner of the bakery. He wasn't impressed at being disturbed at home but once he knew it was a missing person case, he was most gracious.'

'Yes, he returned to the bakery and checked through recent footage because he recognised Bonner's face from the photo we sent. He says he's been in a few times in the past couple of weeks.'

'This video is recorded on his phone because he had no clue how to download it. He's going to keep watching to see if there's more, but this has to be helpful,' Phoebe pointed at the screen. 'You'll see Bonner come into view through the front door first.'

The copy of the copy wasn't crystal clear but good enough to show Marcus Bonner at the counter, initially a few people back then working his way to the front as they were served. He spent most of the time scrolling on a phone but looked directly at the young woman behind the counter, almost straight into the camera which was positioned to face the door. He spoke and then waited, hand on the counter tapping it with his fingers as he read something on his phone in his other hand.

'Can you pause?'

The footage froze.

'And zoom in to his arm. When we met him he wore a suit. His forearms are bare and I want to see that tattoo.'

Annette seemed to struggle with it but Phoebe took over and had the close-up Liz wanted. She took a photo with her own phone, heart racing. 'Thanks, keep going.'

Bonner paid for his order, which was in a box with the bakery logo, then left.

'When was this?'

'Yesterday, just before they closed at three.' Annette changed the footage to that from an outside camera. 'The owner also sent this.'

The perspective was from a corner window and covered the bakery door, a few outdoor tables, and part of the footpath. Marcus Bonner stepped outside and glanced around, appeared to see someone he knew and stopped to speak to them. The other person was a man but his back was turned to the camera from the seat he had at the furthest table. Bonner listened intently to him, nodding his head, then spoke briefly and left.

'Play it back, please.'

There was something about the seated man… Liz was seeing things. The tattoo must be responsible for her jumping to conclusions.

Hamish watched intently. 'He knew someone well enough to stop and talk. No smiles or handshake. But not antagonist either.'

'Would you mind asking Candace to come and view both of these and give her your thoughts?'

He nodded and immediately went to find her.

'Phoebe, do you feel confident about sitting at Meg's desk? Taking over from me and watch for any alerts?'

'Oh. Oh, yes. I can. Right now?'

Liz went to collect her laptop. 'If you don't mind. Or grab a drink first. Meg might be another half hour or more but if anything pops up on those monitors, send Hamish for her immediately.'

Phoebe plonked onto the seat behind the workstation.

'What's happening, Liz?' Annette asked. 'Are you going somewhere?'

Back at her own desk, Liz packed her laptop into her briefcase and slung the handle over her shoulder, then collected her handbag. 'I am. Once Pete is around, or Ben, would you ask them to phone me?'

'Sure, but where are you going?'

'And please ask Candace to run the floor until Ben or Meg are back. I'll update everyone soon.' Not willing to wait long enough for Candace to emerge and talk her out of leaving, Liz ignored the confusion on Annette's face and let herself out.

She was still in the garage, waiting for the roller door to lift when Candace rang and for a second, Liz considered letting it go to voicemail. But she'd abandoned everyone with barely a word and worrying them was not her intention.

'Sorry I didn't stay long enough to speak to you, Candace.'

'You obviously have somewhere to be.'

'Yes. No. You will think I've lost my mind.'

The soft chuckle from Candace instantly reassured Liz. She drove out and navigated to the street.

'No judgement from me. You really should know that by now. And I know *you* well enough to understand you've either connected some dots or are following a hunch. I've taken a quick look at the footage and if I'm not wrong, that tattoo has you thinking about your father.'

Good grief she is good at this.

Not for the first time, Liz longed to pour her heart out to the other woman. Talk about the man who'd abandoned her and then stolen not one, but two young girls in some sick fantasy world where they would be the perfect daughter he had lost.

A car horn blared and Liz slammed on the brakes. She'd almost driven in front of a light truck.

'What was that?'

'Just traffic, Candace. But yes, the tattoo is the same as one of my father's and the one on Tony Shaw's back. Perhaps you can let Ben know? It might help if he sees those two clips.'

'Already sent them. There's no point you going to the Bonner Gallery. Not without back up.'

'I'm not.'

She hadn't even considered it.

'I see.'

Liz wound her way through several narrow streets. Not long and she'd be on the Bolte Bridge.

'Candace, you can track me. I'm going to Rye.'

'Which was my second guess. What do you need from me?'

A helicopter? A bigger team? Exact location of Lyndall?

'You already have. Look, this truly is just a hunch but I've learned to trust myself.'

'Good. Phone if you need me.'

The line disconnected.

In all of her years as a police officer, even working with decent cops like Vince and her old boss, Terry, she'd never experienced the level of trust and support as in these few days.

Liz turned onto the road which would take her to the Mornington Peninsula and accelerated.

Ben and Reuben sat in the observation room, watching Shaw read through the agreement for the third time.

'He's stalling us.' Reuben shifted his chair to better see Ben. 'What if we cut him loose?'

'I'm listening.'

'Tell him we've come into some intel from another source and that he's free to go.'

'Why would he believe us?'

After Shaw had messed them around so much, Ben was at the point of having the man moved to Major Crimes. He just wasn't convinced that would expedite anything.

'We have the painting.'

'Yes, we do.'

'If we lead him to believe we've found something about the painting which will identify Lyndall's location, then perhaps he'll lead us to her. Or to Bonner. Because having it in an undisclosed and secure facility might make Bonner want to do a trade.'

So much depended upon whether Bonner was the right person. Whether the painting was the ultimate target. And whether Lyndall was even alive.

Reuben grinned. 'Besides, I have some fancy little bugs I've been wanting to test on a real criminal. He'll never know he's been tagged and unless he scrubs himself raw with exactly the right mix of chemicals, it won't come off.'

'Is this the clear patch you showed me?'

'Yes. And his phone has already been compromised by us so if he's stupid enough to use it, we'll listen in.'

Shaw was on his feet and tapped the window, holding up the paperwork, still unsigned.

'Shall we give him the bad news together?'

'I've always wanted to see one of these in the flesh, so to speak. Studied them but had no idea I'd find one beneath a layer of oil paint!'

Meg held a minute object with long tweezers beneath a large magnifying glass.

'But will its contents have survived?' Pete had never seen anything so small.

'No reason why not. Microchips like this tiny one are simply a storage device.'

'And the painting?'

Meg carefully placed the chip inside a clear bag and sealed it. 'There's almost no damage to the eye, anyway. If it is needed to use as bait, we should be good.'

They both looked again at The Tides which was on the stainless-steel table. The scanner had quickly located the chip, or at least, imagery at odds with canvas and paint. It was between thick layers of colour where the footprint was in the sand and to look at it now, Pete couldn't tell that Meg had removed what was most likely the reason for Lyndall's abduction.

'What now?'

'We lock these up. I don't have the equipment here to extract whatever is on the chip and wouldn't touch it if I did, not until we have a lot more information about it.'

Pete's mind was going too fast and he took a step back from the table. 'You said bait? For Shaw? Bonner?'

'I'll lock everything up so go find Ben. There'll be a way to contact Bonner.'

He wasted no time getting back to the hub, shooting into the restroom first. On his way back he sniffed the air. Someone had cooked chips. His stomach had long since given up asking for food but now it growled again.

Annette was at her workstation but Phoebe was at Meg's and Candace was in her office for once. Hamish was looking over Annette's shoulder at something. There was nobody else present and the room was quiet.

Candace saw him and waved him toward her.

'Have you spoken to Liz?'

'No, I've come directly from Meg. Where's Liz?'

'Candace! Everyone!'

Phoebe jumped to her feet, the chair rolling backwards. She pointed at a monitor which had a map of the state.

'Look, there's a location.'

Hamish was there first. Everyone crowded around. The image had a pulsating circle with several straight lines pointing to it.

'What is it?' But then it registered and he pushed past Hamish. 'Lyndall's phone, right? Someone please get Meg.'

'I'll go.' Phoebe dashed away.

The circle was in Port Phillip Bay, off the coast of the lower end of Mornington Peninsula. Each line led to land, presumably phone towers which were combining to locate the phone.

'Is it on a boat?' Annette asked.

'I'm here.'

Meg grabbed her chair and slid onto it as Pete moved, her hands already reaching for mouse and keyboard. 'This is good. This is very, very good.' She did something which changed the screen to a satellite view, similar to map apps on a phone. 'Let me pick up the exact location… cool.' Meg copied a line of longitude and latitude and moved it into a search box on a different monitor. 'This is live. This is good except we're nowhere near it.'

She zoomed in until only the circle and the coast were in the same image.

'That's a couple of kilometres off Blairgowrie Beach,' Pete said.

'Actually, it is closer to Rye Beach. Looks like the South Channel Pile Light.'

'Sorry, what?' Hamish looked confused.

'Old lighthouse. Not used, got moved from its original spot and rebuilt. Protected from visitors.'

Candace gave a short laugh. 'Clever woman, our Liz.'

Pete straightened and looked at her. 'She's gone to Rye.'

'She has.'

THIRTY

The phone was on the table between Lyndall and Marcus. It was off again after only a minute or two thanks to the battery going flat. Marcus had called one of his boats over and someone handed him a portable power bank and now, they waited.

'These phones are stupid. Look how long until it begins charging and restarts, even.' Marcus stood and began to prowl. 'It better hurry.' He stopped at a window and stared out into the night.

He'd arrived a while ago, his mood unreadable.

She was starving and quickly ate the stone-cold burger and chips from some takeaway place. Her need for nutrition outweighed a desire to throw the crappy food at his face. All the while he'd sat watching her. Not angry. Not even impatient. More like he was resigned.

When she'd finished, he reached over and touched her face. She yanked her head back to avoid his hand.

'Oh, my dear Nora. How different our lives would be had you not stolen from me. What we've lost. The love we once shared, gone forever. The clever arrangement to fulfil our jobs… mine and Alain's. Perhaps you might have followed your other dream and become an Olympic medallist for shooting. Such a waste of a talent.'

'I didn't steal from you, Marcus. The painting is mine.'

His face darkened. 'Where is it? I'm not willing to wait any more.'

'Before I help you, I need to know this is over. Once you have the painting, you'll never look for me again. You'll never contact me or go near anyone I know.'

Marcus nodded.

'And there's something else.'

'Money? I can give you whatever amount you want.'

And it will never bring my children back.

'Not money... Marcus, I just need to know...' her voice faltered. Asking him this was to risk knowing the worst. But if he truly was going to disappear again, and this time forever, then it was her only chance.

'You wish to know about Claude?'

Her hands began to shake and she shoved them beneath the table.

'Perhaps you think of me as a monster but I kept my promise. He would never come to harm unless you exposed my operation and that of my masters. I had hoped you would find me to return the chip and take your son back into your life, yet you chose not to. Instead, you created an elaborate diversion which sent me searching for you through Europe while all along, you were living in the same state as my home.'

Rather than debate her choices, Lyndall pressed him. 'He is a young man now. Able to make his own decisions. Once you have The Tides—'

'What, Nora? I should pluck him from his life for the second time and tell him his beloved mother is alive and was hiding from him? What cruelty. And you assume I even know his location after so much time so no.' Marcus slammed his fist on the table. 'No!'

Fingers gripping each other, Lyndall gave a slight nod.

It was enough to calm the man and he took a long breath.

I have to control my emotions. Mel and Vince need me to fix this mess.

'But he will stay safe? Claude. You promise me this… please, Marcus.'

'I promise you.'

'I can take you to The Tides.'

Marcus leaned his arms on the table. 'And there lies a problem. Your house is under guard. Despite this, your stupid neighbour went on some kind of alcohol-induced bender and let himself in not long ago.'

'To my house? Didn't the guards stop him?'

'They had gone for a walk or something. He was yelling at the sky then came inside with a beer bottle and staggered all over. I'm guessing he's in love with you to act so foolish at his age. He was in the hallway near your bedroom and lost his balance. Fool fell against a wall.'

'I hope he did no damage! If so, I'll be asking him to pay to repair it.'

Marcus opened his phone and turned it. 'See for yourself.'

The footage was interesting on several levels. The most alarming was seeing there were several cameras not of Lyndall's in place. Another was the panic room door being ajar exactly how she'd hoped it would default to. And then, when he left the room after putting a hand through the correct wall in the correct place, he muttered about needing a vodka. The man hated vodka with a vengeance.

This was wonderful. It was the work of Liz and her faith in the system she'd put in place so long ago was validated.

'Marcus, if a drunk man could bypass the guards then I certainly can. Get me home and I'll retrieve The Tides.'

Marcus burst into loud, raucous laughter.

Doing her best to look distraught, Lyndall went as far as to drop her head onto her hands, which she'd pulled up from beneath the table.

'Come on, Nora. I'm not your stupid, lovesick neighbour. I'll go to the house but you'll tell me how to safely get in and where the painting is.'

'But it won't matter because there's a code. For a safe.'

She raised her eyes. Marcus was frowning, his whole face uncertain.

'Where is the safe?'

'Hidden inside the panic room. It opens either with face recognition and both palms, or there's a code to open it.'

'Give me the code.'

'I would. But this isn't some code you memorise, Marcus! It is custom designed to change on every attempt and will completely lock itself up if three attempts fail.'

'Are you deliberately not making sense? I have people near that cottage of your neighbour and with one phone call I can have people there.'

'Threatening me isn't changing the facts. What I'm saying is you either take me along and use my biometrics or I show you how to use the code. But that only works if you still have my phone. My other phone, Marcus, which I know you took from the gun box.'

His hand slid into a pocket and he tossed it onto the table. 'This one? It isn't a smart phone so how would it possibly do what you say?'

Lyndall hadn't thought this through well enough. The intention was to get him to take her to the house. That phone of hers was good for making calls and sending texts and little else. Other than a small list of numbers on a note program.

'Don't let its appearance fool you, Marcus.'

He turned it on and after a moment of darkness, the small screen lit up. 'What's the password.'

'Claude. All capitals.'

Marcus shot her a look then used the password. 'What now. Where do I look?'

'May I?' She held out her hand. 'It isn't as though I could phone anyone to help with you inches away. Is it?'

He passed it across.

She used the keypad to locate the note and it opened but then the screen went black.

'What did you do!' Marcus snatched the phone away. 'I swear, Nora, if this was some trick—'

'Get a grip. Did you not see the battery flashing? It just needs charging.'

With a grunt, Marcus pushed his chair back and strode to the door. 'Watch your tone, Nora.' He gestured at the boat which had retreated to its usual fifty or so metres distance.

The speedboat which brought Marcus from shore was tied up at the bottom of the steps and its two occupants were outside the building, smoking. It looked fast, but getting control of it felt impossible.

'What will happen next, Marcus? Once you have the codes and I explain how to find the safe?'

In a minute or two the phone would be charged enough to use. Lyndall had to move soon because she didn't believe for a second this man was going to simply let her go free.

'I've been thinking about that. My plan was to leave you here until I had the painting then call off my boat. It would only be a day or two before some sightseer or the like got close enough for you to get their attention. But it appears I've come to the attention of your would-be rescuers and have to adjust my timing.'

Best news in days. Now I just need to stay alive a bit longer.

'Nothing bad will happen to you, Nora. We have a deal.'

The phone lit up and Marcus pushed it across the table.

'Now, the codes.'

THIRTY-ONE

Liz left the bakery, its owner locking the door behind her and returning to his search of many days' worth of footage. He was charming, if bemused by the attention on his little business. She'd been there for a while as Meg connected remotely to his system which was fortunately modern. He'd been accommodating with information, even printing out a duplicate receipt for the sale to Bonner, which so far was the only one caught on camera. The other man, the one seated outside, had not entered the bakery and no amount of checking cameras showed his face. But watching the exchange on the original recording revealed surprise on Bonner's face when he saw the other man, who'd left, in the same direction, a moment later.

She'd met with a couple of local uniform officers arranged by Ben and they were visiting whatever shops were still open so late with Bonner's photograph and the one of Lyndall from Vince's phone.

Marcus Bonner had been careless. He'd felt safe in this small town where nobody knew him. Just another face in a crowd in a community accustomed to strangers, thanks to its popularity as a holiday destination. Had Tony Shaw not been interviewed and let slip the information about authentic French croissants on the Peninsula, then she wouldn't be here right now.

'But where are *you*, Lyndall?'

Liz crossed the road and down to the beach. It was a lovely stretch of golden sand with several boat ramps at intervals and a long pier. She'd been here on occasion and knew it was a safe beach for swimming. But that was during the day.

Clouds moved across the sky, covering and uncovering an almost full moon not far above the horizon. There was no storm forecast, nor was there much humidity, just the residual warmth from the day. The beach was deserted and waves pounded the shore as the tide turned. In the distance, the lights of Melbourne reminded Liz how far away help was, should she need it.

Pete rang and as she answered, Liz walked onto the pier.

'I'm caught up in roadworks,' he said. 'Night works, which inconveniently began half an hour ago.'

'And I'm still waiting on a boat to arrive. How can we not get our hands on anything on short notice?'

'Might be something to do with the short notice? Seriously though, there's two water units travelling down from Williamstown but the wind is chopping up the water and making the trip slower than expected.'

'There's hardly a breeze here,' Liz said. 'I've rung a few charter places locally but nobody wants to come out so late. At this rate I'll commandeer something.'

'Right. Excellent idea, Lizzie. Steal a boat, get it out to this abandoned lighthouse, take down the bad guys, rescue Lyndall.'

'And be back in time for a late dinner somewhere. Pete... do you think Lyndall's out there? So close to land but unable to leave? We don't even know if she can swim.'

'All we know is that her phone signal came from there or very close to it. Once for a minute tops, and then for a few more. Now, if she had it surely she'd send a message or call? But it's more likely Bonner is hiding out there and probably waiting for pick up to get him out of Aussie waters. Turning it on might have been to check if she'd any messages he needed to know about.'

Liz wasn't so sure. She'd researched the South Channel Pile Light while in the bakery and it was a clever place to hide an unwilling person. Lyndall was resourceful and Bonner would know that. Keeping her somewhere so isolated was a smart move.

At the end of the pier the wind was picking up and so were the waves. Somewhere out in the dark was Lyndall's phone. Hopefully Lyndall as well.

'Moving again, Liz. Where shall we meet?'

'Carpark at the supermarket. I'm on the pier right now.'

'See you in fifteen.'

She stayed there, gazing into the night. Three kilometres away, a light blinked and Liz knew it was the source of the phone signal. It might not be used as a beacon now but its lights still served as a guide in the bay. Police vessels would have no trouble reaching it. But would they arrive too late?

Reuben's call galvanised Liz into action. Thank goodness the carpark was only a few minutes away.

'I'm with Hamish on speaker, Liz. We're not far behind Pete but I'm taking a slight detour.'

'To get me a boat?'

He chuckled and for some reason the sound helped Liz's mood calm.

'I am serious.'

'And yes, that's precisely what we're doing. Almost. I have a friend in Tootgarook who has a love of jet skis and happens to keep several. He's agreed to meet me with three and we'll come round to Rye Beach.'

Liz drew in a deep breath of relief. This was something at least.

'Three?'

'I assume you want to come for a little ride.'

'Wouldn't miss it.'

'Good. What if I text you once we're a few minutes away and let you know where we'll be?'

Hamish spoke in the background but Liz couldn't hear. She ran over the road between cars.

'Hamish just heard from Meg. Tony Shaw has taken off in the direction of Lyndall's house, according to his new tracker. Even more positive is that she was able to listen into a phone call he made just after Ben dropped him off at his house.'

'How?'

'The tracker is a bit special. It lets us listen to the wearer's conversations.'

'What was said? Do you know who he called?'

'He didn't use a name and the call was brief, but he said he'd been held and questioned by a bunch of idiots who had no idea who they were dealing with.'

Silly man. Reuben doesn't seem the type to tolerate name calling.

'He said he'd stayed firm against aggressive interrogation so this just confirms his status as a liar.' Reuben sounded pleased, if anything. 'Then he listened to the other end for a while and said… hang on, Hamish do you have it on your phone?'

'Hey, Liz. I have the transcription and his words were… I'll get into that room, boss and if there is a safe I'll find it.'

'Oh my goodness. A safe? I'll confirm with Vince that there isn't one but that might mean Lyndall has told them that. She might still be alive.'

'Yep, that's our thinking. Ben's advised the security guards to stand down but do you want to let Vince Carter know?'

'I'll phone him. I don't want him anywhere near the place right now.'

'And Liz? I know you don't have all the intel yet… I doubt if any of us do, but what I know is positive and nobody goes home tonight without Lyndall.'

She ended the call feeling hopeful at last.

Reuben was right that she didn't have all the latest intel yet.

Her sudden exodus from the hub meant the team had to pick up some of her work and for that she was sorry. But they'd already pursued so many leads with no results that she'd had to follow her instincts. And they were frightening instincts because they led to her father.

There was a familiarity about the man seated outside the bakery in the footage. The same width of shoulders and muscular but lean torso were all she had to go by. That and the tattoo on Marcus Bonner's forearm, which looked eerily similar to her father's. On the drive down from Melbourne her mind had gone round and around, speculating on why three men – two connected to Lyndall's abduction – had the same tattoo which Liz had previously linked to an obscure white supremacist group.

She turned into the carpark and not seeing Pete, rang Vince's number.

'Any news, Liz?'

'Some. And I am sorry to call so late.'

'Not exactly sleeping. What does 'some' mean?'

'Before I forget, do you know if Lyndall has a safe?'

'No, she doesn't. Mind you, that's only from my knowledge so I guess anything is possible. What news is there?'

'Lyndall's other phone came on briefly and we're close to getting to where it originated. We don't know that she's in the same place, so don't expect anything yet.'

'Understood. That's promising.'

'It is. You also need to know there may be some disturbance on Lyndall's property shortly. The man who allegedly installed the panic room button? We've had him in custody for hours and have some good information but he's been allowed to leave and—'

'No, Lizzie why?'

'Because he's wearing a tracker and is the best chance we

have of getting a firm location on Lyndall. That's why I'm calling, Vince. He's moving in your general direction.'

'Then I'll be waiting for him.'

'You will not.'

Pete drove in and parked.

'We need him to show his hand and that of his boss. The security guards are on alert and will stay out of his way unless he attempts to cause damage. Either you lock yourself in the cottage and stay put, or I'll send someone to collect you.'

'You wouldn't.'

Out of the vehicle, Pete locked it and hurried toward Liz.

'Oh, I will, Vince. But while a member of my team is babysitting you, they could be helping find Lyndall. And any movement around her property might be enough to send this man into hiding. So what will it be?'

Pete stopped nearby, both eyes raised at Liz's firm tone.

'Yeah, fine. Okay, I'll turn the lights off and stay inside.'

'And I'll update you the minute I have news.' She ran a hand through her hair. 'We're getting close, mate. Just hang in there.'

'Hate this. Hate waiting. Stay safe, Lizzie.'

She slid the phone into her pocket hoping Pete wouldn't make some smart-mouthed remark.

'Gotta be tough on Vince. Guessing you told him Shaw's heading his way?'

Liz fought an urge to hug Pete for being understanding and decent. 'He'll sit tight but I guarantee he'll be watching.'

'Let's get a coffee somewhere and make a plan.'

They found takeaway coffee at the service station and headed for the beach. In the short time she'd been away, the tide had risen further and the wind was strengthening. Partway along the pier they sat on a bench and sipped their drinks.

Liz repeated the conversation she'd had with Reuben.

'Hamish can stay here and I'll come with you both,' Pete said.

'And before you say I'm picking on him, I'm not. He's a better shot if it comes to a long-range target and I have a jet ski, so will be in my element.'

'You what?'

He laughed at her surprise.

'Where do you even keep it?'

Pete lived in a flat in the western suburbs, nowhere near a beach.

'Storage unit.'

'I guess you never really know a person.' Liz smiled at him. She always envisioned Pete as a surfer so she wasn't far off. 'A bit like Annette. I've known her for years but never knew she had a kid.'

'Nah. She doesn't have any kids.'

That couldn't be right. One of Annette's reasons for leaving the hub yesterday was to arrange care for her child. And then again to buy more oat milk… of which they had plenty. Liz had to have misunderstood her about the child, but how? This was unsettling.

'What do you know about what Meg found in the painting?' Pete asked.

'Nothing. I was gone before you both returned to the hub. She found something *in* the painting? Under the painting?'

'The tiniest microchip ever, Liz. Something out of a spy movie right down to it being planted between layers of oil paint. And there's no way to tell without a decent magnifier that the paint was disturbed, so it still has a use.'

Liz finished the coffee and got up to throw the cup in a nearby bin.

'Ben isn't telling anyone higher up about the chip just yet. He's worried about leaks after Bonner took off.'

'Wait, he'd told his bosses we were going to pick up Bonner?'

'He's had to send updates as part of keeping control of the investigation. Not about The Tides though. The painting and the microchip are locked up and until he works out the appropriate authority to contact about the latter, it is staying put. The painting however…'

'Bait? Is that why Shaw was released?'

Pete opened his phone. 'Meg cut the feed from all the cameras in the house for a few minutes and we asked one of the security guards to go into the panic room and leave a message on the damaged wall. Even though he's searching for a safe, he won't miss this.'

He turned the screen.

On a large piece of paper, stuck in clear sight above the damaged wall, words were drawn in thick marker.

We have The Tides.

Below it was a mobile phone number.

'Either Bonner will see it via a camera, now they're back on, or else we're making it very easy for Shaw to get inside and find this. We'll be listening in when he tells his master that Lyndall has to stay safe in order to get what he wants.' Pete stood and stretched. 'If Lyndall is out on that lighthouse, Bonner will probably want to move her and he's going to find out what happens when you mess with her friends.'

THIRTY-TWO
~DAY THREE~

Midnight ticked over and the wind hadn't dropped but much of the cloud was gone, making visibility better from the end of the pier. It was the sound of the jet skis which pulled Liz from dark thoughts which had no resolutions. She found herself at the end of the pier again.

So much depended upon other people.

Some of them criminals.

And the team, the integrity of it. Liz agreed with Candace that conversations needed to be had and perhaps, more information about everyone's history clarified. Just not right now, when a woman's life was in the balance.

She met up with Pete, and Hamish who'd approached from the beach end, both carrying drone cases. Pete was on the phone and, leaving his case, stepped onto a platform, still talking. Hamish stopped near Liz and picked up the second case.

'Aren't you on a jet ski?'

'Drove the BearCat over. We need to get a drone up and see if Lyndall is in that structure. If so, I'm going to sort out some weapons and stay on land to give proper cover for you three. Imran's friend is on the third jet ski and the two of them have someone picking them up to go home. Reuben insisted they not stay around.'

Pete was off the phone and helped secure the three jet skis as they bumped against the platform. Liz stayed back, not wanting to engage with civilians as nerves played games with her stomach and mind. There were handshakes and a brief conversation and then Hamish was escorting two men off the pier.

Reuben climbed up with a life jacket in his hand. 'You doing alright?'

'Sure am. This is one of the best holiday spots in the state and I'm here. After midnight. And not because there's a picnic blanket or bottle of something special… nope, just some smelly jet skis and the risk of being shot by an evil art dealer.'

He threw back his head and laughed.

Something in Liz broke. She was a strong woman. A strong human. A tough cop. But things were crap right now and her own sense of humour was long gone.

She abruptly turned away to rub her eyes. To weep here and now was unthinkable.

A firm hand squeezed her shoulder and Reuben's mouth was close to her ear. 'Next time we're here, let me bring the wine and we'll celebrate getting Lyndall safely back to her loved ones.'

It was the last thing she'd expected him to say and it would never happen because she didn't go out with colleagues, but for a moment the image of a sunny day with a warm sea, cold wine and good company pushed away all the negatives.

Liz turned. 'Thank you.' The control was back in place.

Reuben nodded, his eyes on hers. 'Hold the thought, okay? Pete's looking at us in a particularly odd way.'

Unintentional laughter bubbled up.

'Much better. Shall we catch some bad dudes?' He handed her the life jacket. 'We'll start to head out in the right direction while Hamish gets a drone up.

Pete's phone was ringing again as they reached him on the platform and after he answered, he put it onto speaker.

'Ben? I have Liz and Reuben here. Sorry for the wind in the background.'

'We can hear you. There's news. Tony Shaw broke into Lyndall's house. Turns out Vince was too busy thinking about vodka to turn the secondary locks on the sliding door.' Ben chuckled. Everyone knew now about the word 'vodka' being a keyword. 'Anyway, he wasted no time going to the panic room and initially stood there looking around before seeing the paper.'

'Looking for the non-existent safe.'

She is alive. She's playing Bonner.

'So, then right in front of us, Shaw makes another phone call.'

Liz held her breath.

'Two, in fact. First was to relay the info about the message from us. It turned into a lot of him trying to speak while someone yelled at him. Couldn't pick up the words but the tone was furious. Eventually there was a break and Shaw said he would meet them at the drop-off point.'

'Do you think he meant the pier in Williamstown?'

'Possibly, Pete.'

'And the second call?' Liz forced the words out.

Meg chimed in. 'This is good intel, guys. Shaw left the property, drove a few kilometres and parked somewhere. He made a call and left a message which only said 'the tide is turning' then hung up. A few minutes later he gets a call. This one was pretty much one-sided from the side we can't hear, but there were some interesting comments from Shaw.'

Liz wanted to sit. Her legs were shaking from a mix of exhaustion and nervous energy and she set her feet a bit apart and braced herself against the slight rocking of the platform.

'Ben, can you read the transcript?'

'Sure. This was after he answered and listening for almost sixty seconds. *I told Bonner the cops have the artwork and left a phone number. Figure they want to trade for Nora. He blew up. Said he's had enough of dealing with your decisions and wants me to be at the pier to help him do a trade.* Then he listened again before saying *I'm with you, not Bonner.'*

Pete and Reuben looked at each other, and then Liz.

'Ben… are you saying somebody is running Bonner? It isn't all him behind Lyndall's abduction?' Liz asked.

Candace replied. 'Since we saw the footage of the man seated outside the bakery, I've adjusted my profile of Bonner to someone who wants to control outcomes but is himself controlled by another person. I feel, from watching the footage over and over, that Bonner didn't expect to see that man and was put on the back foot, so to speak, by his presence.'

'Any idea who this man is?' Reuben asked.

Liz took a step back from the outstretched phone. Her own thoughts couldn't be right.

Pete picked up her disquiet, his eyes narrowing but he didn't say a word.

'Phoebe and Annette are working hard to narrow down some names from Lyndall's life as Nora Egan. So far there's no person who comes up in her background and in Bonner's or even Alain's,' Candace said. 'We have discovered where Nora and Alain met though. It was at a shooting club. Both were contenders for Olympic selection in various rifle events.'

'Wait, so have we approached this all wrong?' Pete asked. 'We've assumed Nora might have been an assassin but what if it was Alain?'

'Or both,' Ben said. 'Either way, it looks as if she might be moved back to the pier for pick up by Shaw, so I'm putting a team together to head there. I'm calling Hamish back so Reuben can get out a drone up first and then if necessary, get out there yourselves..'

'And stay safe!' Meg called.

Taking Hamish from the team in Rye wasn't ideal but Ben was low on bodies and everything pointed to Lyndall being returned to the pier. Having his best shooter a hundred kilometres away wouldn't help anyone if the action moved to Melbourne.

'Meg's sending you the coordinates to meet the helicopter. Bring whatever you need for the operation and Reuben will collect the vehicle later.'

'Will do. I'm not entirely happy leaving them alone here.'

'If anything changes we'll turn you around. Get going so you can meet your ride on time.' Ben disconnected the call.

He agreed with Hamish. Nobody was comfortable with working under these conditions, with a split team and so little to go on. There was every chance he was making the wrong decisions yet the choices were limited. With so much at stake he'd been forced to request the attendance of one of the CIRT teams. Critical Incident Response Teams were small, rapid-response units with highly trained personnel who would support Ben's people. And the water units were making headway toward the South Channel Pile Light so might be in a position to intercept Bonner.

'Are you ready, Ben?' Meg had changed into black pants and top and held a heavy jacket in one hand, the ever-present laptop bag in the other. 'Annette says she'll be at the unit in a second or two.'

'Almost. Go downstairs and I'll grab my stuff.'

Meg waved to the room and let herself out. There was only Phoebe and Candace left and both wore the faces of people pushed to their limits. This was a huge learning curve for Ben and for Operation Nobody. Going forward he needed changes in staff levels and to put some basic rules in place to protect them from this level of exhaustion but for now he was thankful each and every person put Lyndall's needs ahead of their own. It was more than he'd expected to ask of them.

'Go, Ben. Phoebe and I will keep things running and ensure communications continue.'

Hearing her name, Phoebe looked up from her seat at Meg's workstation. She offered a smile and Ben saw the strength she brought to the team. Her nature wasn't aligned with the demands of such a job but she had delivered, and more than once. If anything, Phoebe was beginning to look like she belonged.

Candace followed him to his office where he collected what he needed.

'Watch out for unexpected attack from land or sea,' Candace said. 'Liz didn't say a word when we spoke about Bonner having a master but based on the tattoos on him and Shaw, I know she suspects her father is involved. And physically, the man at the bakery might well be Kyle Moorland.'

'I will be aware and will talk to the others. Kyle's description, including a photograph and short brief, have gone to CIRT. They've had past experience chasing him so should the opportunity arise, I believe they'll make it their business to capture the bastard.'

'The next couple of hours are critical,' Candace said. Her eyes were earnest. 'We all believe in you, Ben.'

That meant the world and as he ran down the stairs to the carpark, Ben committed to live up to the faith placed in him.

In the distance, the blinking lights in the sky were the helicopter coming to collect Hamish. While it could easily have flown low over the South Channel Pile Light, instead it deviated to avoid being identified as a police unit.

Liz felt utterly helpless.

She paced up and down the pier, or at least, the furthest twenty metres. Reuben and Pete had their focus on the drone launched only a few minutes ago. There was a screen open and Reuben sat, cross-legged, before it, guiding the small craft as low to the water as he dared. Pete used long range binoculars to watch its progress.

And I can do nothing. Nothing.

She was second-guessing everything. Her decision to

abandon the team and drive here without a plan was unprofessional. The churning thoughts about her father. And her worries concerning Hamish and Annette. Because if one of them was on her father's payroll, then Lyndall's life was at risk more than anyone realised.

'Lizzie!'

She ran to where the men were, her eyes drawn to the screen which showed what the drone saw.

'It is well back from the structure, almost at its limits to see, and we have problems to solve.' Reuben manoeuvred the controls and a shape in the water gradually moved into view. 'Boat number one. I took a shot of it and zoomed in and it is badged up as Parks Victoria.'

'I've got Phoebe chasing up someone in the organisation to confirm this doesn't belong to them,' Pete lowered the binoculars. 'It is a clever way to keep the usual sightseers away. All they'd need to do is make something up about extending the approach zone and avoid a real Parks boat fronting up.'

'Other issue is a second boat. Harder to see because its small and against the structure but it looks fast.'

'So people *are* out there… can you see into the building?'

'Barely.'

Again, the imagery changed, the screen almost black until the drone stabilised from wherever Reuben had sent it. The angle was just above the surface of the sea and the South Channel Pile Light rose from water. There were windows around the structure and shadowy movement behind them. The focus sharpened as one figure stood pressed against the glass, staring out.

Wearing pyjamas, hair loose around her shoulders, palms against the window, Lyndall had a look of utter terror.

THIRTY-THREE

Age had changed Lyndall. Her body was heavier and not as responsive as even ten years ago. She could still climb a fence and lug huge bags of livestock feed and repair a gate but whether swimming to shore from here was remotely possible remained to be seen. Right now it felt like her only hope, assuming she could find a way to get into the water.

On the upside, her willpower was stronger than ever. And age hadn't hurt her eyesight and as she stared in the direction of Rye Beach, Lyndall saw something. Not in the sea but just above it. As she focused on it, the small shape vanished.

'I told you to sit down, Nora!'

Marcus had ranted and raged and thrown a chair after a phone call so she'd removed herself from his immediate line of fury. Now, she returned to the table.

His face and neck were bright red. Perhaps he would suffer a stroke or heart attack and while his men attended him, she could slip out. Him dying was not something she wanted though. Lyndall doubted she had the ability to locate her son and once she was out of this mess, would torture Marcus if need be to get a confession about everything he'd done. Jean-Paul deserved justice. So did Claude.

Wishful thinking. You're far from safe.

'You lied.'

'Absolutely not. I gave you the codes to access the safe and—'

'There is no safe!'

Lyndall rolled her eyes and leaned back in her chair. 'How hard did your man look?'

'Enough to see a message from your police friends.' He turned the screen of his phone. 'This was stuck to the wall in your panic room. Care to explain?'

The words were clear – **We have The Tides.** And a phone number. And behind it was a hole in the wall.

Goosebumps rose on her arms.

'Is it genuine? The painting is in my safe so how exactly did anyone find it, let alone open it? I'd be asking your man a few questions because this sounds like someone else is wrestling for control.'

It was a calculated risk, the words she was using. Marcus was a control freak and she knew she'd hit his soft underbelly when his colour heightened even more.

'You could get him to go back into my house and watch him more closely.'

'I watched him before.'

'Then did you see him search for the safe? Did *he* put the paper there?'

'I have no idea who put it there but someone cared enough about you to go to great lengths to retrieve the one thing I want.'

He hit the table with both palms.

Lyndall kept still. Baiting him was a dangerous game.

When his phone rang, he lurched to his feet and turned his back to answer.

Taking a long, slow breath, Lyndall focused on his conversation. The phone was hard against his ear but she could tell it was a male voice on the other end. He listened, his spare hand curling into a fist until he had the opportunity to speak.

'Well, I've changed my mind since speaking to Shaw. If they

want an exchange then make it on my terms. They can come here where I've got men in place and have multiple exit options.'

Whoever had called was his boss, Lyndall was certain. She'd been aware of a chain of command when Alain's real purpose in life came to the forefront but Marcus was the only person who'd been visible. Probably to remind her of their own history.

'I'm telling you, that is a mistake. They come to us or I shoot her here and now.' Marcus deliberately swung back to stare at Lyndall. 'She's a couple of metres away. Still thinks she can take me on and win.'

Whatever the other man said made Marcus laugh suddenly. His body relaxed a bit and he nodded.

'Fine. This is all upsetting, losing my gallery and my identity being exposed, so forgive my mood. If this gets us the painting then we'll do it your way, but your person inside that team had better be giving you the right information.' On that curious note, he terminated the call.

Do you mean the police? The ones looking for me?

Was there no end to the insidious reach of Marcus and his masters? It had to be how he'd found her in the first place… a tame copper who knew Liz. Or Vince. The one thing she was certain was that once Pete McNamara heard of this he would stop at nothing to uncover them. He was a fine police officer and a solid human.

Marcus let himself out and yelled to his men who were back on the speedboat a few metres away, gesturing for them to come closer. If Lyndall understood what was going to happen, he would shortly force her onto that boat – in pyjamas and socks – and potentially get her killed if there was an exchange of gun fire at the pier. There was only one course of action in her mind and just as risky but her life would be in her own hands, not that of a monster.

'We're going.' Marcus strode in. 'If you do what you're told, you might just survive this. I'll tie your hands.'

She stood and wrapped her arms around herself, looking as scared as she could muster. 'Do you have a lifejacket?'

'What on earth for? The boat isn't going to sink.'

'Boats sink all the time and I don't swim, Marcus.'

He crossed the distance and grabbed her chin, forcing her to look into his eyes so close she could smell his foul breath.

'Everyone can swim, Nora.'

'I never learnt. And I have every right to fear the sea, particularly this bay, after what happened to my husband and son.'

Marcus sighed. 'For goodness sake. Look, there's no lifejackets but I won't tie your hands. That way you can hold onto the side. I'm not about to let you drown. You, my old lover, are my insurance.' He kissed her lips, rough and thankfully quick, then stepped away.

He was on the phone again, facing away, and she rubbed her mouth on her top.

With all her heart, Lyndall hoped she would survive this if only to destroy Marcus Bonner.

THIRTY-FOUR

Engines off, the jet skis dipped and rose with the current.

Any other time, Liz would have been laughing aloud as she skimmed through the night sea, wind in her hair and moonlight to show her the way. The experience was surreal and when she looked at Pete at one point, his face was alight with the thrill. Now they'd stopped about a kilometre from the building.

All of them had binoculars and both men had rifles on their backs. Liz had her handgun and they wore flack vests beneath lifejackets.

'There's some movement with the Parks boat,' Reuben said. 'Looks like they're moving toward Melbourne. I'll text Ben so he can take care of them.'

Phoebe had confirmed that Parks Victoria had no knowledge of a boat patrolling the area for the past two days.

Liz used her binoculars to look for Lyndall. The windows were empty and the light which had been on in there – most likely a lantern or the like – abruptly extinguished.

'Did you see that? The light is off inside.' Liz kept scanning. 'Wait on… the speed boat is at the bottom of the steps.'

'Got it,' Pete said. 'We're on the wrong side to see what's happening. Might do a loop around.'

'Won't our motors alert them?' Liz lowered the binoculars. 'We need to see where Lyndall is first.'

'Which we can't from here.' Pete started his motor. 'I'll tiptoe over.'

He went slowly, the jet ski less than quiet but probably too far from the building to cause alarm.

Liz's phone vibrated and she answered. 'Candace. What's up?'

'I can see on the tracker that although you are close to where Lyndall's phone came on, it now appears to be moving away from you.'

'What? It's on again? Where is it?'

'According to the map, about two kilometres north-west of you and travelling toward the city.'

Liz relayed the information to Reuben.

'It has to be on the Parks boat.' He changed the direction he was looking in to scan for it.

'So is Lyndall onboard as well?'

'No way to tell but I've spoken to Ben and he's got the water police units onto it. They are well aware of what they might be facing, but it might pay for one of you to get close.' There was a tone of anxiety in Candace's voice Liz had never heard. 'I think you should follow and let Reuben deal with the speedboat.'

'Why?'

'Because... Liz, just take care. Please watch yourself out there.'

Beneath her, the water sloshed against the machine and around her, the wind – although much reduced – carried sounds and smells. For a moment none of it mattered other than the woman on the other end of the phone who was worried about her wellbeing. Liz was unused to being cared about, certainly by other women. But out here was another woman who needed her full attention.

'Candace? I'm going to bring Lyndall home, okay? Knowing you and Phoebe are watching over us makes this possible.'

'And we will be here for as long as it takes.'

Phone back in a pocket, Liz moved closer to Reuben. 'Would you shadow the other boat, please? I'm going to wait until I hear from Pete and if he can't see Lyndall on the speedboat, will send him after you.'

'And if he can?'

'Then he and I will make a plan.'

'Not happy about leaving you.'

Unsure how she felt about being alone on a machine she'd only used a few times, at a juncture which would change lives, the strangest calm descended on Liz.

'We can hardly celebrate rescuing Lyndall with a bottle of wine on Rye Pier, can we, if we don't rescue her. I can manage.'

Reuben's expression said otherwise but for a moment, there was a blaze in his eyes which acknowledged her reference to his earlier words. 'I'll go and shadow but I truly do not believe she's on that boat. So expect to see me soon.'

With that, he was gone into the night.

Liz was alone.

Who knew what sea creatures lurked below.

THIRTY-FIVE

Lyndall made a small show of being afraid to step from the lowest stair onto the speedboat. One of the men took pity on her and supported her arms as she climbed in.

'I get motion sick,' she whispered to him.

He helped her to a seat at the back. 'Throw up over the side.' He moved up to the cockpit seat and started the motor.

The speedboat was sleek and one she'd love to have skippered under different circumstances. Lyndall was a decent sailor but wasn't in a position to overpower three thugs and Marcus. Appearing pathetic made her less of a threat.

Marcus was taking another phone call, standing upon the steps and staring into the night. Unnoticed, Lyndall carefully undid the buttons on her pyjama top, thankful for her old-fashioned sleeping habit of wearing a singlet underneath. This done, she wrapped one arm against her torso to keep the front together, gripping the rail along the side of the boat with the other.

While the motor idled, Lyndall got her bearings.

From this angle she could see straight under the structure which rose from the sea on numerous thick, timber poles.

Beneath it was a timber platform of sorts which didn't completely fill the space. There was sufficient room to swim below but not for a boat to follow. Although she could dive in right now, there were three other people here who would stop at nothing to find her.

I have to judge this perfectly.

Off the phone, Marcus stepped onto the boat and braced himself as it rocked. He glanced at Lyndall then barked at his driver.

'Change of plan. Head for St Andrews Beach and I'll get you the exact co-ordinates soon.'

'That's a dangerous and slow run at night, boss. Too many hazards including The Rip.'

'You'll find a way to speed things up if you want to make the return trip.'

The driver shook his head but changed something on a screen he had open. A sea chart blinked on and he studied it for a moment.

Marcus flopped onto the seat to the left of the driver and looked back at Lyndall. 'I'm not handing you over to Shaw. He can take the heat which is waiting for him back in the city and I've arranged to swap you for the painting at a place where I have the upper hand. Hold tight because it'll get bumpy.'

His sneer might have bothered Lyndall but her mind was in overdrive. The only way by boat to St Andrews Beach was around Point Nepean through the narrow entry to the bay. The Rip was a notorious stretch which had claimed many boats over the years and for a small speedboat to navigate it at night, and possibly at speed, was to court danger. Marcus must have a way to escape after the exchange, unless he expected the speedboat to simply take him out to sea.

How did he know Shaw was effectively walking into a trap?

The motor roared and the speedboat pulled away from the structure where Lyndall had spent more than two days. It turned in an arc so tight that the boat listed and the surface of the water was only inches from Lyndall's side.

Using all of her strength, she threw herself out.

THIRTY-SIX

'She's on the speedboat, Liz!' Pete's voice was hard to hear over a sudden roar. 'I'm going there now. Get Reuben back.'

The line cut out and Liz phoned Reuben.

It took a minute for him to answer and he had to shout above the noise of his jet ski. 'I'm close to the Parks boat.'

'Lyndall is on the speedboat.' Liz had her binoculars trained on the structure. 'Okay, its moving away. Oh crap!'

'What?'

'Reuben, it is turning the other way. Toward Sorrento I guess.'

'On my way.'

Liz called the information in to Candace, keeping it short and requesting the helicopter with Hamish turn around and track Pete and Reuben for a location. If Bonner was moving Lyndall to a new location then did he even intend to swap her for the painting?

A message came up on her phone from Ben.

Bonner wants to meet me to do exchange. St Andrews Beach. Return to land. Co-ordinates coming. Will phone en route but need you over there.

• • •

Returning to land now.

The jet ski had drifted closer to the structure and for the first time, Liz could view it easily without binoculars. There was a visible wash around it… a wide circle like one from a boat.

The speedboat was still there, prowling so slowly that the motor sounds were minimal. Someone was flashing a bright light across the water and under the building.

Did Lyndall escape?

Liz listened intently for either of the jet skis. Nobody was close. Pete had eyes on it so had he lost them, or was he like her, at a distance to observe what had turned the boat back? Using the binoculars, she tried to find Lyndall as the speedboat disappeared around the far side again.

'Come on, come on,' she muttered.

Reuben had to be getting close now unless he'd gone in a more direct route toward Sorrento and then the last few kilometres of the Peninsula. Or had he and Pete been sent to shore as well?

'So I'm all alone out here.'

Liz sent messages to both men and neither responded.

She started the jet ski, letting it idle to make sure she hadn't alerted anyone in the speedboat. Then, as carefully as she could, Liz opened the throttle enough to get forward motion and moved closer.

Her phone lit up with a message from Pete.

Reuben and I are onto the speedboat. Stop moving.

Liz cut the motor and yanked the handles to change direction. She was about two hundred metres from the structure and raised the binoculars as the speedboat once again came into view.

There were three people visible. One was Marcus Bonner, holding a large flashlight and training it around the timber poles. Another was driving while the third was on the bow, peering into the water. This man suddenly yelled something which wasn't clear to Liz but Bonner moved fast, reaching on the other side of the boat and scooping something out.

He held it up.

It was clothing and looked exactly like the pyjama top Lyndall wore when Bonner had stolen her from her home.

THIRTY-SEVEN

You foolish woman, you're going to drown.

Lyndall's lungs were screaming for air and her ears rang and her eyes stung. She'd swum downwards as far as she could bear and then toward the legs of the structure, gripping the slimy, barnacle-encrusted timber as best she could as she'd slowly ascended.

Tilting her face back to expose the least of herself as possible, she gasped for oxygen.

She was under the platform and thought about climbing onto it but then the speedboat approached.

She'd hoped for longer before they missed her.

Marcus was calling her name.

A shark might take her and she'd go willingly before surrendering to this monstrous man. But it gave her an idea of where the boat was as it circled – further away at first and then narrowing the gap with each rotation. He had a flashlight but wasn't near enough to see her. Not yet.

Before the speedboat returned she was certain she'd heard other crafts out here. Smaller. And one which was slow and had the sound of a fishing trawler about it.

I'm going mad. Next I'll be seeing mermaids.

Lyndall slowed and shallowed her breathing, watching the light come closer. If she didn't move soon, Marcus would find her and while he might be reluctant to get into the water to retrieve her, one of his men would have no choice. Waiting until the boat had just passed, she again dipped beneath the surface and swam away from the structure.

This time she had to come up for breath more quickly, which she took while dog-paddling and looking back. Still no sign of the speedboat. She turned her head to find shore. Lights twinkled in the distance in a long row. All she had to do was swim.

There was a shout behind her and then Marcus was screaming her name over and over. Too afraid to look, Lyndall forced herself beneath the water yet again, kicking hard to get far enough down to evade a flashlight, should they have spotted her.

She had to get to land.

Melanie's sweet face needed kissing. So did Vince's.

I just have to swim. Just swim.

THIRTY-EIGHT

Pete was only a hundred metres from the speedboat, using a small paddle and the currents. He owned the same model and knew where to look for small mercies such as this. It was slow going but he had the advantage of stealth.

He'd lost sight of the speedboat when it initially arced away from its mooring and that was something he was furious with himself over.

Lyndall was on that damned thing a minute earlier and then, when he'd caught up enough to see again, she was gone from her seat. His heart had hit his stomach and he'd hesitated, unsure for a second whether to go and look for her or to follow. There was a chance she'd simply slid onto the floor of the boat due to its sharp turn.

So, he'd followed.

It was a short trip and took all his skills with a jet ski to avoid being seen when the boat curved back the way it came. It was bad enough not using lights let alone dealing with other vessels doing the same.

He'd got a message from Ben and ignored it. Instead, he'd been texting back and forward with Reuben, who was taking a wide berth to find a guard point between the lighthouse and the direct way to leave the bay. Reuben was an excellent shot and had assured Pete he wouldn't hesitate to use his rifle if it came to protecting Lyndall, or Liz.

Pete had noticed her moving closer for a while and finally messaged her to stop. She did. And then the speedboat came around again and Bonner pulled something out of the water.

'No, no, no.'

He grabbed his phone and dialled Reuben.

'They've fished Lyndall's pj top out of the sea. We need to find her.'

'I'm heading over.'

Pete turned on the lights of his jet ski and powered the throttle.

THIRTY-NINE

Hearing the jet ski so close made Liz jump. Pete was heading directly at the speedboat. And from the dark, another arrived. Reuben, also at full throttle.

Marcus screamed at his driver, who powered the boat so suddenly that the man on the bow fell into the sea. It didn't wait for him, and while the driver was weaving a path between the two jet skis, Marcus had found a rifle and was bracing himself to shoot.

In seconds, all three vessels had gone, leaving only a churning sea in their wake and the residual sound of their motors.

A shot.

Then another.

Liz dialled Ben and turned on the lights of the jet ski.

'Liz, can I call you—'

'Sorry, no. Lyndall appears to have gone overboard from the speedboat. Pete and Reuben are in pursuit of it which has just left the South Channel Pile Light going south-west. Shots have been fired but out of my sight.'

'Understood. Where are you?'

'Two hundred metres north of the Pile Light and

commencing a search for Lyndall. I need urgent assistance and so do our guys.'

'Helicopter is already on its way. We'll update Hamish and water police.'

'Please warn them Lyndall may be somewhere in the sea, without a life vest. There's one of Bonner's men also in the water and I'm going to get him first.'

'You'll have help in minutes.'

'Gotta go.'

Bonner's man was at the bottom of the steps, swearing and shaking his fist at the dark. Liz got within a couple of metres of his position.

She aimed her gun in his direction and held handcuffs in the air. 'Listen to me. Put one of these on and go sit at the top of the steps and attach the other to a rail. If you mess me around and I need to do it myself I'll make it my business to add years to your sentence. Understand.'

Face grim, he nodded, and when she tossed them over, did exactly what she said, dropping onto the top step.

Liz did a slow circuit of the structure. 'Lyndall! It's Liz and it's safe!'

She didn't expect an answer because many minutes had passed since Lyndall went into the water. Liz was convinced it was on purpose and that she'd shed her pyjama top as a sign. If she'd been hit by the speedboat her body would likely be visible, along with blood, and there were neither.

You're swimming to shore.

Liz followed the most direct route, slow and steady and stopping every fifty metres or so to call for Lyndall and use her flashlight. She was more than two kilometres from the structure when a helicopter roared over the top of her, so close to the water that it left the jet ski rocking. Hamish had the door open and raised his hand to her. It was travelling incredibly fast and should catch up with Pete and Reuben soon.

Please be okay. Both of you.

She had to keep the fears about the gunshots in the back of her mind. It wasn't her job and both of them were outstanding at theirs.

From here, the pier was less than a kilometre away. Could Lyndall have swum so far in the time? Even someone who regularly did ocean swimming might not cover this distance so fast, particularly at night. Let alone having been confined for two days and not dressed for swimming.

She retraced her path but this time zig-zagged across a wide channel.

A boat loomed in the darkness. Not the speedboat but not a police unit. The motor chugged as Liz closed the distance, recognising the shape of a fishing trawler. It was old and small with no name or registration in the usual places.

'Police! I need assistance finding a person overboard.' She called as loudly as possible over the sound of the engines.

Wearing wet weather gear which almost covered him from head to foot, a man waved his arm over his head in recognition. The motor changed as the vessel slowed further.

'Have you seen anyone in the water?'

'Eh? Wodder?' The accent was impossible to guess and the way the man held himself spoke of great age. "Thees un?'

He gestured toward the stern where there was a low gate and as Liz manoeuvred her craft to it, he shuffled along, hunched over, and pushed it open. It was only half a metre or so above Liz and a pair of legs appeared through the opening.

Soaking wet legs wearing pyjamas.

The man was grunting as he helped the person to sit upright.

'Lyndall! Oh my god, Lyndall.'

A weary but familiar face smiled down at her.

'Can you give me a lift?'

With a lot of help from the old fisherman, Lyndall finally made it onto the jet ski and locked her arms around Liz like she'd never let go, head against Liz's back. She was wearing an oversize jumper which reeked of fish and diesel but Liz didn't care.

The fisherman closed the gate.

'What is your name?' Liz called.

'Eh?' He shrugged.

'Thank you.'

With a wave, he turned away and disappeared from view. Liz moved the jet ski away and then turned it so she could took a few photographs of the trawler. He needed to be acknowledged for what he'd done tonight. Then she phoned Candace.

'Liz! All I know is there were shots fired!'

'I've got her, Candace. Lyndall is safe.'

The words felt surreal but the woman gripping her was very real.

'Thank God. Where are you?'

'On our way to Rye Pier. Can you please arrange some assistance to meet us? An ambulance to check her over.'

'Don't need an ambulance.' Lyndall muttered.

'Get to shore and I'll take care of it.'

Liz tucked the phone away. 'I'll go slowly. Just hold on please.'

'Go fast. I didn't get much of a ride in the speedboat.'

That made Liz laugh aloud.

'Yes, ma'am.'

FORTY

Seeing a message flash up on his phone that Lyndall was safe almost brought Pete to tears. It wasn't the time or place so instead he uttered a small word of thanks to whoever was listening.

He was at the point of having to stop this insane chase along the coastline because the conditions were becoming too dangerous the closer they got to the tip of the peninsula.

Reuben pulled alongside him and gestured to their right and up, where the police helicopter was gaining ground. He nodded and held up a hand to indicate for them to stop and pulled back on the power.

They'd been ducking and weaving to keep the speedboat in sight but not be shot and not once had the opportunity arisen to take their own shots. But now that his hands were free, Pete swung the rifle off his back, prepped it and trained it on the rapidly moving speedboat. It was still in range and he fired and missed.

Not far from him, Reuben did exactly the same. And missed.

'He's not getting away!' Pete yelled his frustration and aimed again.

Another miss.

But Reuben took his time, even as the target reached the end of range. This one had an immediate result with the driver dropping to the bottom of the boat. Bonner grabbed a rail to stay upright as the boat lurched, then got to the cockpit and cut the motor.

'Legend, mate.' Pete nosed his jet ski forward again but not as fast.

The helicopter hovered above the speedboat and a brilliant circle of light flooded the sea around it. Bonner's arm shaded his eyes but then his other arm came up with his rifle and in a second he was aiming into the light.

In one motion, Pete and Reuben fired and another shot came from the helicopter.

Bonner's body jerked and fell backwards.

As if in slow motion, the helicopter dropped its height by half. Hamish was half-out of the door, secured by a harness, rifle pointed on the boat below. And then he looked across to the jet skis and raised his thumb.

Liz hadn't left the end of the pier since paramedics had taken Lyndall to safety off the beach. She couldn't see a damned thing from here but Ben had instructed her not to go back out on the water.

She burned with adrenaline and almost dropped her phone when it rang.

'You found her, Lizzie. I'll never forget this.'

'Oh, Vince, I could hardly believe my eyes but yes, she's safe and as far as I know is unharmed. Exhausted and hungry and angry.'

Vince chuckled. 'Just got off a phone call with her and yes, all of that. But she is beyond grateful to you and your team and so am I. Even shithead.'

Liz gazed out to sea.

Come on, dude. I need a call from you.

'Liz? He's good, isn't he?'

'You know Pete, off in the middle of trouble. I'm sure he's fine though.'

'Crap. Okay, I'll get off the phone but let me know.'

Another call came through as she disconnected from Vince.

Meg's voice was cheery. 'Good thing you're alive. And good work finding our Lyndall.'

'Except, I didn't. Not in the water anyway. A fisherman picked her up.'

'Well we shall throw him a party as well. I rang because you have two jet skis on their way to the pier. There's a security guard coming down to watch them overnight before we spruce them up, refill their tanks, and return them to their lovely owner.'

Relief flooded every part of Liz and she sank onto the floor. 'Oh thank goodness.'

'Yes, wouldn't want to replace all that hardware,' Meg laughed. 'Or them. Probably.'

'What about Bonner?'

'To be confirmed but we will know after the autopsy whether it was Pete, Reuben, or Hamish who fired the kill shot. My bet is on Hamish.'

'Then, it's over.'

'One hopes. More or less, anyway.'

'I might see if Lyndall is still here. She doesn't want to go anywhere other than home.'

Lyndall sat on the back step of the ambulance wearing dry clothes and talking quietly on the phone. When she saw Liz, she excused herself from the call and held her arms open.

Liz embraced her, sitting at her side and letting the other woman shed tears. The paramedic left them alone and for a while they stayed that way. Then Lyndall straightened and wiped her eyes.

'That never happened.'

'No idea what you mean. I have some news.'

'They caught Marcus?'

'Unofficially… Marcus Bonner is dead. He can never harm you again.'

Instead of the relief she expected on Lyndall's face, there was a sudden grief. Surely not for that dreadful excuse of a human. But Lyndall regained her composure.

'My son, Claude, is still living. I fear that Marcus is the only person to know his whereabouts.'

And we just took away your chance to be reunited.

'Perhaps. You won't know any of this because we've not had a chance to talk yet, but I happen to be working with an elite group of people who make it their business to fix things. They are the reason we found where Bonner was holding you. That and your cryptic clues. Good grief, next time leave written instructions!'

Lyndall's laugh was hollow.

'No, really. We are smart but there were moments we had no idea what you were going on about.' But Liz smiled. 'My point is, that if Claude is to be found, then you know the right people to begin a search. All is not lost.'

It was almost dawn and Liz was back at the end of the pier. This time it was to watch the sun rise, knowing she'd been part of something incredible.

Later, after the team slept and recharged, there'd be briefings and Liz worried about what would come out of them. Her instincts insisted that Bonner had received intel which surely only someone in the team, or closely connected, would know.

Lyndall was home after a thorough check up. Vince was up at her house and the security patrol were staying for another day, or for as long as Lyndall wanted.

Pete was the only person left in Rye and he'd gone in search of food, which seemed impossible at this time of morning. She'd suggested he look through the window at the bakery in case the owner was still in there.

They were safe. The team. Lyndall.

For once, the bad guys were dead or arrested.

And for today she could stop looking over her shoulder.

When her phone rang she answered without looking, knowing it would be Pete complaining about the lack of open cafés.

But there was a long silence on the other end broken only by a familiar sound. A chugging of an engine… a fishing boat. Liz's heart turned to ice.

'Elizabeth. I hope your friend Lyndall is quite recovered.'

'Dad?'

'Wodda? Eh?'

She squeezed her eyes shut against rising despair.

'Didn't even recognise your own father. You could have climbed aboard and given me a hug.'

Her eyes flew open. 'Arrested you, is what you mean.'

'Not nice. I rescued your friend from the deep, dark ocean.'

'Did you put her there in the first place? *You* are the brains behind all of this, aren't you?'

'That's more like it. A bit of recognition.'

'We need to meet, Dad. Face to face.'

'And we will, Elizabeth. A word of warning. You might have won this time but if you believe the tides have turned… such an appropriate phrase… be prepared. Leave the past alone, you and your team, because there will be no more favours. No more chances. Your Operation Nobody? Back off, or I'll ensure nobody lives. Nice talk. Let's do it again.'

He was gone.

'Hey, Liz. I found some coffee.'

She couldn't turn around to greet Pete. Not yet.

The first rays of sunshine touched the sea, out near the South Channel Pile Light.

EPILOGUE

One week later

Vince hadn't released Lyndall's hand since they'd sat on one sofa, facing Liz and Ben on the other. There was a tray between them all with hot drinks and slices of apple pie, made by Lyndall and Melanie, from Vince's apples.

If that isn't a man in love, then what is?

Lyndall's eyes were bright again and she'd been to a hairdresser and sported a short bob which clearly wanted to revert to curls. She'd made herself available for interviews and line-ups and filled in gaps about her abduction, as well as some of her history.

Outside, grey skies and persistent rain matched the sombre tone of the meeting.

'Please have some pie,' Lyndall said. She seemed unwilling to move, her fingers entwined with Vince's. 'Might as well eat while we discuss the future.'

Ben spent a minute putting pie onto four plates, offering one to Liz and taking one himself. But none of them made a move to taste it.

'You're safe from any prosecution, Lyndall,' Ben said. 'There is no suggestion you had any part in or knowledge of your husband's role as an assassin until after the third killing and then you foiled the fourth. That took courage.'

'I had to protect my children. Yet I failed.'

Liz couldn't bear the grief which she'd seen flare up several times in the past few days. Lyndall's rigidly controlled emotions were now unbottled and tears shed often. Candace was working with her but it was a long road to healing.

'You didn't fail, Lyndall. From everything I've heard about your past, you were against a force too dark and too powerful for any other outcome and I know you've said you should have gone to the French authorities, but there is no way of knowing if you would have been believed and every chance the head of this disgusting organisation had their own people in positions of power. Infiltration is clearly one of the hallmarks of the group.'

Just like with us, and the police, and who knows where else.

'Lizzie's right,' Vince said. 'You fled the country with two children and the only safety net you could find. The microchip. A bargaining tool.'

'Fat lot of good it did.'

Ben leaned forward. 'Now that we know the contents, no wonder Marcus and his people wanted it back. It names dozens of the European operatives and many will still be in play. This will make a difference, Lyndall.'

Sadly for Liz, none of the data retrieved included information outside of Europe. No hierarchy in Australia. No mention of Marcus or of Kyle.

'I'm in awe of you,' Ben said. 'You discovered your husband was more than an art dealer and amateur shooter and when you dug deeper, learnt of the existence of the list kept on the microchip. Stealing it from Marcus was an act of courage and embedding it into a painting was inspired. You couldn't foresee the lengths he and Alain would go to retrieve it.'

Alain had followed Lyndall and the children to Australia and pleaded with her for the return of the microchip. A point had come where he chose his family over his employer and that was when he and Jean-Paul were taken and murdered.

Marcus changed tactics, promising Lyndall a large sum of money to create a new life for herself and Claude in exchange for the painting. After waiting at the agreed meeting place for hours, Lyndall returned home to find her youngest son gone and the friend minding him deceased.

'They wanted it, but someone else decided to play god,' Lyndall said. 'I phoned the police. I was frantic to find Claude and terrified, seeing my friend dead. And a police officer arrived, just one. He handed me a bag and told me to disappear. The bag was filled with cash and a letter. Meg has it now and you know the contents. I was to never reveal The Tides until someone came for it and as long as I followed the instructions, Claude would grow up safe and happy.'

Tears dripped down her face and Vince pulled her into his arms.

'Ben, please.' Liz couldn't bear this any longer.

'Go on.'

'Lyndall, do you remember me saying that all is not lost? That my team wouldn't give up?'

She had Lyndall's full attention, and Vince's.

'We didn't want to raise your hopes but earlier today, Meg found him.'

Shaking her head, Lyndall pushed herself to her feet and stomped away. She got as far as the kitchen then turned back and stopped, arms crossed. 'Lizzie...'

'What do you want to know?'

'Is he safe?'

'Yes.'

'Will he stay safe if I make contact?'

Vince went to Lyndall, close but not touching. She glanced at him then back at Liz.

'Will knowing I am alive put Claude in danger?'

'We don't know. Until we find my father, we just can't be certain of anything. I am so sorry.'

'Then don't say any more about him. Not yet. Let me think.' Lyndall reached her hand out to Vince, who took it. 'Find him, Liz. Ben. Because until you do, none of us can rest easy and I am so, so tired of running.'

'Lyndall is one of the toughest humans I've ever met,' Ben said. 'And so are you.'

'I agree about her but I don't feel anything… actually, I feel so angry. She needs to reunite with her son or at the very least, see him with her own eyes from a distance. We could facilitate that.'

'We could but we won't.'

They stood outside the SUV parked near Lyndall's house. In the distance, the donkeys were braying, but in welcome as Vince and Lyndall wandered to their paddock.

'Be as angry as you need, Liz, but channel it into our team. We're under threat from within, as well as out.'

'Do you think Hamish works for my father?'

Ben grimaced. 'I do not want to consider the possibility but the anecdotal evidence is mounting. Even down to him having the shot which killed Marcus because it is likely Kyle wanted him gone.'

'So what do we do, Ben? If he is planted he's hardly going to crumble during interrogation.'

'Agree. I want to set up a meeting with Candace and Pete and us, away from headquarters or any bugging opportunities. Hate doing it but we might need to set Hamish on a path and see what comes of it. But not today.'

They finally climbed into the vehicle.

'I'm heading back home for a couple of days, Liz. I need to see Ellie and Michael and breathe air which doesn't have the stench of criminals.' He started the motor and headed for the driveway.

Liz gazed out of the window at the peaceful paddocks. They'd done good. Lyndall was home. An organised crime cartel was exposed... at least part of it. The team, for the most part, was coming together. Operation Nobody was truly underway and their next steps were crucial for its future. Tonight she'd take her sister out for dinner and they would laugh and tell each other stories and people-watch.

And then we're going to find Kyle.

———

Next in the series is Lest Nobody Lives

NEXT IN THE SERIES

This time it is personal...

DS Liz Moorland is hunting her father and at last there is an end in sight. The team at Operation Nobody is focused on finding him *and* solving a puzzling old double murder, but are the two cases connected?

Book 4 in the DS Liz Moorland series is the ultimate game of cat and mouse with a gripping and fast-paced search for justice.

Lest Nobody Lives

AFTERWORD

The choice of using a real landmark - the South Channel Pile Light - meant I had to take some liberties with it for the sake of the story but I hope I've still kept the 'feel' of it intact.

In reality, this structure is regularly visited by Parks Victoria as well as local tour operators and those wishing to dive and take photos of seals and seabirds. My understanding is that only officials are permitted within a certain distance so in real life, Lyndall being held there would quickly have been discovered.

I am in awe of Parks Victoria and the history of the structure and encourage you to visit their website if you are just as intrigued.

ACKNOWLEDGMENTS

My huge thanks to you, my reader. This book took me so much longer than anticipated and for the first time ever, release day had to be pushed back. I want to thank you for hanging in there and being so patient.

Two of my author friends were so helpful and generous with information about different parts of the story - thank you both Simon Michael Prior and Fiona Tarr. If you enjoy my stories I am sure you will love theirs so please do check them out.

Finally, for the first time I worked with editor and dear friend Susan Mackie who went above and beyond to meet my ridiculously tight deadline even though she was travelling for part of it. She is another author I recommend who writes gorgeous small town fiction, so please do look her up.

ABOUT THE AUTHOR

Phillipa lives just outside a beautiful town in country Victoria, Australia. She also lives in the many worlds of her imagination and stockpiles stories beside her laptop.

She writes from the heart about love, dreams, secrets, discovery, the sea, the world as she knows it… or wishes it could be. She loves happy endings, heart-pounding suspense, and characters who stay with you long after the final page.

With a passion for music, the ocean, animals, nature, reading, and writing, she is often found in the vegetable garden pondering a new story.

Phillipa's website is www.phillipaclark.com

ALSO BY PHILLIPA NEFRI CLARK

Detective Liz Moorland

Lest We Forgive

Lest Bridges Burn

Lest Tides Turn

Lest Nobody Lives

Connected to this series through several characters is

Last Known Contact

Rivers End Romantic Women's Fiction

The Stationmaster's Cottage

Jasmine Sea

The Secrets of Palmerston House

The Christmas Key

Taming the Wind

Temple River Romantic Women's Fiction

The Cottage at Whisper Lake

The Bookstore at Rivers End

The House at Angel's Beach

The Secrets of Willow Bay

Charlotte Dean Mysteries

Christmas Crime in Kingfisher Falls

Book Club Murder in Kingfisher Falls

Cold Case Murder in Kingfisher Falls

Plan to Murder in Kingfisher Falls

Festive Felony in Kingfisher Falls

Daphne Jones Mysteries

Daph on the Beach

Time of Daph

Till Daph Do Us Part

The Shadow of Daph

Tales of Life and Daph

Bindarra Creek Rural Fiction

A Perfect Danger

Tangled by Tinsel

Maple Gardens Matchmakers

The Heart Match

The Christmas Match

The Menu Match

The Cookie Match

Doctor Grok's Peculiar Shop Short Story Collection

Simple Words for Troubled Times

(Short non-fiction happiness and comfort book)

www.ingramcontent.com/pod-product-compliance
Lightning Source LLC
Chambersburg PA
CBHW011034190726
48290CB00011B/2838